Lake Bride

Holiday Brides Book 5
A Sweet Contemporary Romance
by
USA Today Bestselling Author
SHANNA HATFIELD

Lake Bride
Holiday Brides Book 5

Copyright ©2022 by Shanna Hatfield

ISBN: 9798837728990

All rights reserved. No part of this publication may be reproduced, distributed, downloaded, decompiled, reverse engineered, transmitted, or stored in or introduced into any information storage and retrieval system, in any form or by any means, including photocopying, recording, or other electronic or mechanical methods, now known or hereafter invented, without the written permission of the author, except in the case of brief quotations embodied in reviews and certain other noncommercial uses permitted by copyright law. Please purchase only authorized editions.

For permission requests, please contact the author, with a subject line of "permission request" at the email address below or through her website.

Shanna Hatfield
shanna@shannahatfield.com

This is a work of fiction. Names, characters, businesses, places, events, and incidents either are the product of the author's imagination or are used in a fictitious manner. Any resemblance to actual persons, living or dead, business establishments, or actual events is purely coincidental.

Cover Design: Shanna Hatfield

Published by Wholesome Hearts Publishing, LLC.
wholesomeheartspublishing@gmail.com

*To the Sentinels -
Thank you for your service
and standing guard so faithfully.*

Books by Shanna Hatfield

FICTION

CONTEMPORARY

Holiday Brides
Valentine Bride
Summer Bride
Easter Bride
Lilac Bride
Lake Bride

Rodeo Romance
The Christmas Cowboy
Wrestling Christmas
Capturing Christmas
Barreling Through Christmas
Chasing Christmas
Racing Christmas
Keeping Christmas
Roping Christmas
Remembering Christmas

Grass Valley Cowboys
The Cowboy's Christmas Plan
The Cowboy's Spring Romance
The Cowboy's Summer Love
The Cowboy's Autumn Fall
The Cowboy's New Heart
The Cowboy's Last Goodbye

Summer Creek
Catching the Cowboy
Rescuing the Rancher
Protecting the Princess

Women of Tenacity
Heart of Clay
Heart of Hope
Heart of Love

HISTORICAL

Pendleton Petticoats
Dacey   *Bertie*
Aundy   *Millie*
Caterina   *Dally*
Ilsa   *Quinn*
Marnie   *Evie*
Lacey   *Sadie*

Baker City Brides
Tad's Treasure
Crumpets and Cowpies
Thimbles and Thistles
Corsets and Cuffs
Bobbins and Boots
Lightning and Lawmen
Dumplings and Dynamite

Hearts of the War
Garden of Her Heart
Home of Her Heart
Dream of Her Heart

Hardman Holidays
The Christmas Bargain
The Christmas Token
The Christmas Calamity
The Christmas Vow
The Christmas Quandary
The Christmas Confection
The Christmas Melody
The Christmas Ring
The Christmas Wish

Holiday Express
Holiday Hope
Holiday Heart
Holiday Home
Holiday Love

Chapter One

Wavy-edged crimson leaves from the Persian ironwood trees growing in the columbarium skittered across the pathway, coaxed into an autumnal dance by a gusty breath of mid-October air.

Bridger Holt watched the breeze mingle the leaves with those from maple, magnolia, oak, and dogwood trees before he continued on his walk around Arlington National Cemetery. Arlington wasn't just a place to bury the dead. The history of America was etched into each and every headstone.

For the past two years, the cemetery had become his home, of sorts, as he served as one of the guards of the Tomb of the Unknown Soldier.

Twenty-four months of service as a sentinel had taught him more than he would have imagined possible. Some of the most valuable lessons were in his studies of the people, both living and deceased, at the cemetery.

Bridger watched as a flock of tourists exited a large bus, expressions filled with the anticipation they held in exploring what he thought of as a national monument and treasure. Millions of tourists wandered among the graves at Arlington every year. Most of them abided by the signs that requested all visitors conduct themselves with respect and dignity. The few who spoke far too loudly or behaved obnoxiously made him want to shake some sense into them.

He tipped his head in respect to four ancient, stoop-shouldered men as they shuffled toward the graves of comrades fallen in World War II. He'd seen the older gents there often enough to recognize them. He was sure they were getting in one last visit before cold winter weather set in and forced them to stay away until spring.

The cheerful call of chickadees teased Bridger's ears and drew out his smile as he meandered past a towering old cottonwood tree. He'd only gone a few yards when he stopped to observe what appeared to be a group of grandchildren leaving a spray of mums on the grave of a decorated Gulf War hero.

Bridger quietly continued on his walk, making note of a rowdy group of tourists he'd report to security before he went on duty. He'd never been a big people person, but he'd learned to tolerate most visitors. He much preferred those who came in silent deference to the solemn atmosphere of Arlington than those who acted like they were at a carnival instead of a cemetery.

He nodded to a woman who was one of the official cemetery photographers as she snapped photos of the fall foliage. She lowered her camera and hurried toward him.

"Sergeant Holt! I'm so glad I ran into you," Felice Rogers said with a flirty smile. She pulled a manila envelope from the camera bag hanging off her left shoulder and held it out to him.

"What's this?" Bridger asked, accepting the envelope with a bit of caution. Felice had made it abundantly clear she'd be interested in dating him, but after his past disastrous relationships, Bridger had zero interest in getting involved with anyone. Not while he was still enlisted. Maybe six months from now, when he reached the end of his service and returned to life as a civilian, he'd consider it. Maybe. But certainly not now.

"Just some photos I took I thought you might like. I heard this is your last day as a guard." Felice took a step forward and placed her hand on his arm.

Bridger fought the urge to shrug off her touch. Instead, he held perfectly still, dredging up a half-hearted smile along with a few words of gratitude. "Thanks, Miss Rogers. I'm sure I'll enjoy the photos." He edged backward. "Are you shooting anything particular this morning?"

"No. I thought I'd wander around and see what I could find."

Bridger jutted his chin toward the historic Arlington House that was more than two hundred years old. "I saw that cagey little fox by Arlington House earlier. You might be able to catch him in a photo or two. I think he's been hiding in the boxwood hedges near the old amphitheater."

"I'll go check it out. Thanks for the tip." Felice dropped her hand and shifted the bag on her shoulder. "I'm sure I'll see you around, Sergeant Holt, but in case I don't, I wish you all the best."

"Thanks, Miss Rogers. The same to you. Take good care of yourself, and thanks again for the photos."

"You're welcome," she said, then hurried off in the direction of Arlington House, a home that had been constructed by George Washington's step-grandson.

There was such an abundance of history at the cemetery. After years of feeling adrift and lost, being in a place that had such deep roots had helped Bridger find at least a few parts of himself since he'd become one of the tomb guards.

He shoved his hands into his pockets and meandered along a little-used pathway. Overhead, the blue sky provided a spectacular backdrop to the colorful jewel-toned trees that had yet to shed all their leaves. When the breeze kicked up, the leaves created their own music in a whispering tune. The birds in the trees contributed to the song, while the hum of a leaf blower in the distance added a steady beat. A symphony of autumn.

Amused with his fanciful thoughts, Bridger glanced at his watch and hastened his step. He still had plenty of time to get ready before his shift, but he didn't want to be late. He walked by a group of tourists but stopped when he realized they were lost and a long way from the section they were trying to find.

"The tram will pick you up right there in about five minutes," Bridger said, pointing to one of the stops the tram made around the cemetery. The sprawling acres were far too much for many people to walk.

"Thank you," the man in the group reached out to shake Bridger's hand.

After returning the handshake, he resumed his walk. He started past the Korean War Memorial Contemplative Bench, then stopped. He'd read it dozens of times in the past two years, but pain gripped his heart each time he thought about the words penned by author Herman

Wouk that were engraved on the stone. "'The beginning of the end of war lies in remembrance.' That might be, but I'd much rather forget," Bridger whispered to himself.

"It's hard to forget and remember, isn't it?" a voice asked, startling him.

He spun around and glowered at the petite, elegant figure sitting on a red and blue plaid woolen shawl spread on the grass across from the bench.

"Mrs. Parks! I didn't see you there," Bridger said, removing the ball cap he wore to cover his short, mostly shorn hair that had to be trimmed almost daily to meet tomb guard standards. "How are you?"

"Well enough, I suppose," the woman said, smiling at him and patting the shawl beside her.

Bridger sank down next to her and tugged the hat back on his head. "Hard to believe it's the middle of October, isn't it?"

"It is, but what a glorious autumn we're having." Mrs. Parks reached over and squeezed his hand.

If anyone else had initiated the intimate contact, Bridger would have pulled away and walked off. But he'd come to know and admire Emmy Parks. She faithfully came to the cemetery on the tenth day of each month, often spending an hour sitting on the grass in this exact spot, reminiscing about the day she'd met her husband, an officer who'd been killed in Vietnam.

"Tell me again about the day you met your husband." Bridger leaned forward with his forearms braced on his upraised knees. He'd heard the story many times, but Mrs. Parks loved to tell it, and he wouldn't deprive her of the joy she seemed to derive in sharing how she met her husband.

She gave him a studying glance, as though she gauged his sincerity. At his encouraging nod, she smiled and released a sigh that seemed to hold a wealth of emotion.

"It was a sunny day, much like this one, only it was spring. April. I'd come to put flowers on my uncle's grave. He'd been killed in Korea and was my mama's only sibling—her beloved baby brother. Uncle Jack was nearer my age than Mama's. Anyway, I promised my mother I'd bring over a vase full of flowers to leave at his grave because our lilacs had bloomed early that year. They were delightfully fragrant." She breathed deeply, as though she could still smell the perfume of the flowers.

"And you met him then?" Bridger prompted.

Mrs. Parks got a faraway look in her soft blue eyes. "I did. I'm not sure how I managed it, but I'd gotten myself completely lost. I turned around right there under the tree behind the bench and bumped into Peter. He was such a handsome, strapping young man, and he caught my arms before I could fall. Somehow, I managed not to drop the vase of flowers. He was here to visit his oldest brother, who'd also been killed in Korea. It just seemed natural to go find the two graves together. Then he took me out for a slice of pie, and we wed two months later."

"So, pie is the way to woo a girl?" Bridger asked with a crooked grin.

"The right girl, dear boy. You woo the right girl with a slice of delicious pie." Mrs. Parks offered him a long glance. "Any luck finding her?"

Bridger shook his head and leaned back, bracing the palms of his hands on the blanket behind him. "Nope. Mostly because I'm not looking."

Mrs. Parks laughed and bumped against his side. "One of these days the right girl is going to show up when you least expect it and knock you right out of your boots, Sergeant Holt."

"Well, if I come across a girl who can do that, I'll likely let her catch me."

"That's the spirit," Mrs. Parks teased.

"Did you already visit your husband?" he asked, abruptly changing the subject.

"Not yet. I was rather hoping if I waited, you might just happen along, and here you are. Do you have time to go with me to pay him a visit?"

"Always." Bridger hopped up and offered Mrs. Parks a hand as she gracefully rose to her feet. He assumed she had to be in her seventies, maybe even approaching her eighties, although she could have passed for someone younger. He tucked the envelope of photos from Felice under his arm, folded the shawl and draped it over his left arm, and then offered Mrs. Parks his right.

Together, they made their way to the plot where her husband's remains were buried. Bridger had read the headstone many times, but he read it once more.

"Peter James Parks. Medal of Honor. Colonel, US Army. Died bravely June 7, 1969. Beloved husband and father."

Mrs. Parks ran her hand reverently over the standard-issue headstone. "Our son Petey never got to meet his papa. Peter had a short leave, and nine months later Petey arrived. Six months after that, Peter was gone."

"And you raised three children on your own?" Bridger asked, although he knew the answer. Esteem filled him for this plucky little woman who had experienced such anguish and pain. War heroes, in his opinion, weren't limited to those who fought and died in battle. They included the spouses and families left to carry on without their loved ones.

"I did," she said, looking up at him with a nod. "I had to. What other choice did I have? The children needed me. In caring for them, I discovered it helped ease the burden of my grief." She rubbed her hand over the top of the headstone again. "Not a day goes by that I don't miss Peter."

"I understand, Mrs. Parks. I really do." There were a few people Bridger missed every single day. Rather than dwell on the ragged wounds in his heart that refused to heal, he glanced at his watch.

"You need to go, don't you, darling?" Mrs. Parks reached out for the shawl he still held.

"I do. I'm on duty at the top of the hour."

"Today is the day, isn't it?" Mrs. Parks asked, studying him. "Your last day as a sentinel of the tomb?"

"It is. Are you going to come watch the guard change?"

She nodded. "I'll be there. Now, go on and get ready. I'll see you later."

In an uncharacteristic move for him, Bridger leaned down and pressed a kiss to the woman's velvety cheek, inhaling a subtle floral fragrance that reminded him of days gone by.

Mrs. Parks blushed but appeared pleased by the attention. "Go on with you, Sergeant. You've got no business smooching on old ladies when you have to get ready for your duty."

"Yes, ma'am," he said, doffing his hat to her, then headed toward the Tomb of the Unknown Soldier. Dressed in plain clothes, he looked like any other tourist visiting the cemetery with the exception of his military bearing and haircut hidden beneath his ball cap.

He made his way down to the guard quarters located beneath the Memorial Amphitheater and changed into his uniform. Two new trainees were there to brush away specks of lint before he was inspected to make sure every detail of the uniform came within a miniscule fraction of an inch to perfection.

That was part of the sentinel creed, a standard of perfection. It was something he strove to uphold, at least when it came to his duty.

His personal life was far from perfect, but he refused to think about it.

Bridger settled his hat on his dark brown head, pulled on his spotless white gloves, then moistened them with a spray bottle of water to be able to keep a better grip on his rifle. He then slipped on a regulation pair of sunglasses. They cut down on the glare from the marble of the tomb plaza. He thought the glasses also helped the sentinels look more aloof and formidable.

He gave himself one more glance in the full-length mirror, starting at the toes of his gleaming military dress shoes and working his way up the blue wool pants with the gold stripe down the side of each leg and over the dark blue jacket belted at his trim waist. His gray-eyed gaze lingered, for just a moment, on the Tomb Guard Identification Badge. He'd received it nine months after becoming a sentinel at the tomb. It was hard-won, but he was proud of the laurel wreath pin attached to his right pocket, denoting him as a member of an elite group.

Bridger felt a swell of emotion as he turned from the mirror and made his way to the steps that would take him upstairs to the tomb he'd guarded through searing heat and freezing sleet. He'd kept guard in pouring rain, a late winter blizzard, and hail the size of walnuts that pelted him so hard his shoulders and arms had bruises for two weeks. But he'd never wavered in his duty or his dedication to doing this job that was more about honor than work.

Back straight and posture erect, Bridger made his way up the steps onto the plaza and through the changing of the guard procedure that involved a white-glove inspection of the rifle he carried. The gun had to be as clean and shining as the rest of his uniform, even though it could be used with deadly force if necessary.

He recalled spending thirteen hours preparing his uniform before his first shift as a sentinel. With practice, it now only took him about four to polish everything from the brass on his jacket to his shoes, giving them a high shine, as well as pressing each article of clothing. Stray threads were singed with a lighter and lint was removed with masking tape.

His life as a guard of the tomb was about meeting a standard of perfection. And in this, his last shift as a guard, he had no intention of doing anything less.

Once the commanding officer completed the changing of the guard ceremony, Bridger began the fluid walk of a sentinel down the long mat in front of the tomb.

In shifts with the other guards on duty, he spent the next twenty-four hours guarding the tomb. He marched twenty-one steps across the mat, passing the grave markers in front of each of the unknown soldiers. He paused and faced east for twenty-one seconds, then turned north for another twenty-one seconds before moving his rifle to the shoulder nearest the tourists watching his every move. The movement of the rifle symbolized his willingness to stand between the tomb and any threat that might be made, much as the twenty-one steps and twenty-one-second intervals alluded to the military's highest ceremonial honor—the twenty-one-gun salute.

As he walked and paused in movements he'd made hundreds of times in the last two years, Bridger reflected on his service as a sentinel. The job wasn't for everyone. Of the few who made it through the required training, some would then quit when they could no longer deal with the rigorous attention to detail every aspect of the duty required. Tomb guards weren't supposed to talk during their walk unless a situation arose in which safety became an issue, which suited Bridger just fine. The less talking involved in any situation, the happier it generally made him.

When his commanding officer had suggested he apply for the duty, he'd thought the guy was nuts. Now, he was grateful for the man's insistent urging that he pursue the possibility. With his CO's blessing, Bridger had transferred to the 3rd U.S. Infantry Regiment, traditionally known as The Old Guard, the oldest active-duty infantry unit in the Army. Members of the unit had been serving the nation since 1784.

Training to be a guard had been rigorous and sometimes seemed relentless. Bridger had not only passed, but he also thrived on the duty, a service he saw as a great privilege.

Bridger had six more months before he would either reenlist or leave the Army. Although it was all he'd known or done since he'd graduated from high school, it was time for him to move on. Part of his transition back into what he thought of as normal life was leaving behind the tight-knit group of sentinels and serving in other capacities during his remaining time in the Army.

It had been such a wonderful opportunity to be counted in with the soldiers who had guarded the tomb for decades, beginning in 1926. Not a single moment, not one, had gone by without a guard on duty since 1937. Since April 6, 1948, all the guards had been members of The Old Guard.

Bridger couldn't speak for the other sentinels, but for him, the opportunity had given him time to learn things about himself he might never have otherwise explored. Mostly, he focused on giving the unknown soldiers the respect they deserved for their sacrifices.

Pulled from his musings by the appearance of the guard who would next go on shift as he made his way up the last steps onto the plaza, Bridger felt a deep pang of emotion in his heart as he realized this was the last time he'd march across the mat. Deliberate in his motions, he straightened his already perfect posture and lifted his chin just a fraction as he made the final walk across the mat.

The commanding officer inspected the new guard's weapon and uniform with scrutiny, then turned to face the crowd gathered to watch the flawlessly executed steps involved in the changing of the guard.

"Today is the last day Sergeant Bridger Holt will serve as a guard of the Tomb of the Unknown Soldier. We wish him well in all his future endeavors. Sergeant Holt will take a moment to place flowers on the graves in a sign of respect to the Unknowns."

Bridger hated being the center of attention, but he felt a deep need to offer his best to the remains of the men in the unknown graves. Men who had given their all and inspired Bridger through their sacrifices to give his all, or at least try to give it, every day.

Several of his fellow guards had come out on the plaza to watch. His closest friend and fellow guard, Quinten Walker, took Bridger's rifle. Quinten handed him the three roses Bridger had purchased to lay on the graves and left below in the guard quarters in a bottle of water so they would stay fresh.

While a private played "Taps" and the spectators gaped with undisguised interest, Bridger saluted the tomb, then laid a rose on each grave. When he finished, he reclaimed his rifle, turned to face the tomb once again, saluted for twenty-one seconds, then made his way off the plaza.

In the quarters below ground, his fellow guards slapped him on the back and shook his hand, offering words of congratulations. The commanding officer in charge nodded at Bridger and then loudly cleared his throat.

"Today is Sergeant Holt's last day as one of the guards. You've honorably filled your post, Holt. You've never once complained. You've often gone above the call of duty. No one will forget when you volunteered to walk an extra shift in the hailstorm last spring. You've lived up to the standard of perfection and then some. We all wish you well as you transition to your new post."

Quinten grinned and thumped Bridger on the back. "Holt is giving up a post of dignity to go strut around with the peacocks on parade."

Bridger glowered at his friend as the other sentinels laughed. His new duties would include participating in official ceremonies, marching in parades, and putting a good face on The Old Guard unit.

"Speech! Speech!" a few of the guards chanted.

Bridger had no more desire to give a speech than he did to be in the spotlight, but it seemed he didn't have much choice in the matter.

He glanced at Quinten, then his CO, before he removed his hat and sunglasses. "When I started training two years ago, I had no idea how this post would change me, how much it would teach me. It has been the greatest honor of my life to serve as a guard of the Tomb of the Unknown Soldier and an experience I'll never forget. Thank you for this opportunity to give the unknowns my best."

The commanding officer offered him an approving look; then two guards walked forward, carrying a big sheet cake.

Two hours later, after Bridger had eaten two pieces of cake with ice cream and enjoyed a fruity punch concoction made by an officer's wife, he changed into his civilian clothes. It wasn't until then he recalled the photos Miss Rogers had given him the previous morning.

Bridger pulled three glossy photos from the envelope, all of them showing him marching as a guard. One was of him walking in the snow. One was a spring day with the hint of trees in bloom behind him. The third was a photo that showcased the colorful array of fall leaves in the background.

Pleased to have the photos as a keepsake, he returned them to the envelope and packed it with the rest of his belongings, then carried the duffel bag upstairs. He watched the changing of the guard from where a group of tourists gathered behind the fenced area that kept visitors from getting too close to the tomb. Back in the 1920s, before anyone began guarding the tomb, some people had been disrespectful, using the area for picnics and whatnot, instead of honoring the soldier who had given his all in service to his country.

Bridger observed with admiration what he thought of as an elaborate military ballet as the officer on duty inspected the guard's weapon and uniform. When the ceremony concluded, Bridger turned and walked through the cemetery, heading for the nearby base where he chose to live.

With each step, he felt as though a vital, important chapter of his life had come to a close.

Bridger's problem, he realized, was that he wasn't ready for it to end.

Chapter Two

Six months later

"Well, Keith, this is it," Bridger said, kneeling in front of the grave of the man who had been his best friend from the first day they'd met at boot camp.

Keith Bryant had been outgoing, friendly, and fearless right up until he'd been killed three years ago overseas in a war zone. One moment they'd been side by side, fighting against a group of terrorists. The next, Keith had taken an improvised explosive device to the chest and was gone before either of them could blink.

Bridger knew the world would be a better place if he'd been the one who'd died and Keith had survived. His thoughts on that subject hadn't changed once since his friend had died. They never would. He'd replayed the moment over and over in his mind, trying to recall if there had been any warning of what was coming; if he could have shoved Keith out of the way and saved him.

Shaking off his memories, Bridger brushed his hand over the top of Keith's headstone. The magnolia tree nearby was in full bloom, and a few petals had dropped onto the stone. Bridger was glad Keith had been buried at Arlington, even if he hadn't been able to attend the service. He'd been in a medically-induced coma, recovering from the injuries he'd received that horrible day when Keith had been killed.

But since he'd been stationed in Arlington, he'd visited Keith's grave almost every week.

Bridger had just completed his last day in the Army. As of thirty minutes ago, he was once again a civilian. He glanced up at the sunny April sky, wishing he had some direction or purpose for his life. He'd received a few job offers, but nothing that excited him. He wasn't certain he wanted to remain in the area, but he didn't know where else to go.

Everything he owned that wasn't in storage in his parents' attic was crammed into the two duffel bags he carried with him. Despite his attempts to make some sort of plan for his future, he hadn't been able to do it. People probably thought he was nuts, not that he cared.

The only plan he had in mind was to spend tonight in a nice hotel, then go apartment hunting tomorrow. He didn't need much space, but he wanted to find somewhere quiet. Somewhere neighbors would leave him alone and not ask questions. Bridger had endured the past six months in a battalion with The Old Guard that conducted memorial affairs for fallen comrades as well as ceremonies and participated in special events as representatives of the Army. The memorial events were something he was comfortable doing, but he hated being "a face of the Army," as his commanding officer called their duties.

Bridger liked quiet. Peace. People not in his face or pelting him with a hundred questions he had no interest in answering. He had enjoyed the time he'd filled in with the Caisson Platoon. Horses and riders trained constantly to be able to do their duty with immaculate precision when it was time for the horses to pull a flag-draped casket on a black artillery caisson to Arlington National Cemetery.

Summers spent at his uncle's farm had given him an opportunity to learn to ride and a love of horses. He had a way with animals and had no trouble stepping into the role of a rider of one of the horses while a permanent replacement was trained.

Maybe he'd head out West. Get a job on a ranch somewhere. He wouldn't mind working around horses or cattle. Or even on a farm. The thought of running a tractor up and down a field held far more appeal than an office job.

"Guess this will be goodbye for a while, Keith. I'm officially finished with my Army career. Too bad I never figured out what I wanted to be when I grew up. You'd think at twenty-seven I'd finally have my act together. Seems like without you around to keep me in line, everything just fell apart."

Bridger swallowed hard as emotion washed over him. If he wasn't careful, he'd be bawling like a baby before long. He drew in a long, cleansing breath, brushed a few magnolia petals away from the base of the headstone, then stood. "Wherever I end up, I'll be thinking about you, buddy."

He turned and made his way over to watch the changing of the guard. He had no idea when or if he'd return to the cemetery and wanted to see it one last time.

When the ceremony wrapped up, he waited a few minutes until the crowd dispersed. He picked up his bags and was about to leave when Quinten hurried over to him. Bridger knew he was on shift today but hadn't expected to see him.

"Hey, what are you doing over here?" he asked quietly when Quinten moved beside him.

"Your CO has been trying to find you, Holt. You have an urgent call from your dad. Your family has been trying to reach you all day. The CO called our office to see if you might have dropped in to say goodbye. The message is for you to call your dad ASAP."

Bridger had turned off his phone when he reported for duty that morning and hadn't bothered to turn it back on. He took it from his pocket and turned it on, seeing he had a dozen text messages and sixteen missed calls.

"Come down to the quarters to call," Quinten said, leading the way to the quarters below ground.

Bridger pushed a button and listened as the phone rang once, twice. On the third ring, a voice he recognized answered.

"This is Jason," his father spoke in his smooth banker tone.

Bridger swallowed a sigh. "Hey, Dad. It's Bridger. My phone's been off all day, but I heard you were trying to get in touch. Is everyone okay? Did something happen?" He could think of nothing short of death or catastrophe driving his parents to reach out to him. They'd been completely and thoroughly disappointed in him when he'd joined the Army right after he graduated from high school instead of going to college and pursuing what they viewed as an acceptable career. They'd never had a close or good relationship, but his blatant refusal to go to college drove a wedge between them the size of the Grand Canyon.

"It's Uncle Wally, Bridger. He had a heart attack this morning. He's in the hospital in Altoona, but they don't think he'll make it through the night."

"I'm on my way."

Bridger shoved the phone into his pocket and picked up his bags. Before he made it to the door, Quinten rushed up to him.

"Everything okay?" his friend asked.

"No. My uncle is in the hospital. Dad said it's not looking good. I need to see him."

"Is this the uncle you spent summers with on his farm?"

"Yep." Bridger set down both bags and held out a hand to Quinten. "Thanks for finding me, and for being a good friend, Quint. I'll miss seeing you around."

"Take care of yourself, Holt. Promise you'll keep in touch."

Bridger nodded once. He wasn't someone who wrote letters, or even sent text messages with any frequency, but he would try to keep in touch with Quinten. After losing Keith, Quinten had been the only person Bridger had allowed himself to truly be friends with. "I'll do my best."

"Good. You need a ride somewhere?"

Bridger nodded. "Actually, that would be great."

"Hang on a second."

Quinten disappeared and returned a few minutes later. "Felice Rogers will give you a ride."

At Bridger's scowl, Quinten grinned. "I saw her taking photos earlier and assumed she was probably still here. She'll meet you at the south gate in five minutes."

"Thanks, man." Bridger gave Quinten a brotherly hug, grabbed his bags, and left.

Although everything in him wanted to sprint across the cemetery, he kept his steps to a respectful pace until he reached the gate where Felice waited for him in her car.

He tossed the bags in the back and slid onto the front passenger seat. "Thanks for giving me a ride, Miss Rogers."

"You're welcome. Where to?"

Bridger had considered flying to Pennsylvania, but by the time he got to the airport, found a flight, then got a rental car on the other end of the trip, he figured it would be faster to drive.

"The nearest car rental agency."

Felice Rogers pulled into traffic. "You don't have a vehicle?"

Bridger shook his head. "Nope. I haven't needed one while I've been in the service."

"I guess that makes sense. Didn't I hear you are about to wrap up your time in the Army?"

In no mood for idle conversation, Bridger forced himself to be polite. Felice was doing him a huge favor. "Today was my last day."

"You're still in uniform," she observed.

"Yep. Haven't yet had time to change." Bridger had planned to go find a hotel room before he changed. Now, it looked like he'd be wearing his uniform for a while longer.

Her eyebrows lifted, but she didn't say anything as she turned down a side street and pulled into the parking lot of a car rental agency.

"Want me to wait for you?"

"No, but thank you." Bridger got out, then retrieved his bags from the back. He bent his knees and looked inside the car through the still open passenger door. "I appreciate the ride, Miss Rogers. I don't think I mentioned it, but I am incredibly grateful for the photos you took of me working as a guard. It was kind of you to print them out. They mean a lot to me. So, thanks."

She smiled. "You're welcome, Bridger. I hope you find something or someone in life who brings you joy."

Bridger thought it was an odd thing for her to say, but he offered an almost smile, closed her car door, and rushed into the office.

He was able to rent an SUV and was soon heading toward Altoona, Pennsylvania, where members of the Holt family had lived since the mid-1800s.

Bridger's particular branch of the Holt family tree had stretched out to Oregon where his great-great-great-grandparents had lived in the small town of Holiday. Evan Holt had been the town's first doctor, and his wife, Henley, had worked as his nurse and assistant.

For reasons Bridger didn't know or understand, his great-grandfather had left Oregon and returned to Pennsylvania. Uncle Wally now owned what had once been Evan's property in the small town of Holiday located in the eastern half of the state.

The entire drive to Altoona, Bridger prayed he'd reach the hospital before his uncle passed. Uncle Wally had been such a bright spot in Bridger's childhood. During the school year, he put up with his parents' ceaseless demands for him to perform like a trained circus monkey. But during summer vacations he'd been given a reprieve and sent to his uncle's farm for three glorious months. His younger brother, Ross, had gone only once and had lasted just three days before he begged, whined, and pleaded to be sent home. Bridger had been delighted to see him leave. He once again had his beloved uncle and the farm all to himself, except for the cousins who popped in and out with regularity.

If Bridger had been given a choice, he would have remained with his uncle on the farm that had once belonged to his great-grandparents. It was the only place he'd ever really felt at home and could just be himself.

Wallace Holt, a lifelong bachelor, was actually Bridger's great-uncle. But to Bridger, he'd always just been Uncle Wally.

It was his uncle who had taught him about farming, hunting, survival skills, basic mechanics, and carpentry. The Army had filled in the rest of the gaps until Bridger felt like he could be a jack of all trades even if he was a master of none. The fact that he didn't excel at any one thing, didn't have a burning passion for any career path, was probably the reason he had no idea what to do next with his life.

He took an exit off the freeway and made his way to the hospital, pulling into the first open parking space he found, then running to the lobby. He got Wally's room number and directions on how to find it from the receptionist at the front desk.

He entered the room to find no one there with the dying man. Did no one care enough about Uncle Wally to keep him company in his last hours of life?

Bridger quietly crossed the room and stood by the bed, assured by the beeping machines and the laborious sound of Wally's breathing that he was still alive. Barely.

Gently, Bridger lifted Wally's hand in his, holding the scarred, arthritis-gnarled fingers as though they were made of glass.

"Hey, Uncle Wally. It's Bridger. Your favorite nephew." Bridger waited for a response. Not even Wally's eyelids fluttered in recognition. "Uncle Wally. It's Bridger. Bridger Holt. Your nephew. The one you taught to spit and fight, and fish and farm. Remember the summer you took me to the cabin in Holiday and we spent a week on the lake, fishing and exploring? I think those trout we caught and cooked over the campfire were the best I've ever eaten. I know I haven't said it often, or at all, Uncle Wally, but I wouldn't have survived my childhood without you. The thought of spending the summers with you got me through the rest of the year. The happiest memories I have are of the days I spent with you at the farm and in Holiday. Thank you for that, Uncle Wally. For taking a lost boy and making him feel seen and loved. I'll never forget you or the good times we had together. I love you, Uncle Wally. Always will."

Bridger almost yelped in surprise when his uncle's eyes opened. Although they looked cloudy and confused, he blinked twice at Bridger. Then he felt a slight pressure on his hand, as though his uncle were trying to squeeze it.

"I love you, Uncle Wally. So much. You've been a friend, an uncle, a grandpa, and a father all rolled into one. Thank you for that, and for always making me feel like I had a home to come back to with you."

The noises produced by the various machines hooked up to his uncle changed. Bridger had spent enough time in hospitals to know the sound wasn't good. He pushed the nurse's call button, then leaned close to his uncle.

"Go with God and be in peace, Uncle Wally," he whispered as a nurse rushed into the room along with one of Bridger's cousins. "You are loved."

"Bridger!" His cousin Madelyn waited until he released Wally's hand and carefully placed it on the bed to give him a hug. She brushed at her tears when she realized Uncle Wally had drawn his last breath.

To some, Uncle Wally might have seemed eccentric or odd, but Bridger had loved the old coot without reserve. A few of his cousins, mainly Madelyn, had been fond of Uncle Wally, even if they hadn't spent as much time with him as Bridger had.

Regretfully, Bridger had hardly seen his uncle in the last handful of years. He'd been overseas for three tours of duty, then injured. He had come back to the farm for two weeks before he began training to become one of the tomb sentinels. That was the last time he'd seen his uncle, although he did try to call him a few times a month just to see how the old guy was doing.

He'd just spoken to his uncle a week ago. They'd talked about Bridger's uncertain plans for the future. Uncle Wally had encouraged him to come to the farm until he figured out what it was he wanted to do next in life.

Bridger stood back with Madelyn and watched as the doctor declared an official time of death, then noted it on the chart.

"He was waiting for you to get here," Madelyn said, wrapping her arm around Bridger's and standing closer to him than he was accustomed. He'd always been uncomfortable with people in his personal space. In this particular, painful moment, though, it felt comforting to have his cousin close. "You were always his favorite of any of us, Bridge."

"Uncle Wally was special." Bridger didn't know how else to explain his feelings about the man who had shaped so much of the person he'd grown into.

"He was, but so are you. Your folks were here earlier with Mom and Dad." Madelyn leaned her head against his arm. "I'm so glad you came, Bridger."

"Me too. I'm grateful I got here in time to tell him goodbye."

"You needed that closure." Madelyn patted his arm and then stepped back as another nurse entered the room and whispered something to the doctor. He nodded and followed her out the door.

"Stay as long as you like," said the nurse who'd come in with Madelyn. "I'm very sorry for your loss."

"Thank you," Madelyn said, smiling at the woman as she left the room. She faced Bridger with a questioning look. "Do you want to stay longer or leave?"

Instead of answering, Bridger walked over to the bed, bent down and kissed his uncle's forehead, then turned to his cousin. "I'm ready to go. Did Uncle Wally have anything we need to take with us?"

"No. He was in his pajamas when the ambulance brought him in." Madelyn picked up the purse she'd set on a chair and slipped the strap over her shoulder. "Are you going to stay with Aunt Rosalind and Uncle Jason?"

Bridger gave a derisive snort. "Not unless forced under duress."

Madelyn grinned and grabbed onto his arm again as they left the room and made their way over to the elevator. "You can stay with us. If you'd rather, I'm sure it would have pleased Uncle Wally to have you stay at the farm. Until the will is read, you have as much right to be there as anyone."

"Staying at the farm sounds like the best plan."

Madelyn nodded. "At least come to my house for dinner. Mark promised to have it ready as soon as I get home. I'll send him a text letting him know we are on our way. Do you remember how to find my place? Do you need a ride?"

"I have a rental, but thanks. I think I remember the way to your house, but maybe I'll just follow you." Bridger glanced down at his cousin, deciding she didn't look much different now that she was all grown up, married, and a mother of two than she had when they were kids playing together at Uncle Wally's farm. "I'll walk you to your car."

In silence, they crossed the parking lot. It turned out Madelyn's car was only four spaces away from Bridger's rental. He held her door, jogged back to the SUV, and then followed her to her house. Her husband had a hot meal waiting, and Madelyn's two little girls kept them entertained.

"Thanks for dinner and this evening, Maddie," Bridger said, giving his cousin another hug as he stood at the door.

"Of course, Bridger. If you need anything, give me a call. You do still have my number, don't you?"

Bridger shook his head and took his phone from his pocket. He handed it to Madelyn. "You'd better just add your info. I had to get a new phone a few years ago and lost all my contacts."

She added her information, sent herself a text, then handed the phone back to him. "I think our folks are planning to meet for breakfast to discuss arrangements for Uncle Wally. Anyone who wants to be involved is invited."

"Okay." Bridger waved, then left, uncertain if he was ready to wade into the midst of his family, especially when his heart ached from the loss of his beloved uncle.

The next morning, he sat on the porch at the farm drinking a cup of coffee made in Uncle Wally's ancient percolator and watching the sun rise. The last thing he wanted to do was face his parents, but out of respect for Uncle Wally and the old man's wishes, he planned to join the breakfast hosted at his aunt and uncle's home.

With reluctance, he finished his coffee and headed out to meet with his challenging family.

Five days later, after listening to them argue and fight, Bridger was ready to run away and never speak to his parents or his father's siblings again. If he'd been twelve, he might have.

His parents and Madelyn's had argued about everything. Everything. First, they couldn't agree on a day for Uncle Wally's service. Then there was the great debate about the coffin and funeral programs. He thought his mother and Aunt Therese might slug it out when it came time to decide on the flowers. It seemed to him, and Madelyn, that they were purposely trying to be difficult.

Somehow, they made it through the service without any fists flying.

Now, as Bridger sat in the attorney's office with his parents and his dad's three siblings, he wanted to be anywhere but there. Of his eleven cousins, he was the only one who had been requested by Uncle Wally's lawyer to attend the reading that was scheduled two weeks after the man's burial.

He ignored Aunt Therese's glacial glares as the attorney took a seat at his big oak desk and riffled through a file folder of papers. He took out two envelopes and set them aside, then cleared his throat and read the will.

The farm had been left to a distant cousin who owned the neighboring property, with the stipulation it could never be sold to anyone outside the Holt family. The cousin was out of town at a cattlemen's meeting; otherwise, Trent would have been there.

Bridger watched as his mother's lips formed a thin, hard line. No doubt, she was calculating the high price she could have gotten out of the farm and the commission she would have earned, since she sold real estate for a living.

Uncle Wally had left an equal sum of one hundred thousand dollars to Bridger's father and each of his siblings. He'd also left specific items to each of Bridger's cousins.

"And to Bridger Holt," the attorney read, "I leave the cabin and property in Holiday, along with all the contents of the cabin as well as the trunk in my bedroom at the farm."

Bridger felt every eye in the room settle on him as he gaped at the attorney. He hadn't expected this, hadn't really expected anything. He was a great-nephew to Wally, not immediate family.

"That can't be right," Aunt Therese yelled, leaning forward and slapping the corner of the attorney's desk.

The attorney offered her a cool, dismissive glare over the top rim of his glasses. "I assure you, Mrs. Holt, it is exactly as Wally directed. He wanted Bridger to have the Oregon property. Now, if you'll all remain seated, there is paperwork to be signed. First, though, I am under orders from Wally to walk Bridger out before we get to that."

Bridger stood from his chair and watched as the attorney stuffed all the papers back in the folder, picked it up along with the two envelopes, then motioned for Bridger to join him at the door.

Once they left the office, the attorney walked down a short hallway.

"Step in here, son," the attorney said, moving into a small office that was empty. "I just need your signature on a few papers. Wally made it clear he didn't want you to linger while the rest of them argue and fight over the will."

Bridger took the pen the attorney held out, signed where the man indicated, and handed the pen back to him.

"These are your copies." The attorney handed him a folded sheaf of papers. "And these are for you." He gave Bridger the two envelopes. "Wally left them for you. He also told me to tell you to go to the house and get the trunk out of his room before anyone starts pilfering the contents. You might have someone call your cousin Trent and let him know what was decided so he can be forewarned about the vultures circling. That's how your uncle referred to that bunch of ingrates in my conference room." The attorney tipped his head toward the room where the sound of angry voices carried through the wall.

"Thank you, sir. I appreciate this and all you've done for Uncle Wally. He mentioned you a few times and said you were one of the few people he trusted to manage his stuff."

The attorney chuckled. "Wally never liked the term 'managing affairs.' It was always his stuff." The man patted Bridger on the shoulder. "Take care, son. Wally was so proud of you, of your service. Thank you for the sacrifices you've made for our country."

Bridger felt emotion clog his throat and found it impossible to speak. He reached out and shook the attorney's hand, nodded to him once in parting, then rushed out of the building to his pickup. He'd turned in the rental SUV and purchased a used extended cab pickup with low miles from the dealership one of his father's cousins owned. Regardless of what happened in his future, he knew he'd need a mode of transportation.

Without a moment of hesitation, he sped out to the farm and went straight to Uncle Wally's bedroom. Beneath the window, buried under a stack of old blankets, was a big flat-topped trunk. Bridger took a moment to unfasten the leather straps from the buckles and push open the lid. It appeared to hold a variety of items, including a few framed photos of Bridger when he was a little boy. A note taped inside the lid caught his eye, and he carefully peeled off the tape from the crumbling wallpaper lining the trunk.

Dear Bridger,

When you leave the farm, take this with you. It has history you should know along with things you'll need. Our summers together were some of the best days of my life.

I love you, kid.
Be strong. Be brave. Be kind. And be you.
All my best,
Uncle Walls
P.S. Make sure you take my box of fishing tackle with you and my fishing poles. No one else will appreciate them the way you do.

Grief, raw and strong, rolled over Bridger, but he shoved it down and set the note from his uncle back inside the trunk, fastened the buckles, and hauled it out to his pickup. Afraid someone might try to steal it out of the back, he pushed up the back seat and slid the trunk in, then rushed into the house.

It didn't take him long to change out of the pressed slacks and polo shirt he'd worn to the attorney's office and into a pair of jeans, a T-shirt, and a pair of worn cowboy boots. He packed his duffel bags, carried them out to the pickup, then went to the storage building near the shop where Uncle Wally kept his fishing gear. Bridger located the tackle box and the fishing poles, adding them to his things in the pickup.

He ran back inside, stripped the sheets from the bed he'd been sleeping in, the room Uncle Wally had always said was his, and set them in the washing machine on a quick cycle, then returned to his room. There were a few things there he wanted to keep. Things that reminded him of his summers at the farm, like some rocks he'd collected and a chess board his uncle had helped him make out of wood. They'd spent many hours on the porch playing chess and eating ice cream as the sun set.

After locating a box to load everything in, he packed his treasures and carried them to the pickup, put the sheets in the dryer, then dusted his room, cleaned the bathroom, and remade the bed once the sheets were dry.

He was just headed out the door when he saw his father's car pulling up outside.

A groan escaped him before he could swallow it. He'd hoped to make a clean getaway, but it appeared he'd have to face Jason and Rosalind Holt whether he liked it or not. His father, an investment banker, and his mother, who fancied herself quite the socialite as well as a shrewd real estate agent, had never understood Bridger. They'd eventually declared him hopeless and pinned all their aspirations for greatness on his brother, Ross, who lived in New York City and did something on Wall Street with stocks and investments. Ross hadn't liked Uncle Wally or the farm and had spent his summers honing his ability to talk people out of their hard-earned money, or so it seemed to Bridger. Ross was a natural salesman and used that along with his sleek good looks to manipulate people.

Bridger knew his brother made a lot of money, but he was certain Ross sometimes made it at the expense of someone else's livelihood.

He closed the door to the house, locking it behind him, and walked down the porch steps as his father helped his mother out of the car. Together, they stormed toward him, as though he'd committed a crime against them.

"What are you doing?" his mother demanded as Bridger stood with his hands shoved into the back pockets of his jeans.

"Leaving. Why?"

His mother narrowed her gaze and took another step toward him, invading his personal space. She was well aware it made him uncomfortable, which was why she did it.

Bridger forced himself to remain relaxed, although inwardly he felt tense and coiled, like a tightly wound spring. He kept his expression bland and gave his mother a vague look.

"You aren't fooling me, young man." His mother's long, manicured finger shook in his face. "Wallace Holt was an eccentric lunatic. Therese thinks the will can be challenged based on the loss of his mental faculties."

Bridger wanted to shout that the ones who needed their heads examined were his mom and Aunt Therese, but kept his mouth shut.

"We want the cabin," his father said, stepping beside Rosalind. "Roz thinks it's probably worth at least a couple hundred thousand. That's more than we inherited from Wallace."

Bridger wondered how these two greedy, selfish people could possibly be his parents. Somewhere along the line, the honorable Holt genes had been diluted. From what he'd learned about his family history, Doctor Evan Holt had been a kind, caring man, well-loved in the community of Holiday. His children had been the same. Liked. Respected. Generous. Compassionate.

Perhaps it was just his father and his siblings that seemed to be the bad seeds. Bridger had always thought his paternal grandmother was mean and crabby. Maybe that's where the problem had stemmed.

He was glad he and Madelyn seemed to have inherited more of the Holt DNA than what had been passed along from their belligerent grandmother.

Disappointed in his parents, Bridger straightened to his full six-foot-two-inch height and widened his stance, knowing he could appear imposing when he did. He caught his father's gaze and held it until the older man looked like he wanted to squirm under Bridger's scrutiny.

"I'll only say this once, so please pay attention," Bridger said in an authoritative tone. "I'm not giving you the cabin. Uncle Wally left it to me, and I'm keeping it.

If you want to battle out who gets all of this," Bridger swung his arm in a wide arc to indicate the farm and its contents, "be my guest. We all know Uncle Wally was of a sound mind. If it comes down to testifying he was, I will. I spoke with him a week before he passed away. There wasn't a thing wrong with his mind, and there never has been. You have my number if you come to your senses and stop acting like money-grubbing morons. Until then, don't expect to hear from me. And before you or the others get any ideas about packing anything off the place, don't. There's an inventoried list of everything, down to the last package of seeds in the garden shed. If something comes up missing, I'm sure the sheriff will know exactly who to start questioning."

His mother's mouth fell open in astonishment, and his father looked as though he thought about punching him. While they floundered, Bridger stalked over to his pickup and left before he told his parents what he really thought of them.

He headed into town and drove to Madelyn's house where he parked on the street in front of the yard. Bridger jogged across the sidewalk and up the porch steps. He rang the doorbell, then impatiently rang it again.

"Coming!" he heard Madelyn call before the door swung open.

"Bridger! What are you doing here?" She stepped back and motioned for him to enter the house. "You look upset. What's wrong?"

"You knew about the will being read today?" he asked as he followed Madelyn down the hallway into her sunny kitchen. She poured a glass of milk for him and set it on the table in the breakfast nook, along with a plate of chocolate chip cookies, still warm from the oven.

"Yes, Mom called and told me about the will. She and Aunt Rosalind think they can get Uncle Wally declared incompetent. All I have to say is good luck with that." Madelyn sank onto the chair across from him. "Did you really inherit the cabin in Oregon?"

"I did." Bridger ate a cookie in two bites, then took another, chasing it down with a big gulp of milk before he spoke again. "I'm going there."

"What? Where?" Madelyn frowned as she caught his train of thought. "To Oregon? You're going to that dilapidated old cabin?"

Bridger nodded and ate a third cookie.

"I have nowhere else to go and no place I need to be. The summer Uncle Wally took me there was one of the best I ever had." A shrug rolled off his shoulders. "I guess I want to see it again, maybe spend a little time alone."

Madelyn reached across the table and placed her hand on his arm, patting him gently. "We've been so wrapped up in Uncle Wally's passing, that none of us have stopped to ask how you are. How you're doing with all the changes in your life. It has to be hard to walk away from everything familiar from your years spent in the Army and start something new."

"It's been different," Bridger said, feeling evasive. He wasn't going to tell Madelyn how hard it had been to leave the routine and order of being a soldier. Then he'd come back to Pennsylvania only to lose his favorite relative and be caught in the middle of family turmoil. None of it was what he wanted. Since he had no obligations or responsibilities here, the moment he'd learned the cabin was now his, he'd decided he'd go to Oregon and spend some time there.

Although he hadn't thought about it at the time, the Army had been a good place for him to hide away from things he didn't want to face. When he'd been a tomb sentinel, it had become his entire life. Then the duties of the past six months had kept him too busy to think of much else but what he needed to take care of each day.

Now, though, he needed time and space to figure out what to do with his life. To unpack all the baggage he'd been dragging around for years and get rid of it once and for all. He couldn't do that around his obnoxious family. However, he hoped he'd gain clarity at the remote cabin, where he could be alone with his thoughts.

"Bridge, you have to promise you won't become a hermit and grow a beard that's two feet long. You might think otherwise, but you need to be around people, at least once in a while. I won't let you leave unless you promise to occasionally go into a town and socialize."

He grinned at his cousin. There was no possibility she could stop him if he wanted to storm out the door, but it was cute she thought that she could. He held up his right hand, like he was making a pledge. "I promise I won't become a beard-wearing hermit who loses his mind from spending too much time in his own head."

"And ..." Maddie prompted.

"And I promise I will socialize on occasion. I'll even send you a text from time to time."

"Good." Maddie picked up a cookie and took a bite, brushed the crumbs away from her mouth with a paper napkin she pulled from a holder on the table, and then gave him a studying look. "Do you need anything? Is there anything we can do to help you? I just hate to see you run off when you've hardly been back any time."

"I've been back long enough to know our parents have gotten worse instead of better as they've aged. I want no part of whatever trouble they are going to stir up over Uncle Wally's will. You'd think they'd all be happy with the money he left them."

Madelyn toyed with a broken piece of cookie before popping it in her mouth. "It wouldn't have mattered what he left them. It would never be enough." She sighed and looked at him again. "I don't blame you for leaving. Do you have room for a stowaway in your truck?"

Bridger grinned. "I'd be happy to have you along, Maddie, but your husband and children might not appreciate it. Besides, you have to stay here and keep me updated on all the trouble our parents are going to cause. Do you think anyone let Trent know he inherited the farm?"

"I sent him and Christina a text as soon as I heard from Mom. They are on their way back. Trent asked me to call a locksmith and have them change or add locks to all the doors on the house, shop, and barn. By the time they get home, he figures the relatives will have packed off anything worth keeping."

"It's possible, but I may have led Mom and Dad to believe there's an inventoried list of everything at the farm and if anything was missing, the sheriff would pay them a visit."

Madelyn giggled. "Is there a list?"

"Not that I know of, but our parents don't need to know that little detail. Actually, I did start a list the other day when I considered something like this happening. I only made it through the first floor of the house, though."

"That's more than anyone else would have done."

Bridger finished the half-eaten cookie in his hand, drained the glass of milk, then stood. "I'd better get going. I'm hoping to make it to Chicago yet today."

"So, you're driving across the country?" Madelyn asked as she hopped up and stuffed several cookies into a resealable plastic bag.

"That's my plan."

"I'll pack a snack for you, and I won't take no for an answer." Madelyn yanked open the refrigerator door and began setting out sandwich makings. "You haven't had that pickup long. Do you think it might break down on you?"

"I doubt it, but if it does, I'll fix it. I'll stop and buy one of those big crossover truck toolboxes to sit in the back of the pickup bed. I should have some tools on hand, and those boxes lock, so it would be a good place to keep what I need."

"You should stow a few gallons of water in there, and maybe a tow rope. Jumper cables. A full-size jack. Mark attempted to change the tire on his pickup once with the jack that came with it and vowed he'd never try that again."

Bridger wondered if his cousin thought he was completely stupid or had just been in the Army so long he no longer remembered how to do anything. At any rate, he decided not to take her comments as an insult, but to instead be grateful she cared about him. He had few enough people who did these days.

His parents had barely spoken to him the day he'd gone to their house to sort through the belongings he'd stored in their attic. He'd hauled most of it to a Goodwill store. The few things he'd wanted to keep, he'd packed in a box and brought back to the farm. Now that box was stuffed into the back seat of the pickup, ready to travel to Oregon. He was glad he'd left nothing at his parents' home.

"Will this be enough?" Madelyn quickly stuffed two sandwiches, an apple, a small bag of grapes, two snack-sized bags of chips, and three candy bars along with the cookies into an insulated lunch bag.

"How much food do you think I can eat in a day, Maddie?" he asked, then smirked at her. "It looks great. Thank you for doing this for me."

"You're welcome." Madelyn zipped the lunch bag shut and handed it to him.

Bridger decided to ignore the *Paw Patrol* screen print on the outside of it. He hoped he wasn't depriving one of Madelyn's girls of their favorite lunch bag. He gave Madelyn a hug and stepped back.

"Keep me posted. I will gladly fly back and testify if things go that far with the will."

"They won't. Mom and Aunt Rosalind are full of hot air and nonsense, as Uncle Wally would have said."

"That they are." Bridger walked to the front door and opened it, then looked back at Madelyn. "Thanks for everything, Maddie. I might even miss you."

She laughed and wrapped her arms around him, giving him a tight hug. "You know you will. Just don't forget your promises and keep in touch once in a while so I don't worry that you were eaten by bears or mistaken for a sasquatch."

Bridger chuckled. "I promise." He hurried down the steps and out to his pickup. He waved to Madelyn as she leaned against a porch post, then turned around and left.

Before he hit the freeway, he stopped and purchased a heavy lockable box for the back of his pickup that stretched from one side to the other. He added a toolbox full of new tools, a towing rope, chains, jumper cables, a good jack, and a wheel wrench. Then, because he liked to be prepared, he purchased a first-aid kit, duct tape, three gallons of water, two flashlights with extra batteries, and a fire extinguisher. He filled a bag with energy drinks and protein bars at a convenience store, filled the pickup and a couple of small gas cans with fuel, then started driving west.

Bridger wasn't tired when he reached Chicago that evening, so he kept driving until he got to Cedar Rapids, Iowa, and got a room at a roadside motel. It wasn't fancy, but it was clean, and he fell asleep not long after his head hit the pillow.

He awoke early the next morning, showered, and ate a quick breakfast of pastries and a banana served in the motel's lobby before he continued on his trip.

When he reached Omaha, he drove around until he found the cemetery where one of his ancestors had been buried after being stabbed in a fight in a saloon. The man had been the father of Evan Holt's wife. From what Uncle Wally had shared, Henley's father had been a professional gambler and was killed during a card game.

Bridger spent thirty minutes wandering through the old cemetery before he found the headstone. Oddly, it bore the name Henley's father used, which was John Jones, and his real name, Asher Tarleton. Bridger thought the name sounded like it belonged to a character from a *Gone with the Wind* sequel. He left a bouquet of daisies on the grave, then got back on the road. He'd never driven through South Dakota before and decided to take a little side trip to see Mount Rushmore. A sense of pride and patriotism filled him as he stared up at the carved faces of the presidents.

Deciding he wasn't in a rush, he spent two days exploring the Badlands and surrounding areas. He snapped a photo at sunset of the sky and the mountains ablaze with color. Before he could change his mind, he sent it to Madelyn, letting her know he was well and had eaten the last cookie she'd sent along that morning.

From there, he headed to Yellowstone National Park, another place he'd never visited but had always wanted to see. He checked out all the popular tourist destinations, then spent another day quietly observing the wildlife in the area. He happened to be close enough to take a few photos of a grizzly bear wandering across the road, seemingly unaware of the tourists madly snapping pictures with their phones and cameras. He also took several photos of bison and a few of elk.

When he texted the grizzly photo to Madelyn, she immediately replied.

Be careful! You'd better not be an appetizer on his dinner menu! Glad you are having a good time.

Bridger grinned at her message, then tucked the phone into his pocket. After watching two idiot tourists nearly get killed when they got between a bison mama and her baby, he decided it was time to leave.

He drove through Idaho and stopped to visit the Craters of the Moon National Monument. It covered more than fifty-thousand acres and featured lava flows that spread out like an ocean with islands made of cinder cones and sagebrush. The landscape was weird and fascinating, like something out of a sci-fi movie.

Bridger snapped a bunch of photos, knowing Madelyn's oldest would love seeing the rock formations. He stopped to read a sign that offered the informative details that the park covered more than a thousand miles, roughly the size of Rhode Island, and the bulk of the lava flows that made up the monument could be seen from space.

"Now that's cool," Bridger said to himself as he wandered through the museum exhibits.

Since it was early afternoon, he drove on to Boise, where he got a room in a nice hotel, ate a steak dinner at a nearby steakhouse the front-desk agent recommended, then wandered into a massive sporting goods store his Uncle Wally would have loved.

Bridger bought a pair of hiking boots, three pairs of cargo pants, and several moisture-wicking T-shirts before he headed back to the hotel, where he soaked his tired muscles in the jetted tub in his room while watching an old western on the television.

He felt downright indulgent as he crawled between the crisp sheets of the king-sized bed and fell asleep.

Exhaustion kept him sleeping longer than he'd expected, but excitement tugged him from the bed and on his way to Holiday the next morning.

Three hours later, he stopped to fuel up his pickup in Holiday and tried to figure out how to get to the cabin. The town looked far different than he recalled from his visit so many years ago. Buildings that had sat empty and forlorn then now bustled with business.

He parked his pickup on a side street and wandered into Sunni Buns Bakery, where delicious aromas hung in the air.

Bridger admired the architecture of the old building as he made his way to the counter, where he ordered a Cuban sandwich and a glass of huckleberry lemonade. He remembered having huckleberry ice cream when he'd come with Uncle Wally to Holiday. A vague memory of his uncle talking about picking berries in the mountains floated through his thoughts.

He took a seat at a table by a sunny window and sipped the sweet, tart drink as he waited for his sandwich.

A beautiful woman with dark hair and eyes snapping with life brought a plate to his table and set it down with a smile. "Thank you for coming to Sunni Buns Bakery. I'm Sunni, and I hope you enjoy your meal."

"I'm sure I will. It looks great. Thank you." Bridger nodded politely at the sandwich that had been cut into quarters. He lifted one quarter and took a bite. The bread had been buttered and toasted, but the inside was soft, pillowing the spicy pulled pork, smoky slices of ham, crisp dill pickle, and gooey melted cheese. Bridger took a bigger bite and tried not to moan in pleasure, although he did close his eyes to better savor the delicious flavors.

When he opened them, he noticed a serving of pasta salad with olives and marinated veggies on the plate, along with artfully arranged slices of fresh apples and peaches. It didn't take long to wolf down his meal, finishing every last crumb.

He was draining the glass of lemonade when Sunni appeared at his table again.

"Might I assume it was to your liking?" Sunni asked with a knowing grin.

"You might assume that," he said, smiling at the woman. He'd noticed the wedding ring on her hand and thought her husband was an incredibly fortunate man to have a lovely wife who could cook. "That was one of the best sandwiches I've ever had, and everything else was great too."

"Did you save room for dessert? I have an assortment of cookies or my signature cinnamon buns. I also have lemon bars and strawberry cheesecake today."

Bridger felt like he might explode, but he hadn't eaten a lemon bar in years. "I'll take a lemon bar now and a cinnamon bun to go, please."

"You've got it."

After he'd enjoyed every bite of the lemon bar and Sunni had brought him the cinnamon bun packed in a take-out container along with his bill, he took his credit card up to the counter to pay for his meal. Sunni smiled as she rang up his ticket. "Are you passing through or here for a visit?"

"A visit. My uncle owned a cabin out by the lake, but it's been so long since I've been here, I'm not certain how to find it."

"Which lake?" Sunni asked, giving him an observant look as she handed his receipt to him.

"As far as I know, it was called Holiday Lake. My great-great-great-grandpa was the first doctor in Holiday."

Sunni gaped at him a moment before she seemed to recover her wits. "You're related to Doctor Evan Holt?"

Bridger nodded, wondering why he'd mentioned that. He wasn't one who generally shared any personal information with strangers, but for some reason, Sunni's friendly demeanor seemed to loosen his tongue. "I'm Bridger Holt."

"Oh, my word! Wait until I tell Kali, my cousin. She's in charge of all the historical stuff in town. She'll want to speak with you, but we can talk about that another day if we don't scare you off before you even get settled." Sunni drew in a breath that seemed to calm her. "Okay. If you're looking for the Holt cabin, you'll find it not too far from town. Go two blocks north on Main Street, then take a left and follow that road out of town. When you've gone about five miles, you'll see a huge no trespassing sign on the left by a road that looks like no one has driven on it in ages. You have four-wheel drive?"

"I do," Bridger assured her.

"Good. You might need it. Anyway, just follow that path for about a quarter-mile. You can't miss the lake."

"Thank you. And thanks for the good food." Bridger held up the cinnamon bun container.

"You're welcome. I hope you'll come in again soon."

Bridger's sweet tooth would guarantee his return. "You'll likely see me again before long. Thanks again."

Eager to see the cabin that had held such good memories from his past, Bridger hurried out to his pickup.

As he drove out of town, he couldn't help but hope Holiday might become the place he could call home.

Chapter Three

"Sunni wasn't joking about four-wheel drive," Bridger groused as he hit another rut, or maybe it was a tree stump, on his way to the cabin. The path, because it certainly couldn't be called a road, had overgrown bushes covering the tracks, not to mention tree limbs haphazardly tossed across it, looking like the aftermath of a brutal storm.

He bounced over another rut, hit his head on the top of the cab, and decided if the cabin was even half as bad as the path, he was in trouble when it came to accommodations for the night. He'd seen a sign for a hotel in Holiday. He might have to stay there if …

His thoughts derailed when he arrived at the lake to find a new cabin built right on the edge of the lake with a dock off to one side. A set of wooden steps led down to a footbridge that spanned a narrow creek on the upper end of the lake. It looked like something out of a bucolic landscape painting with flowering shrubs planted around the porch.

As he stared out the windshield, he watched four ducks land on the water. Sunlight shimmered across the surface of the lake like crystal prisms in a swaying chandelier. He could see deer on the other side of the lake, hiding in the trees, watchful of a stranger intruding into their paradise.

Bridger was sure he was in the right place, but this cabin wasn't the one his uncle had brought him to that long-ago summer.

He'd decided to wait to read the letters Uncle Wally had left for him until he reached the cabin. Now, he wished he'd read them. Maybe his uncle explained about this cabin that didn't appear to be more than a few years old. Leaves and a few tree branches were on the cedar shake roof, while leaves and debris littered the porch, but the structure itself seemed to be in great condition. It looked solid.

More importantly, it looked welcoming and inviting.

Bridger got out of the pickup, walked over to the porch, and jogged up the steps, then paused at the door with his hand on the knob. Memories of his uncle flooded over him. He leaned his head against the warm wood and said a prayer of thanksgiving for having the time he'd been given with Wally.

Bridger drew in a deep breath, inhaling the scents of pine and clean, woodsy air. He turned the knob, finding the door locked.

He felt like an idiot for assuming the door would just magically open as he retraced his steps to his pickup. He dug out the two letters from Wally, opened the one that had "read first" printed on the front of the envelope, and took out a thick sheaf of papers. Taped to the corner of the top sheet was a house key.

Bridger tucked the papers back into the envelope and returned to the porch. The key slid right in, and the lock clicked as he turned the knob and pushed open the door.

Hesitant but curious, he stepped into the cabin. Sunlight filtered in the windows, illuminating the living area, where big leather couches surrounded a rock fireplace. Pine floors and walls definitely gave the space a cabin feel, as did the old Pendleton blankets draped over the back of the couches. A pine coffee table rested on a cowhide rug. Matching end tables held lamps made from antlers.

A large, framed photo hanging on the wall above a narrow desk shoved against the wall showed Bridger as a little boy. He was holding Uncle Wally's hand, grinning up at the older man in adoration.

If he'd owned any doubts about being in the right place, the photo assured him he'd found Uncle Wally's cabin.

"Wow," Bridger muttered, closing the door behind him.

Dust motes danced in the sunbeams, but the place wasn't filthy. In fact, with only a thin layer of dust on everything, he wondered if someone had cleaned it within the last month or two. He glanced at the fireplace and noticed a switch on the wall near it. He'd seen a large propane tank outside and assumed the fireplace ran on gas. That was a bonus.

He turned and studied the open kitchen floorplan. The pinewood floors carried into the room. The cupboards and cabinets were also pine, stained a shade darker than the floors. The stainless-steel appliances looked brand new. Bridger was sure, with a little cleaning, the quartz countertops would gleam.

A long bar extended across one end of the kitchen, creating a separation from the living room. Rocks similar to those used in the fireplace covered the bottom of the bar facing the living room. Three pine barstools with high backs and thick cushions were pushed beneath the counter's overhang.

Bridger tipped his head back and studied the ceiling that showed off the heavy timbers and wood paneling. He glanced into the living room and noticed a stairway tucked into the corner. He walked up the stairs, hand gliding along the smooth wood of the banister. At the top of the landing, he looked around a large loft space packed with plastic storage tubs and antique trunks. Some of the trunks looked familiar. He'd seen them in the cabin he and his uncle had stayed in the last time they'd come to Holiday together.

He stuck his head inside a doorway and discovered a bedroom with an antique iron bed, a vintage dresser and matching chest of drawers, and a rocking chair tucked beneath the window. The rocker was familiar to him. He recalled sitting in it, listening to his uncle tell stories one evening when it had rained too hard to play outside.

Another doorway drew him into a bathroom with a pedestal sink, a small shower, and a tiny round window set in the wall above the toilet. Bridger leaned forward and looked outside, watching a spotted fawn nibble at a sapling. The pleasure of seeing the deer made him smile and linger at the window before he made his way back downstairs.

He turned down a short hallway and stopped at a closed door. He opened it to find a closet tucked beneath the stairs, where the furnace was located as well as shelves holding cleaning supplies. At least he could clean the place without making a trip into town.

He took two steps down the hallway and entered the main bedroom. It was large, with big windows on two sides of the room. A king-sized bed was covered in a Pendleton woolen blanket that looked quite patriotic. The cobalt base of the blanket featured navy stripes and an Aztec pattern in red, gold, and cream colors. He could picture his uncle choosing the blanket with him in mind. Pillows in a reverse pattern with a red base were tossed across the head of the bed. The bed, dresser, chest of drawers, and a side chair matched and were what he'd consider rustic décor, made of heavy burnished pine with brass knobs and accents. He loved it all and wondered if Uncle Wally had chosen the pieces knowing Bridger would like them.

Bridger stepped into a large bathroom that had an incredible walk-in shower with river rock as the base, slate tiles on the walls, and heavy timbers surrounding the glass door. He'd never seen anything like it. There was also a big garden tub, a sink set into a granite counter, and a closet that held the water heater as well as a stackable washer and dryer. A door between the shower and tub opened to a deck that stretched across the back of the cabin. He liked that he could come straight into the bathroom without tracking mud or messes through the house.

"Great planning, Uncle Walls," Bridger said, shutting the door and returning to the closet where the cleaning supplies were stored. Before he hauled in anything, he knew the place needed to be cleaned. He checked the bed downstairs and found there weren't sheets on it, but discovered a set in a sealed bag on a shelf in the bedroom closet. At least he wouldn't have to wash the sheets before making the bed.

First, though, he found a duster with an extension handle and started at the ceiling, brushing away cobwebs and dust as he worked his way down to the floor. It took him several hours to wipe down the walls, wash the windows, scrub the counters and sinks, mop and vacuum the floors, then sweep the porch and the deck. When he finished, the cabin sparkled. He wiped out the already clean fridge, plugged it in, and made sure it worked, then took a break and ate a protein bar. He chugged two bottles of water he'd picked up at the gas station, then hauled in his belongings.

Before he could really settle in, he'd need groceries, so he drove into Holiday and loaded up on basic supplies. Rather than cook dinner, he ran by the Holiday drive-in where he ordered a double bacon cheeseburger, a double order of crispy golden tots, and a thick chocolate milkshake.

He'd slurped the last of the shake before he turned off the road onto his bumpy lane. Regardless of the cost, the first thing he needed to do was to have someone come in and grade the road, then haul in gravel.

Bridger wasn't penniless. He'd lived frugally and saved every dime he could. Thanks to his father's insistent lessons about money, he'd invested wisely, making a good return on his investments. He wasn't wealthy, but he could take a year off without working and not end up destitute.

He'd get estimates on the projects he thought needed attention first; then he'd see about moving some money around and freeing up funds to cover the expenses.

Bridger parked in the same spot where he'd stopped before. He thought about building a carport or garage near the cabin but decided he didn't want it to mar the landscape. Tomorrow, he intended to climb up the hill where the old cabin used to be and explore what remained. From what he could see, there wasn't anything left up there. He wondered if weather, age, or fire had claimed the cabin the community had built for Evan and Henley Holt when they'd wed.

Quickly carrying in his groceries, he put them away. He'd been surprised the cabin hadn't been overtaken by rodents, but he hadn't found a single sign of a problem. He attributed that to the place being well built and properly sealed.

Just in case, though, he'd picked up a few mouse traps and set them around in strategic places. There was nothing he hated more than discovering a mouse had invaded his space.

By the time he took a shower and pulled on a pair of worn knit shorts that were once part of his Army physical fitness uniform, Bridger was completely exhausted. Instead of falling into the freshly made bed, though, he wandered outside and leaned against a porch rail, staring out into the night and listening to the sounds of crickets chirping and frogs croaking. The evening serenade was one he recalled from when he'd been there with Uncle Wally.

Bridger looked across the lake and was sure he could see a flicker of light. The lake and three hundred acres surrounding it were private property, owned by the Holt family for generations. No one else should be out there. He swiped a hand over his eyes and decided it could be the moon reflecting off the water or something in the trees.

He was too tired to worry about trespassers tonight, even if they did exist.

With one more glance across the lake, Bridger returned inside and made his way to the bedroom he'd decided would be his. He'd left Uncle Wally's letters propped against the lamp on the nightstand. He turned on the lamp, flicked off the overhead light, and sank onto the edge of the bed.

Although sleep tugged at him, he knew it was long past time to read the letters. Part of him had put it off, thinking as long as he didn't read them, then Uncle Wally wasn't really dead. Childish? Perhaps. But he just couldn't bear the thought of his beloved uncle being gone. Not when the man had meant so much to him.

Bridger pulled the papers out of the envelope he'd opened earlier when he'd retrieved the key to the front door. A key he intended to have duplicated right away. He'd leave the spare hidden somewhere outside in case he ever lost the original.

He rested with his back braced against the headboard and smoothed the papers flat against his thigh. Uncle Wally's bold, distinctive penmanship glared at him from the top paper.

Dear Bridger,

If you're reading this, then I'm dead and buried, and you've endured a meeting with the attorney and the relatives that I'm sure was most unpleasant. I swear, all four of my brother's children inherited the worst traits their mother possessed. Not to speak ill of the dead, but your grandmother was one mean ol' biddy.

Bridger grinned. He sure wouldn't argue the point. Not when he knew it to be true.

If your parents, or anyone else, try to convince you I'd lost my marbles and the cabin belongs to them, just pop them right in the nose. Actually, if you do that with your dad, I'd kinda like to be there to see it. Jason has been too big for his britches since he was twelve.

Anyway, you're probably wondering about things. Why I left the farm to Trent and money to the ingrates that are my nieces and nephews. Why I left you the cabin.

Trent is a good man, one who works hard, and I know he'll keep the farm in the family, as it should be. If I'd left it to your father, or one of the others, they'd have sold it so fast, dust wouldn't have time to settle in the house.

"Agreed, Uncle Walls." Bridger could picture his mother dragging clients out there the same afternoon the will was read if she and his dad had inherited it.

I know your father and the rest of them will act like a bunch of donkey's derrieres over their inheritance, but it is what it is. I should have left them bupkis, but my conscience would have bugged me about it. I left something I thought would be meaningful to each of your cousins.

One of the best summers I've had was the one we went to Holiday and stayed at the lake in the old cabin. It was such fun for me to experience everything through your eyes, Bridger. You were always such a clever, curious, smart boy. I'm so proud of the man you've become. Don't give up on yourself. One of these days, you'll forgive yourself, even though you should never have placed all that blame on yourself in the first place. What happened over there in that war zone was not your fault, and you did nothing wrong. What you did was heroic, and the government strongly agreed. It was exactly what I would have expected from you.

I hope you'll make time to visit the cabin someday. Maybe you'll even spend a summer there. Four years ago, I went out to check on the property, and the old cabin was falling down on itself. I used as many of the original timbers as possible in constructing the new cabin. You'll see the old wood in the bathroom around the shower. It's also what I had the kitchen cabinets made from.

There are trunks and boxes upstairs in the cabin that hold a wealth of family history. I hope you enjoy getting to know Evan and Henley as real people who once lived and loved there at the lake instead of just names on the family tree.

To answer your next question, no, I'm not dying as I write this letter. At least not that I'm aware. I just figure when a man gets to be my age, it's a good idea to get his stuff in order. (I still hate that term of affairs! Stuff it is!)

Bridger smiled, as though he could almost hear his uncle speaking, and continued reading.

Be safe and well and happy, Bridger. You deserve it and so much more. I'm still holding out hope you'll find a girl to love, one who completes you. Enclosed, you'll find the deed to the property in Holiday along with details about how everything works at the cabin. I've hired a local contractor to check on things every few months. His name and contact information are below. He's been good to work with if you need to hire him for anything.

You've been the son I always wanted and never had, Bridger. Have a wonderful life and know you brought your old uncle a heart full of joy.

Love you, son.
Uncle Walls

Emotion washed over Bridger, and he let it, let his eyes burn, and his throat clog, missing his uncle and the security, stability, and wisdom the man had brought into his life.

After a glance at the paperwork, Bridger decided it might be a good idea to get a safe deposit box in town.

He'd need somewhere secure to keep the papers. Perhaps he'd go into Holiday tomorrow and take care of a few pressing errands.

Before he could talk himself out of it, he opened the second letter from his uncle and read it.

Bridge, my boy!

Don't mourn my passing for long. If you're reading this, I'm dead and gone, and grief won't bring me back, as you well know.

Celebrate life and being alive. Celebrate each day as the gift that it is.

And for goodness sakes, find a good woman to love. Don't be like me and waste your life pining for something you can never have.

Ha! I never told you about Alma, did I? Oh, but she was something. I met her when I was eighteen. Her folks had just moved to town. It was instant love, or so I thought. She promised to write when I enlisted, and she did. For a whole year. Plans were made for us to wed on my next leave. When I returned home, it was to find her married to someone I had once considered my best friend. I never spoke to either of them again. They both died years ago, but that kind of betrayal leaves its mark on a person. I just couldn't ever bring myself to love another.

I know that twit you dated for a while hurt you, but don't let her shallow remarks ruin you for a woman deserving of your love.

Take the advice of a lonely old coot. Find a sweet gal who makes you laugh and smile, one who would never betray you, and hold onto her for the rest of your life.

Be sure you get the trunk that's in my bedroom from the house before the vultures try sneaking off with all my

belongings. Make sure you take everything out, right down to the very bottom.
Love you, Bridge, more than you'll ever know.
Your ol' uncle,
Walls

Bridger had no idea his uncle had once been in love. No wonder he'd remained single. The kind of betrayal Uncle Wally had endured would leave a man questioning the sense of getting involved a second time.

He assumed Uncle Wally's mention of the twit Bridger had dated referred to Valerie. He'd met her when he was on leave and had gone to Florida for a week with some buddies. She was gorgeous, but that's about all he could say for her. He was sure there were lumpy potatoes with a higher IQ. Eventually, she'd told him he was married to the Army, and that she required a man of more substance.

Bridger snorted. He assumed substance meant a fatter bank account. Before Valerie, there'd been Libby. They'd dated for about three months before she'd concluded he wouldn't ever take their relationship seriously. She'd accused him of being emotionally removed from life, whatever that meant.

In high school, he'd dated one of the cheerleaders. Since he'd played football and baseball, they'd been quite the power couple, until he'd left her in tears a few days before graduation. Megan had tossed an ultimatum in his face, telling him if he wouldn't open up and share his feelings, she was through with him. He'd chosen to break up and told Megan she needed to grow up.

Maybe Uncle Wally was right. He needed to find a good woman. If Mrs. Parks had been correct, she'd enjoy a good slice of pie.

Bridger set aside thoughts of his failed love life and contemplated getting up to examine the trunk he'd carried in earlier and left in the living room. The weight of it had nearly made him topple backward off the porch steps. He wondered if Uncle Wally had lined the bottom with bricks or rocks.

Far too weary to dig through it tonight, Bridger set the letters and papers on the nightstand, turned off the light, and scooted down in the comfortable bed. With a sigh of contentment, he was asleep.

Sunlight streaming in the window, along with the cheerful sound of birds chirping, awakened him the next morning.

Bridger opened his eyes, looked around the unfamiliar surroundings, then lazily stretched in bed. It was the best night's sleep he'd had in years. Maybe ever.

Excited to dig into the trunk his uncle had left for him and then do some exploring, Bridger hurried out of bed, dressed in a pair of cargo pants with a T-shirt, and walked into the kitchen. He filled a bowl with cereal, milk, and slices of banana, then sat on the top porch step to eat it. The sunlight on the lake was nearly blinding, but he loved it. Loved the fresh air filled with the scent of the trees. Loved hearing the birds singing their morning greeting and the ducks winging in for a landing on the water. A sound to his left drew his gaze to a bushy-tailed squirrel sitting on a stump, watching him.

Bridger fished a piece of cereal out of the bowl and tossed it toward the stump. The squirrel hopped down and picked up the cereal, racing off with it.

From the corner of his eye, Bridger could see the fawn he'd noticed yesterday nibbling at the leaves of a sapling about a hundred feet away. He wondered where its mother was and why it was hanging around the cabin. If it was an orphan, maybe he should look into getting it some feed. He had no idea what a deer should eat.

After he finished his cereal and washed the bowl, Bridger scooted the trunk over by one of the couches, pushed open the lid, and took a seat.

He'd already read the note, so he set it aside and pulled out a box that had once held cowboy boots. When he lifted the lid, he stared at dozens of black-and-white photos. Some of the people he recognized, like his grandparents and uncle. Others were unfamiliar to him, but names were written on the back of each photograph. He set the photos aside to spend more time with later and took out a thick scrapbook album. It was full of photos, report cards, newspaper clippings, and printed articles of Bridger. He had no idea Uncle Wally had kept all that stuff. Things his own parents should have kept but hadn't.

Bridger set it aside, then pulled out three additional scrapbooks. One was from his grandpa Winn's and Uncle Wally's service in the Army during the Korean War. They'd each served, although Uncle Wally had been in his early twenties, and Grandpa Winn had been nineteen.

The second scrapbook was from World War II. It seemed there were two older brothers who'd served in the war and died. Bridger wondered why no one had ever mentioned them. The last scrapbook was from a Holt who had served during World War I. The photos showed a young man who looked confident and cheeky. Bridger wondered if he had the trademark red hair so many of the Holt family still sported.

There were two more boxes of photos and old letters. A wooden case held postcards with postmarks from the early 1900s. At the bottom of the case, Bridger found a small box that held letters written from John Jones to his sister.

He wanted to go through every letter, every photo, so he left the albums and boxes of letters sitting out, but the trunk would be in the way. He closed the lid and lifted it, but it still felt heavier than he thought it should. He set it back down and looked inside. It was then he realized the bottom should be deeper and began feeling around for a way to lift it up. He finally discovered a spot in the peeling paper inside the trunk and pulled on a tab. One corner of the bottom shifted, and he was able to work his fingers under it to lift out the false panel. Beneath it, sewn onto an old, yellowed petticoat were gold coins. Bridger lifted out the cloth, removed the coins, and counted fifty of them. The dates ranged from the mid-1870s through the early 1880s. The newest one bore a date of 1884.

"Who did these belong to?" he wondered aloud as he looked over the coins again and then back into the trunk. It was then he noticed a sheet of paper in the bottom.

He picked up the parchment paper that seemed as fragile as the paper lining the trunk. The feathery script appeared to be decidedly feminine.

Greetings,

This trunk belonged to Asher Tarleton, my father, known to me only as John Jones, a gambler by trade but a much-loved papa. He left behind several of these coins when he passed. The rest my husband and I added. I stitched them all to an old petticoat so they wouldn't rattle together in the trunk.

Evan and I decided to keep them hidden here in case the day ever comes we need the funds.

If these are found after we've passed, spend them wisely.

With sincerity,
Henley Jones Holt

A shiver rolled over Bridger.

It was one thing to hear about his ancestors and the lives they'd lived in Holiday. But it was something else entirely to hold a letter Henley Holt had written. Bridger snapped a few photos of the coins, then emptied one of the boxes with letters and set them inside. He carefully set Henley's letter and the petticoat back into the trunk. After he inserted the false bottom, he closed the lid and carried the trunk to a spot beneath one of the windows.

Even if the trunk hadn't contained a single thing, knowing it had belonged to Henley's father made it special to Bridger. He ran a hand over the top of it, then looked around at the photos and albums he'd left sitting out. He neatly stacked everything on the dining room table, then returned to his room. After lacing up a pair of hiking boots, he considered going exploring, then decided it might be best to head into town and see to his list of errands first; then he'd have the rest of the day to hike or fish.

He'd already thought of several things he'd wished he'd picked up at the grocery store, and he couldn't help wondering if he could find a small rowboat for sale. He loved the idea of rowing out on the lake to fish. Uncle Wally had rented one the last time they'd come to Holiday.

Bridger shoved his phone and wallet into his pocket, picked up his keys, tugged on a ball cap, then hurried outside with the things he wanted to leave at the bank, including the box of coins. He debated leaving the door unlocked, then decided it was better to be safe than sorry.

He bounced his way back over the rutted path to the road and concluded finding someone to give him a quote on the job of repairing it should take first priority. He thought he remembered the name of the contractor in Uncle Wally's letter. When he got into town, he'd give the man a call.

Bridger glanced at his watch and decided he'd go to the feed store first. He figured someone there would know something about deer. He wanted to get a little feed for the fawn just in case it was on its own. He intended to keep an eye on it for a few days and see if it was alone or had a skittish mother.

He parked at the feed store and headed inside the building that resembled a big barn. A display at the front of the store reminded him that Memorial Day fast approached. The thought of a grill where he could cook steaks and burgers made him veer over to a selection located next to an old wooden wagon holding colorful yard flags and garden statuary.

"Welcome to Milton Feed & Seed. May I help you?" a feminine voice asked from behind him.

Bridger turned around and smiled at a dark-haired young woman wearing a polo shirt with the store's logo emblazoned on the pocket.

"Good morning. I'm thinking about getting a grill. Do you recommend pellet, gas, or charcoal?"

"I prefer gas, just because it's cleaner and faster, but my husband would tell you pellet is the way to go." She shrugged. "I guess it just depends on your patience level."

Bridger grinned. "Gas it is. If you were buying one, which model would you choose?"

The woman walked over and tapped the grill that wasn't the highest or lowest priced. "This one. It comes with a year warranty, gets the job done well, but lacks the fancy bells and whistles only a trained chef would ever use."

Bridger chuckled. "I'd like to get one, please."

"Perfect. I'll have Colt set one out for you. It comes in a box unless you want us to assemble it."

"Box is great." Bridger figured the box and packing around it would keep the grill from getting jostled into a thousand pieces on his terrible road.

"You're new in town, aren't you?" The woman held out her hand to him. "I'm Piper Ford. My husband, Colt, and I own the store."

"It's nice to meet you, Mrs. Ford." He shook her hand and smiled.

"Please, call me Piper. Colt has two brothers in town, and it gets confusing if you start calling all of us Mrs. Ford."

"Piper. I'm Bridger Holt." He watched as her eyes widened; then she smiled.

"You wouldn't, by any chance, be related to the Holt family who lived here when Holiday was a new town, would you?"

Bridger was surprised anyone knew the Holt name and connected it to his ancestors. "Evan and Henley are my great-great-great-grandparents. My uncle owned the cabin out at Holiday Lake, and I recently inherited it. I think I'll spend the summer here." Up to that moment, Bridger hadn't decided what he would do, but the notion of staying in Holiday for the summer felt right.

"I'm so sorry. I assume you recently lost your uncle." Piper offered him a sympathetic look.

"I did. Uncle Wally brought me here when I was twelve. It was the best summer I've ever had."

Piper smiled and nodded her head. "That's wonderful you had that time with him and got to be in Holiday. So, you're staying at the cabin? I haven't been out there myself, but Carson, Colt's brother, mentioned there's a newly built cabin out there."

"Yep. Uncle Wally had it built a few years ago, although I had no idea about it until I arrived yesterday."

"Well, welcome to Holiday. If there is anything we can do to help you, just let us know." Piper's smile broadened and she motioned to someone behind Bridger.

He turned and watched a broad-shouldered cowboy approach. The man had eyes only for Piper, so he assumed he must be her husband.

"Colt, this is Bridger Holt. He's one of the descendants of Doctor Evan and Henley Holt."

"Nice to meet you." Colt stretched out a hand in welcome.

Bridger shook it, finding he may have just met two people who could become friends. "Likewise. This is a great store. Looks like you've got a little bit of everything here."

"We try," Colt said, then bent down and kissed Piper's cheek.

"Bridger wants to buy this grill," she said, placing her hand on the mid-price grill. "He'd prefer one that is boxed. Can you help him load it, Colt?"

"You bet." Colt leaned toward him and dropped his voice to a conspiratorial tone. "Are you sure you don't want me to talk you into one that uses pellets?"

"Thanks, but the gas one will be great. Where can I get tanks of propane?" Colt told him the best place in town to pick up the small portable tanks, then they discussed his horrendous road and who would be good to contact to speak with about repairing it. The name Colt mentioned was the same one in Uncle Wally's letter.

"Oh, I almost forgot. Do you sell feed for deer? There's a fawn at the cabin that seems to be on its own. I wasn't sure what to feed it."

"We have deer pellets, and even blocks of feed that are great for an assortment of wildlife," Piper said, leading the way to the aisle where they had everything from dog food to chicken feed. "Poor baby. Are you sure the mother isn't just hiding?"

"No, but I intend to keep an eye on it. Every time I look outside, it's close by. I assume if the mother were around, it would have disappeared by now."

Colt shook his head when Piper gave him a look Bridger had no hope of interpreting. "No more rescue projects, Piper. Not right now." He glanced over at Bridger. "We're up to our ears in the animals she rescues. We've got horses, rabbits, chickens, dogs, cats, goats, and two pigs. Our most recent acquisition is a one-eyed mule named Ichabod. It's like all the rejects from a barnyard nursery rhyme ended up at our place."

Piper playfully swatted her husband's arm. "It's not that bad."

Colt shrugged, then gave his wife a rascally wink.

Piper helped Bridger choose feed for the fawn while Colt loaded a grill on a flat cart and rolled it up to the cash register. Bridger added some barbecue tools and cedar planks for grilling fish to his purchases.

After Colt helped him load everything, he shook hands with the man.

"Give Grady a call. He'll be able to give you an idea about the road. If he can't take care of it, I'm sure he knows someone who can," Colt said, taking a step toward the door.

"I appreciate it. It was nice to meet you."

"If you find yourself looking for work, let us know. Piper and I have a few part-time openings."

"I'll keep that in mind, Colt. Thanks again." Bridger waved once to the man before he got into his pickup and drove to the bank. It was a few minutes before opening time, so he took out his phone and called the number for Grady Guthry, the contractor his uncle had used and Colt had recommended. Grady agreed to come take a look at the road at two that afternoon.

Bridger went into the bank when it opened and inquired about renting a safe deposit box. The teller referred him to a beautiful red-headed woman sitting behind a desk. A brass plaque on the corner read Katherine Ford. He wondered if she was one of Piper's sisters-in-law.

"Mrs. Ford?" he asked as he moved in front of the desk.

She looked up at him and smiled. "Yes. May I help you?" she asked, rising to her feet.

"I'd like to rent a safe deposit box, please."

The woman smiled and motioned to one of the two chairs in front of her desk. "Of course. I just need you to fill out a few forms."

As she gathered the papers from a file in her desk drawer, Bridger leaned back in the chair. "By any chance, are you related to Mrs. Ford at the feed store?"

The banker nodded her head as she raised her gaze to his. "I am. Piper is my sister-in-law. I married Kaden, the youngest Ford brother." She gave him a studying glance. "Are you new in town?"

"Yes. Bridger Holt." He reached across the desk and shook her hand. At least she didn't question him about being related to the famed Doctor Holt of the town's past.

"It's nice to meet you. Please, call me Katherine." She slid two papers across the desk toward him along with a pen.

He read the form, signed his name, then followed her to the secured room where the boxes were kept. Once she'd taken out the box he'd rented and set it on the table in the room, she backed away. "I'll leave you to do whatever you need to."

"Thanks," Bridger said, then took the deed to the property and the other important documents he'd brought into town with him, along with the box holding the gold coins, and set them inside the box, closed the lid, and locked it, then stepped back into the lobby area.

"Finished?" Katherine asked, rising as he again approached her desk.

"Sure am. Thanks again. It was nice to meet you."

"You as well, Bridger. Welcome to Holiday."

"Thanks. It's nice to be here." Bridger nodded to the woman who looked far too young to be a bank manager, then hurried out to his pickup.

He realized he should have asked Piper and Colt if they knew anyone with a boat for sale but decided he could pursue hunting one down later. He had enough to keep him busy for several days, although the thought of lazing away an afternoon, casting a line into the lake, held a great deal of appeal. Maybe he could look online and see if anyone had a boat for sale.

He left the bank and drove along Main Street, checking out the variety of businesses. He saw several signs for museums and thought he might enjoy exploring them another day.

He turned around when he reached the edge of town and drove back through town to the other end, traveling along a few side streets. Most of the houses looked well cared for. Yards were mowed. Flowers bloomed in beds and pots.

Overall, Holiday looked like a slice of small-town America. A place that he may very well decide to call home.

Bridger turned and drove to the grocery store where he picked up several things he'd forgotten yesterday. He loaded the bags into the back seat of his pickup, then ran by Sunni Buns Bakery where he got a sandwich, pasta salad, and three cookies to go.

Sunni bustled out of the kitchen and saw him waiting for his order at the end of the counter. "You're back!" she said with a grin.

"The food was too good to stay away," he said, smiling at her as she set two plates in front of customers at a table near the front window, then came over to him. "Did you find the cabin?"

"Sure did. I'm glad you mentioned four-wheel drive. The road is terrible."

She nodded. "It is, not that I want to admit to trespassing, but my husband and I drove out there once just to see the lake. I wasn't sure we were going to make it back out. The lake is gorgeous, though, and worth the horrendous drive."

"It is. I imagine you weren't the first or the last to drive out there to take a look."

Sunni grinned. "Definitely not. So, what brings you back into town, besides another sandwich?"

"I needed to pick up some supplies, stop by the bank, that sort of thing. Grady Guthry is coming this afternoon to give me a bid on repairing the road."

"Oh, that's great. Grady's a good guy. He'll give you an honest bid."

"Good to know," Bridger said, accepting the bag that held his food when the server carried it out to him. "Have a nice day, Sunni. I'm sure I'll see you around."

"Well, you're welcome to join us for church on Sunday. You can't miss it. It's the Holiday Community Church."

"Thanks. I'll think about it." Bridger offered her a polite nod, took two steps, then turned back to look at her. "You don't know anyone with a rowboat or a small motorboat for sale, do you?"

"Hmm. Not off the top of my head. I'll ask around."

"Thank you." Bridger nodded to her again; then left.

He drove out of town, eager to return home.
Home.

It had been a long time since he'd thought about a home of his own. Would the cabin become his home? It wasn't like it was far out of town. But it was isolated enough to suit him since he preferred solitude to crowds.

When he turned off the road onto the rough path, he clenched the steering wheel to keep from being tossed around the pickup cab. He hoped the eggs he'd purchased didn't end up scrambled in the carton before he reached the cabin. He parked the pickup in the same spot he'd been using, carried in his groceries, and put them away. As he hauled in the bags, he noticed the fawn napping beneath a maple tree. Two pheasants lingered near it, as though they were keeping watch.

Maybe the feathered babysitters would have better luck than he'd had in determining if the fawn was orphaned.

Bridger walked all the way around the cabin, discovering a small tool shed set back in the trees, not visible from the front of the place. He backed the pickup up to the porch, barely avoiding hitting a stump, and slid the grill out directly onto the wooden floor. There was no way he could have carried it up the steps by himself.

After parking his pickup a second time, he went inside and ate his lunch at the counter. When he finished, he got out two steaks he'd purchased and set them in a resealable bag with a marinade he mixed from basic ingredients. Even though he was stuffed from lunch, his mouth watered just thinking about eating the thick pieces of tender beef. He planned to cook them both tonight and save one to eat tomorrow.

He sat on the couch and searched online for coins that were similar to those he'd found that morning. His eyes almost bugged out of his head at the auction prices he found for similar coins. He'd have to look up the specific details of each coin, but he thought one of them was worth more than a hundred thousand dollars.

"Whoa!" He sat back and tried to wrap his head around the estimated value.

Had Uncle Wally known that? The man had definitely known the coins were in the trunk, otherwise, he wouldn't have mentioned looking down to the bottom, and he wouldn't have made sure Bridger knew to get the trunk out of the house before anyone else tried to claim it.

If the coins were worth as much as he suspected, he could have a small fortune sitting in the safe deposit box at the bank. He was glad he'd taken them there for safekeeping even though he had no intention of selling them. However, if someone broke in and took the trunk, or the cabin caught fire, at least the coins would be safe.

The sound of a motor approaching outside drew him to his feet and out the door. He'd give more thought to the coins later. Right now, he had a road repair project to discuss.

After he and Grady Guthry walked the length of the road, they shook hands on a deal. Grady would email the paperwork in the morning. He had two other jobs he had to complete first, but he promised Bridger he'd get to the road as quickly as he could.

In an effort to be friendly, Bridger offered Grady a bottle of cold water and one of the cookies he'd picked up at the bakery when they returned to the cabin.

"You need a boat," Grady observed as he leaned against a porch post, looking out over the sun glistening on the water.

"A boat, a couple of chairs for the porch, and about a hundred other things I haven't even thought of."

Grady chuckled. "If I hear of someone with a boat for sale, I'll let you know. I'm assuming you want a used one?"

"I do. Just something small I can take out to fish. Even a rowboat would work." Bridger took a long drink of water, then looked at Grady. "Do you know anyone who makes patio chairs? I'm thinking Adirondack chairs, or something with a more rustic feel, would be good for the porch."

"You might ask Piper at the feed store. She has some of that kind of stuff in the garden center."

"I'll check there the next time I'm in town." They watched as a bird swooped down and snagged a fish from the water.

Grady turned to Bridger with a broad grin. "I'll knock five hundred dollars off the project if you give me permission to come fishing out here."

"You'll check with me first before you come? And you promise not to bring a bunch of yahoos out here?" Bridger asked. Grady didn't seem like the kind of guy to hang out with idiots who might do something stupid like burn down the woods around the lake, but he wanted to be sure.

"No yahoos, and I'll call or text before I come out. If I brought anyone, it would likely be my granddad or nephew."

"It's a deal then." Bridger reached out and shook Grady's hand. "You're welcome to come whenever you like."

"Great. Thanks. I've got a bunch of work to finish before I can think about a day of fishing, but maybe once I get your road in shape, I'll make the time." Grady glanced at his watch and pushed away from the porch post. "I'd better get back to town. Thanks for getting in touch. I'll let you know once I can give you the day I'll start the work."

"Perfect. Thanks, Grady. It was great to meet you. I look forward to having a smooth road to drive over."

"Me too, if I'm going to be coming out here to fish." Grady walked down the porch steps, then turned to glance back at the cabin. "Your uncle was a really neat guy. I enjoyed our visits when we spoke on the phone a few times a year, and when I was working on the cabin with him. Did he tell you about reusing a bunch of the logs and timber from the original cabin?"

Bridger nodded. "He mentioned it in a letter. The shower is incredible, and the kitchen cabinets are fantastic."

"It was beautiful old wood. It would have been a shame not to use it. Have you been up to the old cabin site?"

"Not yet. I'll probably explore up there tomorrow."

"Have fun." Grady waved and then left.

Bridger stood on the porch watching him drive away. He heard a noise and turned to see the squirrel sitting on the tree stump again. The fawn had moved from beneath the maple tree to munch on tender shoots of grass while the two pheasants stood guard. What a strange menagerie.

That evening, after Bridger had grilled his steaks to perfection and sat on the porch step to eat one, he saw a light flickering on the other side of the lake in the same place he'd seen it the previous night.

Once, he might have considered it to be the trick of the moon. But twice? Nope. Someone was on his land who had no right to be.

He thought about storming over there to discover who was trespassing, but caution won over indignation. If it was someone looking for trouble or hiding from the law, he knew it would be careless and stupid to creep into their camp in the dark.

The trespasser could be kids camping out. Or even a homeless person.

First thing tomorrow, he intended to find out who was making themselves at home on Holt land.

Chapter Four

Snuggled into her sleeping bag, Shayla Reeves was in no hurry to get up and start the day. After all, today was her last day off. Tomorrow, it was back to the routine of providing nursing care at Golden Skies Retirement Village in Holiday.

Shayla liked that she worked on a rotating schedule of four days on and four days off. The four days on could be brutal or fun, depending on what was going on with the residents at the retirement facility. Shayla spent the majority of her time working in the dementia wing. It broke her heart when the loved ones of her patients came in and left in tears because they were no longer recognized.

There were good things about her job, though. She liked being able to help patients who truly needed someone to be patient and kind with them as they navigated the murky waters of their once clear minds. Shayla had her favorite patients, and being able to make them smile made her days seem worthwhile.

Since the weather had been warm and gorgeous, Shayla had decided to spend her days off camping. She loved being outdoors and craved the fresh air and sunshine when she was working a long shift stuck inside.

Part of the reason she took her patients on walks outside each day was that she thought sunshine and breathing in the mountain air were helpful to their well-being. But another reason she liked to take them on those daily walks was her own need to be outside where she could feel the warmth of the sun on her shoulders or cheeks and where the fresh air could fill her lungs with the faint hint of pine that always seemed to linger on the breeze.

Shayla hadn't grown up in Holiday, but it had been home to her since she graduated from nursing school eight years ago. She'd taken a job at the hospital, working in a variety of positions including the emergency room.

When her friend Fynlee Ford had mentioned the new wing opening at Golden Skies, Shayla had practically jumped up and down in excitement at the opportunity to work there.

Although her friends referred to the facility as HPH, or the Hokey Pokey Hotel, Shayla enjoyed her job and the people she worked with there. Some of the residents, like colorful Matilda Dale and her sidekicks Ruth and Rand Milton, kept things from ever being dull.

Shayla rolled onto her back and smiled as she thought about Matilda and Ruth employing their matchmaking efforts to set her up with the cute doctor who'd joined the staff six months ago. Doctor Zach Huxley was in his early thirties, great with the patients, and pining after the woman he'd been dating in Montana before he moved to Holiday.

Only Matilda and Ruth seemed to be convinced if they shoved Shayla and Zach together, they'd fall madly in love. Shayla considered Zach a friend, but nothing more. They'd made the mistake of going out to dinner once, at Matilda's insistence, and the self-proclaimed matchmaker became twice as determined they belonged together. If Shayla had any brothers, she was sure her feelings for Zach would have easily fit in that category. She knew he had no romantic feelings for her either. Not when he constantly brought up Mindi from Montana. Shayla and Zach were coworkers and friends, but that was it. All it would ever be.

Before Zach, Matilda and Ruth had tried to connect her with Doctor Dawson, but he'd resigned quite suddenly when he married a pharmaceutical representative and moved to Portland right before Thanksgiving.

Shayla knew she wasn't the only one on the receiving end of Matilda and Ruth's efforts. It seemed if anyone in their sphere of contacts happened to be single, the two meddling old women began hatching happily-ever-after schemes.

Most of the time, it was entertaining to watch, as long as it didn't involve Shayla directly.

With a sigh, Shayla opened her eyes, ready to begin her day. At least the weather had been mild. She'd thought about sleeping with the tent flap open last night just to catch more of the breeze, but she hadn't wanted to awaken with a raccoon or goodness knew what else curled up against her side.

Shayla lifted her arms from the sleeping bag and stretched them over her head. The temperature hadn't dropped much last night. The thought of a quick dip in the lake energized her. She shed her clothes, pulling on her hiking boots and an oversized sweatshirt that hit her mid-thigh; then she stepped out of the tent and put coffee on to heat on a little propane stove she'd brought with her. She gathered the supplies she'd need to bathe and ran down to the shore. After leaving her sweatshirt and boots there, along with a big, fluffy towel, she grabbed a bar of soap from its little plastic container and plunged into the water.

The water was chillier than she anticipated. A gasp would have escaped her at the shock the temperature delivered, but the cold water seemed to suck her breath from her chest. Speed was her best bet now. In one fluid movement, she arched her body and dove into the lake. She broke the surface of the water, tossing her hair out of her face, then hurriedly soaped her skin and hair, bobbing down to rinse off the soap. From the time she left the shore to the moment she felt clean, only a few minutes had passed, but she was ready to get out of the water.

Shayla swam to the shore. When her feet touched bottom, she walked out, dropping her soap into its container; then she cocooned her hair in the towel, squeezing out as much water as she could before she wrapped the towel around her. She used her sweatshirt to dry her feet before shoving them into her hiking boots.

She rolled up the sweatshirt, picked up the soap container, and froze in place when she heard something large coming through the trees. Holding her breath, she strained to listen. To try to distinguish if the interloper was human or an animal. She was fairly certain she'd rather face a bear than deal with a two-legged brute up to no good. The thought of someone with nefarious plans catching her in her current state of undress made panic well up inside her.

With careful, quiet movements, she hastened toward her camp, trying to think of what she could use as a weapon that might inflict enough damage to let her get away. The only thing she had at hand was a mag flashlight. She grabbed it off the stump where she'd left it last night and wielded it like a club in her upraised arm as whoever, or whatever, crashed through the brush, heading straight for her. Absently, she wondered if the intruder would take her seriously if she brandished a weapon the same color as Barney the dinosaur.

Maybe it would be a better plan to call one of her friends and ask them to come to her rescue.

By the time someone drove out to where she'd parked on a little-used U.S. Forest Service road and hiked over a hill to reach her, Shayla concluded her dead body would likely be resting at the bottom of the lake.

"Get a grip, girl," Shayla muttered under her breath. Obviously, she needed to stop enjoying so many police dramas on television. Perhaps she should listen to Fynlee and Sage James at HPH and watch a few of the sweet romances on the Hallmark channel.

Shayla glanced at the tent a few yards away, gauging if she had enough time to yank on clothes before the intruder appeared. If she pretended her life depended on it, which it might, she thought she could at least get a pair of pants and a shirt pulled on, which had to be better than a damp towel.

In her haste to reach the tent with her hiking boots untied and flapping loose, she tripped over a fallen tree branch. She would have sprawled on her face if a pair of muscled arms hadn't caught her and kept her upright.

Something zinged up both arms, crossed in her brain, and traveled down to her toes, making goose bumps break out on her skin.

Her gaze traveled from the tanned, bulging bicep in front of her line of vision to a shoulder rounded with muscle, clearly defined by the crisp T-shirt the man wore. She tipped her head back and looked into a face covered by a dark scruff of whiskers. The roguish growth of hair failed to disguise his handsome features. His nose was a little too big and slightly crooked, like it had been broken at some point, but it enhanced his masculine appeal. A mole centered high on his left cheek did nothing to detract from his good looks. Her perusal took in eyes that were more gray than blue, rimmed with thick, dark lashes.

Why did guys always get the incredible eyelashes? Shayla wasn't one who wore a lot of makeup, but she felt naked without at least a few coats of mascara.

She noticed the Army logo on the front of the ball cap tilted back on his short, dark brown hair as he studied her. His expression was unreadable, as though he'd be great at playing poker, although she detected a hint of humor mingling with surprise in his stormy eyes.

He relaxed his hold on her arms, and she took an unsteady step back, letting her gaze rove over him from head to toe. Her would-be assailant looked like he bench-pressed MINI Coopers instead of weights. His T-shirt, ironed with creases on the sleeves no less, molded to his chest, highlighting his sculpted muscles. Thighs the size of small tree trunks strained against the seams of the pressed cargo pants he wore.

Shayla sucked in a breath. She had no idea who the man was or what he was doing at her campsite, but if he planned to kill her, at least she'd die looking at a beautiful creation, and she didn't mean the lake, or the woods.

"Oh, my," she whispered when he reached down and picked up the flashlight she'd dropped, handing it back to her.

His gaze tangled with hers. She decided if he'd planned to do something terrible to her, he wouldn't have placed her makeshift weapon back into her hands. Besides, there was a gentleness about him that she couldn't begin to explain, but knew, to the very depths of her being, it existed.

He might look like he could wrestle a bear and win, but she was no longer afraid of him.

Shayla straightened her awkward posture, tossed the flashlight into the tent on her sleeping bag along with her sweatshirt and soap, and boldly glared at the intruder as she tightened her grip on the towel that had dipped precariously low when she'd tripped.

"Might I inquire as to why you're standing in the middle of my camp?" she asked, trying to sound confident as the breeze blew up the back of the towel.

Rather than answer, he offered her a long, studying glance. She realized she probably looked like a throwback to cavedwellers with her hair in a snarled mess. It always looked like birds might nest in it until she combed out the tangles. Also, she likely had buffalo breath, since she hadn't yet brushed her teeth. Confidence flagging, she tried not to breathe directly on him.

He grinned and took a step back, as though he'd read her mind. Shayla glanced down and hiked the towel up, securing it tightly in her armpit.

It was just her luck to run into a hunky guy when she looked like a waterlogged cat.

"Why are you here?" she asked when he continued to stare at her. Efforts to act nonchalantly failed miserably as hysteria bubbled in her stomach and threatened to claw up her throat.

"I could ask you the same question," he finally said, hiking one dark eyebrow toward his perfectly straight hairline. "Do you realize you're trespassing on private property?"

"What? Isn't this Rockdale Lake? It's open to the public." As Shayla said the words, she realized she'd never actually seen a sign to denote the area as Rockdale Lake. In fact, the road she'd parked on had one tiny Forest Service sign out on the main road, but no others. No campground signs. Nothing.

She'd wondered why she'd never seen anyone else out at the lake the past times she'd camped there. It had seemed odd there were no public restrooms, picnic tables, or other facilities. She'd just assumed it was one of those primitive locations where nothing was provided.

Regardless, it was one of the prettiest lakes she'd ever seen. A grassy knoll stood on one end of the lake with a cabin on the other end near a babbling creek. She assumed the cabin was probably a caretaker's home, or maybe even a place for rent.

"This is not Rockdale Lake. I've never even heard of it. It's Holiday Lake, and you're on private property. I'll have to ask you to pack up and leave." He glanced around, as though expecting her to have someone there with her, but Shayla was alone. Completely alone. In retrospect, it was not the smartest move she'd made, camping off someplace no one would likely ever find her, especially since she'd thought she was somewhere else entirely.

This would be the last time she went off in the woods by herself, at least to an unknown location. The reality of how careless she'd been slammed over her. If this guy had been a serial killer or someone up to no good, she'd be dead, and no one would ever find her body.

The past three years, since she'd Googled nearby lakes, she'd been camping at this particular spot. Then again, it wasn't like she came out every weekend. More like three or four times a year.

The thought of never returning made her sad. Truly, it was one of the most picturesque places she'd ever seen. It was like it had remained untouched by humans and no one dared change it, with the exception of the cabin, dock, and footbridge.

"I'm sorry. I didn't realize I was trespassing, sir. Are you the caretaker of the property?" she asked, edging toward the tent.

"Something like that." He glanced at the coffee about to boil over. "Want me to turn that off?"

"Sure. You might as well have a cup while I get dressed." She took another step toward the tent. "You will give me time to do that much before you chase me off, won't you?"

The man offered her another long look, then nodded once. "I suppose."

The intensity of his gaze, the spark in his eye, made heat simmer in her midsection and spiral out to every extremity. Her cheeks felt like they flamed with embarrassment as she rushed into the tent and yanked on the zipper to close the flap.

She dressed in record time, took a moment to work the tangles out of her hair and braided it, then stepped back out to find the man sitting on a fallen log, sipping coffee from her lone cup.

"Good coffee," he said, taking another sip and then tossing a glance her way. "I didn't mean to frighten you. I noticed your light the past few nights and wanted to make sure someone wasn't over here causing trouble. It really is private property, though."

"I didn't realize, and I'm sorry. I'll get packed up and be on my way soon." Shayla sighed as she looked around. "I'll miss coming out here. It's so peaceful and lovely."

"It is those things, which is why it's important to enforce the private property thing. Otherwise, it would be like every other overrun campground."

"True." She started gathering her things, then looked over at him as he finished the last sip of coffee and set the cup on a stump. "What's your name?"

"Bridger."

"Well, Bridger, I'm Shayla. Shayla Reeves. It's nice to meet you." She held out a hand, determined to be friendly even if the man intimidated her. It wasn't like she was a petite, tiny little thing. She was taller than average for a woman and could hold her own with even the unruliest patients, but this man seemed to tower over her. He had to be a few inches on the other side of six feet tall, and he was brawny. He also owned a presence that seemed to command attention. She almost felt the need to salute him.

Even without the Army ball cap, she would have pegged him as someone in the military. He just had that bearing about him.

"Are you the new groundskeeper or something?" she asked as she dragged her big backpack out of the tent, then began to roll up her sleeping bag.

"Or something," he answered, sounding evasive. He poured the remainder of the coffee in the cup he'd used and handed it to her, then took over breaking down her camp.

Rather than attempt to push him aside, she sat on the log, drank the coffee, and watched in awe as he packed up her possessions with a level of ease and precision that made her feel like she had ten thumbs.

In the time it would have taken her to fold up the pop-up tent and store it in its pouch, he'd packed up everything but the little propane stove and the cup in her hand.

"Where are you parked?" he asked as though he couldn't get her off the land fast enough.

"That way," Shayla pointed toward the hill. "There's a Forest Service road over there with a turnout area where I park. I realize now it was stupid of me to assume this was a public place and not privately owned. My apologies for intruding."

Bridger—a rugged name for a rugged man—shrugged. "I'm sure you didn't intend to trespass."

"I didn't. Honest. It won't happen again. I'm not sure where I'll go camping now, though."

He glanced at her as he removed the heating plate from the propane bottle that made up her camp stove. It wasn't fancy, didn't take much room to pack, and got the job done for one person.

His look said it all. She could practically see him thinking *how are this crazy woman's camping troubles my problem?*

She almost laughed at the thought of a cartoon bubble above his head and hid her mirth by draining the last drop of coffee from the cup. She wiped the cup dry with the hem of her shirt and then tucked it into her backpack. The backpack weighed what felt like a ton, but it was either pack it in one bag she could hoist on her back or make multiple trips to her vehicle.

Bridger tucked her little stove and propane bottle into her backpack. To her astonishment, he hoisted it onto his shoulder, clearly planning to carry it for her.

In slow motion, or so it seemed to her, she watched muscles ripple and bunch as he adjusted the weight of the backpack when he shifted it to his back. The way he moved made it look as though the bag weighed next to nothing, but she'd weighed it before she left the house. It was almost forty pounds. Of course, it was devoid of most food supplies now, which made it lighter, but still. Bridger whoever-he-was could have been swinging around a feather pillow instead of her backpack as he took a few steps and then stopped to glance back at her.

"Coming?" he asked, although it sounded more like a command than a question.

"Yep." Shayla snagged her scattered wits together and walked past him. She led the way through the trees, up the hill, and down the other side to where she'd parked her car.

The entire walk, which took about twenty minutes, Bridger never said a word.

Since he remained mute, so did Shayla.

"There's my car," she said, pointing to where she'd parked her SUV off the road out of the way. The need to point it out was unnecessary since there wasn't another vehicle to be seen for miles around.

"Do you live in Holiday?" Bridger asked in his deep voice. A voice that Shayla wouldn't mind listening to with frequency. The thought of waking up to that voice or falling asleep to it as it caressed her name almost made her trip over a tree root. Thankfully, she caught herself before she required Bridger's assistance a second time.

"I do. I moved here eight years ago for work. It's a great town. I fell in love with it right away. The people are so nice, and it's a really close community. It's grown a lot recently. I'm currently employed at the retirement home in Holiday." When she was nervous, she tended to babble. Like now. She was definitely babbling. "The people there are so friendly. If you're ever in the neighborhood, drop by. It's the only retirement place in town and not hard to find. In fact, they have nice meeting facilities. Many people in town use the conference room for various reasons. There have even been several weddings held in the courtyard too. That's mostly because of the matchmakers. If you aren't married, you might want to avoid letting them know. Matilda and Ruth will have you set up on a date faster than you can run the other direction."

By sheer determination, she pressed her lips together, willing the words to stop pouring out of her mouth.

Bridger didn't appear to be concerned or even notice her nonstop chatter as she stepped behind him and fished her keys from the front pocket of the backpack. She pushed a button on the key fob, and the hatch on the back of her SUV lifted.

She would have relieved him of the backpack, but she didn't know how to do that without making things even more awkward between them. He set the backpack in her vehicle, then stepped back. He moved into a position that looked like an officer had just commanded him to stand "at ease," with his hands behind his back, head and posture straight.

He was definitely a military guy. Not that she'd been around a lot of them, but she watched them in her weekly police shows. Everything about this dude hollered military experience.

"Thanks for carrying my stuff and packing up my camp." Although she wasn't particularly grateful that he'd caught her nearly naked, then insisted she leave immediately, she was glad he'd carried her heavy backpack for her.

A dozen questions tangoed on the end of her tongue, eager to swing out, but she held them back. Bridger was definitely the strong, silent type, not a gregarious soul who dished about his entire life five minutes after meeting him. The way he'd packed up her camp and escorted her to her vehicle made it strikingly clear he wanted her gone.

Now.

She'd been evicted and evacuated without a bit of ceremony.

He tipped his head toward her. "You're welcome, Miss Reeves. Drive safely back to town."

"I will. And please, call me Shayla." Shayla closed the hatch on her SUV and stared at the good-looking, mysterious man. "Would you be willing to tell me your whole name?"

His gaze met hers, and she experienced that same zinging feeling she'd noticed earlier when he'd caught her arms. What was it about this guy that got to her?

"Yes, ma'am. It's Bridger Holt."

She ignored that he'd called her ma'am instead of miss. "Bridger Holt. That's a nice name," she said smiling at him as she nervously toyed with her keys. "Is your wife staying out here with you, Mr. Holt?"

"Nope. No wife. No kids. Just me. Call me Bridger." He gave her another observant look. "Where's your husband?"

"Don't know, since I haven't met the right fella yet." She leaned toward him slightly. "Just don't tip off those matchmakers I mentioned earlier, or I'll never get any peace."

Bridger broke into a smile. It was like sunshine bursting through the clouds on a stormy day. His whole face brightened, and delight twinkled in his eyes. "Maybe I should get their names and numbers, just in case you decide to trespass again."

Shayla offered him a look of mock indignation and fisted her hands on her hips. "You wouldn't dare."

He winked at her and took another step back toward the trees. "It was nice to run into you, Shayla Reeves."

"It was ..." A noise that sounded like a bear barging through the brush cut off her sentence and drew their gazes to a spot across the road. A gangly dog raced into view. It looked like it was mostly a chocolate lab with maybe some German shepherd mixed in. The poor thing was skin and bones and was bleeding from a gash. It whined and woofed, as though it was glad to see a human.

Bridger stiffened and glowered at her. "You were just going to go off and leave your dog? What did you do to the poor guy? Haven't you been feeding him? Look! He's bleeding!"

Shayla narrowed her gaze and opened the back door of her SUV, digging out the first aid kit she kept in a plastic storage box beneath the front seat. "First of all, that is not my dog. I've never seen it before in my life. Second, if it were my dog, he'd be healthy, happy, and content, not looking like he's been abandoned and starved. Third, I'm insulted you think I could treat any living thing with such neglect."

Bridger offered her an apologetic look. "Sorry."

She opened the back of the SUV and set the box down.

Bridger moved close enough he could look over her shoulder into her collection of medical supplies. "Are you a doctor?"

She tried to ignore the warmth of his presence and the fresh, outdoorsy, masculine scent of him. "Nurse."

"Great. I'll catch the dog. You'll treat the cut?" he asked.

"That's my plan." Shayla took out the supplies she needed, set them within easy grasp, then took a bottle of water from the stash she had in the back. She removed the cap and nodded at Bridger.

He hunkered down and pulled something from one of the many pockets of his pants. Shayla realized it was a little bag of jerky. He held out a piece of the dried beef toward the dog and waited.

It only took a few seconds for the dog to snatch the bite of meat, gulp it down, and eagerly wait for more.

Bridger took out another piece and held it out to the animal. When the dog took it, he gently placed a hand on the canine's head.

The dog glanced at Bridger but didn't react, other than to wag his tail. Bridger dumped the rest of the jerky onto his palm and fed it to the dog, placing his arm around the animal to keep it from escaping. He pulled the dog against him, holding it securely.

Shayla knelt down and began washing the dog's wound, although he really needed a bath. The poor thing stunk to high heaven, like he'd rolled in something dead.

Thank goodness the stench wasn't from an infection in his wound. In fact, the wound was so fresh, she was sure the dog had sustained it within the past hour. Most likely, he'd tangled with a sharp stick or something along those lines.

He had no collar, but he seemed like a sweet dog, especially when he kept trying to lick Bridger's chin. Shayla tried not to laugh, but she couldn't hide her grin as the dog managed to drag his slobbers across Bridger's neck.

"Whew! He is ripe!" Bridger wrinkled his nose and held his face up so the dog couldn't reach it with his slobbery tongue.

"He could certainly use a bath," Shayla agreed, taking shallow breaths as she rinsed the wound and decided it wasn't as deep as she originally anticipated. Some ointment applied two to three times daily would be all he needed.

"Stitches aren't required, but he'll need to have ointment applied to the cut for a few days."

"Don't tell me." Bridger shook his head as he continued petting the dog. "He's not my pet. Why don't you take him home with you?"

"No and no. I rent a house, and the landlord has a clear no-pets policy. It's a nice house in a great location with low rent. I'm not doing anything to mess that up. Besides, I spend four very long days at work every week and would hate to think of this poor boy stuck at home, unable to get out. He needs to be with someone who can take him for long walks and let him run off his energy." Shayla wiped her hands on a disposable wipe, then rubbed the dog's head. He looked like he'd found his version of doggy nirvana as he leaned against Bridger. The man scratched behind his ears and beneath the dog's chin.

Since Bridger obviously wanted her gone, and now that she smelled like dog, she was ready to head home. She did have some cleaning and errands she should take care of today, even if she'd rather have spent one more day camping.

She stepped away, wiped her hands again, and returned the medical supplies to the box but left out the tube of ointment. Shayla held it out to Bridger.

He stared at it like it was something diseased.

She waggled it at him. "If you don't want to keep him, I can drop him off at the pound, although I hate to do that."

"No. I'll take care of it." Bridger straightened and took the ointment from her. The way he spoke left her uncertain if he meant he'd adopt the dog and give it the attention he needed, try to find the dog's owner, or if he planned to do something terrible and horrible, like shoot the poor thing. She couldn't quite picture Bridger being that cold-hearted and assured herself leaving the dog with him was the right thing to do as she opened her door and slid behind the wheel.

The dog whined and looked up at her with big, sad eyes as she started the vehicle.

She almost wavered. Almost hopped out and opened the back door for the dog to join her. But she didn't.

When she looked up at Bridger as he stood close enough she could reach out and touch one of those impressive muscles, she saw the slightest hint of a smile on his all too kissable lips.

"Next time you want to go camping on my property, ask first."

Shayla was encouraged he hadn't told her she was never welcome to return. Next time meant she'd see him again. Part of her silently rejoiced at the prospect. "Take good care of our new friend."

"I'll try." Bridger rubbed his hand over the dog's head as he took a step back and shut her door. He lifted a hand and waved once before he whistled to the dog and smacked his hand on his thigh, encouraging the canine to follow him. They took off through the trees.

All the way home, Shayla wondered when she'd have the opportunity to encounter the intriguing Bridger Holt again.

Chapter Five

Bridger glanced down at the pathetic canine that trailed after him as he walked back to the cabin.

As soon as he'd awakened that morning, he'd decided to investigate who was camping on the other side of the lake, if anyone was.

He'd started to head out as the first fingers of light stretched across the sky, then changed his mind, wanting to give the person time to wake up.

After frying three eggs and sausages for his breakfast and drinking a tall glass of orange juice, he'd added a few things he thought might come in handy to the pockets on his cargo pants, like a zip tie, his hunting knife, and a taser gun, along with a few snacks, and a bottle of water. He preferred to be prepared rather than get taken by surprise. If it came down to hand-to-hand combat with an assailant, he was confident in his abilities to triumph, thanks to training and brute strength. However, he wasn't cocky enough to think there weren't unforeseen risks. He'd done his best to have contingency plans in place before he set out on the hike.

He'd breathed in the morning air, so fresh and green and vibrant with spring, as he journeyed around the perimeter of the lake. He followed a trail he assumed was made by deer or other wildlife. As he walked, he wondered if the fawn resting beneath the maple tree was truly an orphan. It hadn't left the cabin that he'd noticed, and he hadn't seen a mother anywhere either. If the fawn was still there this afternoon, he intended to start feeding it.

When Bridger had found the campsite, he'd assumed, because of the small tent and scant supplies, only one person was there. In a quick glance, he'd concluded the person didn't seem up to anything unlawful, other than trespassing. A splashing sound from the lake had drawn him there. He'd mutely stood in the shadows of a big pine tree, watching as a woman walked out of the water with the rising sun behind her, nearly blinding him.

But what he'd seen—golden skin and long legs that went on for days—had left him flustered and feeling like he'd just tried to swallow a mouthful of sawdust. He'd turned around and kept his back to her as she'd dried off. He counted a hundred Mississippi's before he glanced over his shoulder. It had taken a great deal of self-control not to laugh aloud at the vision the woman made with a huge towel wrapped around her and her hair in a tangle of wet snarls. She had a sweatshirt tucked under one arm and wore hiking boots that clump-clumped with each step she took; since she hadn't bothered to lace them up.

It had also taken self-control not to kiss her, with her dewy skin glistening in the early morning light.

Bridger wasn't a ladies' man. Far from it. He wasn't into flings or meaningless encounters. Nevertheless, the sight of the woman's fresh face, with freckles skipping across her nose and a smile on her rosy lips, made him want to sweep her into his arms and see if she tasted as sweet as she looked.

He'd followed her, making enough noise she should have thought a whole herd of elk was about to enter her camp. Then she'd tripped, he'd caught her, and everything in his world had seemed to turn end over end.

A feeling, one completely foreign to him, had settled into his chest as he gazed into mesmerizing brown eyes that snapped with life and energy.

Shayla Reeves wasn't the most beautiful woman he'd ever seen. She leaned more toward cute, but there was something in her lovely smile that transformed her from attractive to breathtaking. Her face was expressive, and her skin smooth and soft, at least what he'd felt when he'd grasped her arms to keep her from falling when she'd tripped. He liked that she was taller, although he stood a good five inches over her.

He hadn't been surprised to learn she was a nurse. She possessed what he'd always thought of as a nurturing spirit. Bridger's grandpa had been like that. He wondered if his ancestor Evan Holt had also been that way.

At any rate, with Shayla standing there in nothing but a towel, and him thinking thoughts he had no business contemplating, he'd decided the best thing to do was get her off his property as fast as possible. When she'd disappeared into the tent to dress, he'd poured a cup of coffee just to keep himself distracted.

As soon as she was dressed, he knew he had to get away from her, but he couldn't very well march off and leave her there, so he'd packed up her camp. He'd had a wealth of experience in breaking down and packing up in a matter of minutes when he was in war zones overseas. He was sure she thought he was rude and pushy, but that was probably for the best. Maybe then she'd stay away from Holiday Lake and him.

He was just here for the summer to get his head on straight and decide what he wanted to do with the rest of his life. He had zero—as in zilch and nada—interest in getting involved in a relationship with anyone or anything.

Except, after finding the half-starved dog, it looked like he was now the caretaker of a needy pet. He'd already decided to adopt the fawn, and he'd been feeding the chatty squirrel.

Bridger had never owned a pet. Growing up, his mother claimed they devalued a property with holes and messes. He and his brother had never even been allowed to have a goldfish. Of course, Uncle Wally had plenty of animals at the farm, but it wasn't the same as owning his own pet.

In truth, the dog looked like he'd be a good one, once he was clean and put on some weight.

It was possible the dog had wandered off from his home, but Bridger figured he'd probably been dumped in the woods. That happened far more often than any decent person cared to consider.

He was sure the dog hadn't belonged to Shayla, but he wanted to test her, see what she'd say. As she'd tenderly cleaned the dog's wound, he'd been assured she was a softie, even if she didn't want to take the dog home with her.

Bridger couldn't bear the thought of the poor canine being taken to the pound where his days would likely be numbered. Most people wanted an adorable puppy, not a full-grown eating and pooping machine.

When Shayla had climbed into her SUV, Bridger had to dredge up every ounce of resistance to keep from leaning inside the open door and kissing her like he longed to do.

Now, as he strode toward the cabin with the dog keeping close to him, he wondered at what moment this morning he'd lost his mind. Because right now, all he wanted was to drive into town, find Shayla, and keep her talking so he could spend hours listening to that sultry voice of hers. That was certifiably insane in his book. He didn't know her, didn't know anything about her. It was foolish to even give her more than a passing thought. He'd do well to forget ever encountering her.

Bridger entered the cabin through the back door, gathered a few things, and changed into an old pair of shorts. He didn't bother with a shirt, assuming his plans would end with him completely soaked and in need of a shower.

He carried his supplies down to the water's edge where it was shallow. The dog trailed after him like he was his new best friend. He doubted the canine would feel the same way after Bridger got through giving him a bath.

"Well, pooch, let's get you cleaned up, then we'll see about feeding you a decent meal. What do you say?"

The dog wagged his tail as he plopped down beside him like he was about to get a treat.

Bridger wasn't sure how to proceed, since he'd never given a dog a bath before, but he removed his shoes, grabbed a bottle of dish soap and a rag, then stepped into the water. Slowly, he backed up, while speaking in low, calm tones to the dog.

"Come on in, pooch. The water is refreshing. You might even catch a fish or two."

The dog sat up and whined, took a few steps forward until his front paw touched water, then he plopped back down and whined some more.

Bridger made a kissing sound and smacked his free hand on his thigh. "Come on, boy. Come on!"

The dog stood and pranced one way then the other before he made another whining sound. All at once, he leaped forward into the water with a splash that soaked Bridger.

He laughed and put a hand on the dog, drawing him closer to him. They weren't in deep water. In fact, the dog could still touch the bottom, so Bridger hurried to squirt soap on his back and start scrubbing. He was careful around the wound, then realized he shouldn't have brought the dog into the lake water. What if there was a parasite or something that got into the cut? Concerned by his error, he determined he'd call the veterinarian in Holiday as soon as he finished the task and see if the vet would need to treat the dog.

Once the mutt got used to the water, he didn't seem to mind the bath. In fact, he acted like a playful puppy by the time Bridger finished scrubbing and rinsing him.

When Bridger walked out of the lake and picked up an old towel, the dog raced over to him, making a happy, yipping sound.

Bridger knelt in the grass and wiped away the water clinging to the dog's coat. Once he was dry, Bridger got the dog to follow him around to the back door of the cabin. In the bathroom, he dabbed the ointment Shayla had given to him over the wound. The dog winced once but didn't try to run or bite him.

"Good boy! You are a trooper." Bridger ruffled the dog's ears and gave him a few good scratches on his back. "How about we set you up with some food and water? If you don't object, I'll bring it in here. That way, it'll be easy to clean up if you spill."

Bridger went to the kitchen and found two plastic bowls that would have to do for the time being. He filled one with water and the second with chunks of beef he'd seasoned to make a stew for dinner that night. He figured the dog needed the protein.

He'd barely set the bowl of meat down when the dog stuck his head in it and started gobbling the meat.

Bridger let him eat in peace while he took a quick shower and changed his clothes. By the time he finished dressing, the dog had eaten all the meat and drank most of the water. Bridger didn't want him to eat too much and make himself sick, but he'd find something else to feed the dog in an hour or so.

Quickly refilling the water bowl, he returned it to the spot by the empty food dish. He then folded a towel in half and laid it on the floor in a patch of sunshine. "Why don't you rest, pooch? We'll talk more in a while."

The dog circled the towel, sniffed it twice, then curled onto it and closed his eyes with what sounded like a contented sigh.

"Have a good nap, buddy." Bridger left the bathroom and went out on the front porch where he looked up the number of the vet and called. The person he spoke with seemed friendly and knowledgeable, assuring him the dog should be fine, but if he began to act sick, to bring him in. The vet encouraged him to continue applying the ointment a few times a day. No one had reported a missing dog, so the vet told him he could probably keep it if he wanted.

Bridger thanked the veterinarian and disconnected the call. He glanced out across the water. A month ago, he was finishing up his last few days in the Army and had no idea what he wanted to do with the rest of his life.

Here he was, in Holiday, at a fantastic cabin on a beautiful lake that belonged to him thanks to Uncle Wally's generosity, and it looked like he was about to become the owner of his first pet.

Unable to hold back his joy, Bridger smiled. The first thing he needed to do was give the dog a name. Maybe build a doghouse, and get one of those nice cedar beds for it. Right after he made another trip to town to pick up dog food.

His smile widened as he considered the possibility of running into Shayla. He sure wouldn't mind seeing her sunny smile again.

Chapter Six

"You're doing great, Mrs. Langley." Shayla patted the bony hand of the patient clinging to her arm. The woman had advancing dementia but remained mobile and able to get around without much difficulty. Twice a day, and sometimes three times if she could work it in, Shayla took Mrs. Langley for a walk around Golden Skies.

The courtyard was one of her favorite places to take patients for walks because it was beautiful in any season. The assortment of plants and flowers meant there was always something blooming. The location in the center of the facility ensured a patient couldn't run off easily.

Shayla pushed in the code to open the doors as they left the dementia wing and guided Mrs. Langley down the hall. She grinned at Fynlee Ford as she stood in the doorway of her office, holding her sweet baby boy. He'd arrived in January during a terrible snowstorm, but Ethan Beaumont Ford seemed to be thriving under the care of his doting parents.

Fynlee, an occupational therapist, had returned from maternity leave on a part-time basis. She worked three days a week at Golden Skies. Carson, her husband, took care of Ethan one day a week. The little one spent another day with his aunts and uncles, who took turns watching him. On the third day, the baby came to work with Fynlee and stayed with her grandmother, Matilda, and Carson's aunt Ruth. The two women lived at Golden Skies and had been best friends for years. Ruth's husband, Rand, also helped out when he wasn't busy with board meetings for the historical society or one of his other community projects. Ruth and Matilda were the notorious matchmakers who just couldn't seem to help themselves when it came to nudging people toward falling in love.

"Good morning, Fynlee." Shayla smiled at her friend and paused in her walk. Mrs. Langley grinned at the baby and reached out, wiggling his foot. Ethan giggled, and the old woman laughed. "Looks like Ethan is set to charm everyone today."

"Always. I'd better take him up to Grams and Aunt Ruth. They have their day with Ethan all planned out."

"It's fabulous they get to spend one day a week with him," Shayla said, pleased to see Mrs. Langley entranced by the baby. All too often, the woman showed no interest in anything.

"They love it, and it's handy for me to be able to dash upstairs to check on him." Fynlee kissed her son's rosy cheek, and the baby chortled, waving his hand in the air. "Enjoy your day, Shayla."

"I will." Shayla took Mrs. Langley's hand in hers, gently pulling the woman forward. "See you later."

Outside, Mrs. Langley wandered around the courtyard, sniffing fragrant blooms and fingering the leaves of a tree. From what Shayla knew, the woman had once been a master gardener and spent inordinate amounts of time coaxing her yard into a fantastic display of blooms.

Dementia was such a strange disease, affecting everyone differently. Shayla wondered if somewhere in Mrs. Langley's mind she remembered her love of flowers.

When the woman took a seat on a chair, face turned to the sun, Shayla joined her. "It's a lovely day, Mrs. Langley. I can't believe how warm it is for it only being May. Then again, June will be here soon."

"I married in June. Beneath the rose arbor. My granny said she'd never seen a more beautiful wedding or bride," Mrs. Langley said, reaching down to pick a sprig of lavender that grew near her chair.

Shayla offered the woman an encouraging look. It wasn't often Mrs. Langley spoke, and when she did it was usually nonsense. At the moment, she seemed lucid, though.

"What color were the roses, Mrs. Langley?" Shayla asked, hoping to keep her patient's mind focused on reality for a few moments.

"Pink. They were pink and delicate, so pretty for a wedding. My aunt had cinnamon pinks growing like wild weeds behind her house. We filled baskets with them and placed them around the yard. The scent was divine." The woman closed her eyes and drew in a deep breath, as though she could still smell the fragrance. When she opened her eyes, she grinned. "A bee lingering by the flowers stung my sister-in-law. She deserved it. That little hussy was never anything but trouble."

Shayla smiled. "Did you have any siblings, Mrs. Langley?"

"Two older brothers and a younger sister. Don was killed at Midway, and Danny died in Germany during World War II. My mama never recovered from losing them, or my daddy. Merlene, my sister, was only five when the war ended." Mrs. Langley sighed. "I sure miss them. Don and Danny were such fun."

"What were some of the things they used to do?"

Mrs. Langley opened her mouth to speak, but before she could a blank look settled in her eyes. Her glance darted around the flowers surrounding them, giving her a lost appearance.

"Let's get you back inside, Mrs. Langley." Shayla helped the woman to her feet and guided her inside.

The morning passed in a blur of activity, and by the time Shayla took her lunch break, the afternoon was half gone.

Sage James, a lovely woman who'd been the receptionist at the facility for several years, popped into the break room and sat down at the table with a glass of water and a snack bag of grapes.

"Want one?" she asked, holding the bag out to Shayla.

"Thanks." Shayla took a grape, bit into the juicy orb, and decided it tasted more like candy than fruit. "Did you get those here in town?"

"Yes. They had a sale at the grocery store when I was there yesterday. These looked too delicious to resist. Shane ate half the bag last night after dinner. He's going through another growth spurt. Justin and I can hardly keep him fed."

Shayla grinned, thinking of Sage's teenage brother she was raising. The boy would be a big man when he finished growing, and a handsome one too. Most importantly, he was a nice kid with a big heart and a good head on his shoulders, thanks to Sage's influence.

"What are Shane's summer plans?"

"He's going to work at the Flying B again this year." Sage popped another grape into her mouth.

The past few summers, Shane had worked for Carson and Fynlee at their ranch. It had been a true learning experience for the boy, but he always seemed eager to work there as soon as school released for the summer.

"You've said how much he loves working at the ranch, and that he's learned more than you could have imagined. Sounds like a win to me."

"It is. Carson keeps him busy and pays a good wage. I don't have to worry about Shane getting bored or into trouble like kids who have nothing to do with their time."

"He's a great kid, Sage. I don't think you have to worry."

"Thank you." Sage sighed. "I know he's a wonderful young man, but I do worry."

Shayla nodded. She had no idea what it would be like to raise a sibling or a child. She'd always thought she'd fall in love and get married, raise a family of her own someday. But the years seemed to be rolling by, and she had no prospects in sight, even though she was getting close to thirty.

A picture of Bridger Holt popped into her head, but she mentally swatted it away. The man wasn't her type. For the most part, she was a lighthearted, upbeat person. She couldn't picture being with someone who rarely smiled and acted so serious all the time. Then again, she'd only spent an hour around him the other day. But what an hour it had been!

She was still mortified he'd caught her wearing nothing but a towel and hiking boots. He probably thought she was some sort of eccentric idiot.

"Did you hear someone moved out to the cabin on Holiday Lake?" Sage asked as she fingered another grape, then slid the bag over to Shayla.

"I did hear that. In fact, I met him the last time I went camping."

Sage stopped with the grape almost in her mouth and lowered her hand. "Do tell."

Shayla shrugged and took three grapes from the bag, setting them next to her half-eaten sandwich. "Apparently, I'm dumber than I give myself credit for sometimes. The past three years when I thought I was camping at Rockdale Lake, I was actually at Holiday Lake."

"What?" Sage asked, giving Shayla a concerned glance. "How did you manage that?"

"I guess I read the map wrong that first time I went out to camp there. I followed a Forest Service road, but evidently, it wasn't the right one. There's a wide spot in the road where several cars could park. From there, it was a relatively easy hike over a hill to the lake."

"But Rockdale Lake is at the big campground about ten miles from here, heading north up the mountain. You don't have to hike to it. There's a big parking area and restrooms with showers."

"Yeah. I kinda looked all that up when I got home after Mr. Holt escorted me off his property."

Sage raised an eyebrow. "Mr. Holt? Is he old? Young? Was he mean? Did he threaten you? I could send Justin to go talk to him."

Shayla shook her head. "No, he wasn't mean. Just surprised me. I thought he was a bear stomping through the woods. Then, in the time it took me to finish drinking a cup of coffee, he packed up my stuff. He carried my backpack and escorted me back to my SUV." Shayla sighed, recalling for the hundredth time how it felt when Bridger's hands connected with her bare arms. It was almost ... electric.

"And?" Sage prompted. "Age? Looks? Did you get his full name?"

"Bridger Holt. He's young. Probably our age, although he acts older. From the way he carries himself and his haircut, I'd say he's military. He never did get around to telling me why he was there, but he made it clear the property was private. He did say the next time I wanted to camp there, to ask first. Oh, and as I was leaving, this starving dog ran up to us. He looked like he'd been dumped in the woods. Bridger tried to get me to keep the dog, but I told him the best I could do was leave it at the pound, so he said he'd take care of it. I've been a little worried about what that meant. You don't think he'd shoot the dog, do you?"

"Did he act like someone who'd do that?" Sage asked, finishing the last grape.

"No. He helped me put some ointment on the dog and seemed interested in it. Bridger, I mean Mr. Holt, seemed like a person who needed a friend, even if the friend has fur and four legs."

"Then the dog is probably fine. Why don't you call and check on it?"

Shayla sighed. "I would if I had Bridger's number. He didn't bother to share it with me."

"Then drive out there on your day off. The dog gives you an excuse, doesn't it?" Sage stood and rinsed her hands at the sink, then grinned at Shayla. "You shouldn't waste opportunities to hang out with a hunky guy who's turned your head."

Shayla scowled. "My head has not been turned, and I never said he was hunky."

Sage laughed. "Nope. You didn't. But the way your face just turned red said all I needed to know. Keep me posted. I'll want to hear more about your mysterious Mr. Holt."

"He's not my mysterious Mr. Holt. He's not my anything."

Sage offered her a knowing look as she stood in the doorway. "You keep telling yourself that, my friend."

Shayla wadded up her paper napkin and tossed it at Sage, listening to the woman laugh as she headed down the hall back to the reception desk.

Just because she couldn't get Bridger out of her head didn't mean she was desperate to see him again. Although Sage did have a point.

Someone should go out there and check on the dog. Who better to make sure the dog's wound was healing than a registered nurse?

Shayla grinned as she walked over and picked up the napkin. On her next day off, she intended to drive out to the lake. The worst that could happen was Bridger would kick her off the property—again.

Chapter Seven

Bridger hustled across the parking lot at the grocery store, grabbed a cart at the door, and rushed inside. Cool air engulfed him and he released a long breath, trying to remember everything on the list that he'd accidentally left on the counter back at the cabin.

Earlier, he'd picked up more dog food at the feed store for Ubu, the name he'd given his adopted canine. Every time he said the name, it made his heart happy—a feeling he'd known far too little of in recent years. Uncle Wally had watched old reruns that ended with a screenshot of a dog with a frisbee and a guy saying "Sit,

Ubu. Sit." Bridger had always liked the name, and it fit his playful dog well.

Ubu loved stopping by to see Piper and Colt at Milton Feed, since they always gave him a treat. It was as if the dog thought they were there just to lavish him with attention. Then again, Piper had a deep love for all animals and had many rescue pets at home.

After the feed store, Bridger had taken Ubu to the veterinarian's office. The vet was going to check the cut that had nearly healed, and give the dog the necessary shots for continued good health since they had no idea if he'd had any shots at all. The vet's assistant assured him he had plenty of time to run to the store while they took care of Ubu.

Bridger started with the produce aisle, choosing a variety of fruits and ingredients for a few salads, and then added several ears of fresh corn to his cart. He hadn't eaten corn on the cob for what seemed like ages and couldn't wait to bite into the golden kernels, dripping with butter.

He chose several pantry staples, grabbed milk and eggs, then loaded up on meat including three packages of steaks, and a pound of smoked sausages. After selecting several small containers of ice cream, and a bag of frozen French fries, he added bottles of juice and soda to the cart and headed for the register. He was nearly there when he remembered he was almost out of laundry soap and turned around. Due only to his quick reflexes, he avoided colliding with Shayla Reeves.

The woman had lingered in his mind during the day and danced through his dreams at night since the morning he'd escorted her off his property. He'd tried convincing himself he didn't need the complications of a relationship and should avoid her.

Yet seeing her in a pair of navy and pink Hawaiian-print scrubs with her messy bun about to slide off one side of her head made him long to drink in the sight of her. To lean on his cart and listen to her talk about everything and nothing. To experience the warmth of her presence. When she glanced up and noticed he was the one who'd nearly bumped into her, she offered him a genuine smile, as though pleased to see him.

A little horizontal line formed above her upper lip as she smiled, and he wondered what she'd do if he kissed it. Or maybe pressed his lips to the mole on her neck, located above a pulse that seemed to be beating quite rapidly.

"Hey, sorry about that, Miss Reeves," Bridger said, backing up so she could push her cart around him. From the contents of her cart, it looked like she'd hit the produce aisle and the ice cream section. He noted she appeared to also enjoy black cherry ice cream.

She shook her head. "I thought you agreed to call me Shayla, and it's not a big deal, Mr. Holt."

"Bridger. And I do apologize. I wasn't paying attention. I left the dog at the vet's and was rushing to get back, but I forgot laundry soap."

Shayla's smile faded and she took a step closer to him. "Is he okay? The dog, I mean. Did his cut get infected? I was sure with it up high on the back of his neck where he couldn't lick it, he'd heal just fine."

"He did heal well. I just took him in for some basic vaccinations since I don't know what he's already been given, if anything." Bridger felt his feet shuffling closer to Shayla, as though his brain and body had disconnected. There was no wisdom at all in dating the woman, especially when he had no idea how long he'd be in Holiday. Besides, he was a loner. Always had been. Likely always would be. Guys like him didn't form attachments, especially not to a sweet girl like Shayla, who was a people person, thriving on personal interactions.

A look of relief settled on her face. A face Bridger was finding more and more beautiful with every passing second.

"I'm so glad he's fine. It's probably a smart idea to have him vaccinated. I don't think it would hurt anything if he ended up having some shots twice."

"That's what the vet said." Bridger forced himself to push his cart a few steps forward. "I should probably get going."

Shayla offered him a studying glance he had no hope of interpreting. "I'm glad you ran into me."

He smiled. "Again, my apologies. At least I didn't break your eggs since you don't have any in the cart."

"Next on my list," she said, still holding his gaze. "Have a great evening, Bridger."

He nodded and rushed off to the aisle with the household supplies, grabbed laundry soap, bleach, and dish soap, then raced back to the check-out line.

As he set items on the conveyor belt, he glanced back and noticed Shayla in line directly behind him. She'd added yogurt, eggs, and cottage cheese to her cart.

"Would you like to come to the cabin on your next day off?" he asked as he set a bag of grapes and a container of strawberries on the conveyor. He felt as surprised as she looked by the invitation.

"Actually, I'd love that. I have the next three days off. Would one of them work for you?"

"Tomorrow." Bridger had no idea what had possessed him to invite her to the cabin, but now that he had, he felt a little frisson of excitement at the prospect of spending time with her.

"What time should I be there?"

"Is nine too early for you?"

Shayla grinned at him as he set the last of his items on the conveyer and then pushed the cart ahead so the bagger could load the groceries. "You're kidding, right? My days usually begin before five."

"Really?" Bridger gave her an appraising glance. He should have known with her outgoing, perky personality she'd be a morning person. He rose early because he liked the quiet, not necessarily because he bounded out of bed eager to begin the day.

"May I bring something?" she asked as she took a step closer to him. One more step and he'd be able to count the number of freckles dotting her nose.

"Nope. But wear your hiking boots. I thought you might like to explore."

Shayla's grin widened, and her eyes sparkled with excitement. "I would. Thank you for the invitation."

"You're welcome." Bridger hurriedly paid for his groceries, then grabbed the handles of the cart. "Have a great night, Shayla."

"I will. I definitely will."

Bridger knew he probably looked like an idiot, but he grinned all the way out to his pickup and was still smiling when he went to pick up Ubu.

Chapter Eight

"Good heavens!" Shayla yelped as her head connected with the roof of her SUV for the third time since she'd turned off the highway onto the path she'd learned was the road to Holiday Lake and Bridger's cabin. She'd stopped by the bakery to pick up something sweet to take with her and mentioned to the owner, Sunni, about Bridger and the lake.

Sunni had pointed out the cookies Bridger seemed to favor when he came in to order something and gave Shayla directions on where to turn to find the lake and Bridger's cabin as she bagged several cookies.

As the vehicle bounced over another rut, or maybe it was a tree root, Shayla started to wonder if she'd misunderstood Sunni's directions.

Just when she was considering finding a place to turn around, she saw the glimmer of water ahead. A dozen yards further and she could see the lake. She parked beside a big pickup, presumably Bridger's.

The hands she'd clenched around the steering wheel hadn't yet relaxed, so she spent a moment gathering her composure and looking out at the incredible scene before her. Towering trees, sunlight skimming the water, and blue skies looked like something from a painting. Bridger waved from where he and the dog walked across the dock back toward the cabin. She noticed a small boat tied to the end of the dock. She hadn't seen it there when she'd camped across the lake and wondered if Bridger had recently acquired it.

Shayla waved, then got out of the vehicle, lifting the bag from Sunni's bakery.

"I come bearing sweets," she said, grinning as the dog bounded over to her and whacked his tail against her legs.

"Look at you, boy. Don't you look all healthy and happy?" Shayla bent down and gave the dog a few good rubs along his back and behind his ears before she glanced up at Bridger. "He's like a completely different dog. You must be feeding him well for him to fill out this much in just a few weeks."

"He's been a bottomless pit when it comes to eating, but the vet said he's making up for lost time. He runs and plays so much I'm not worried about him getting heavy." Bridger smacked his hand against his thigh twice, and the dog went to sit beside him.

Shayla was impressed. "It appears you've already started obedience training."

"We're trying. I have a friend who worked with military dogs and picked up a few things from him." Bridger ruffled the dog's ears, and the canine looked like he was about to smile.

"Did you name him?" Shayla asked as the three of them started down the short path to the cabin.

"Ubu." Bridger cast a glimpse her way and shrugged. "Remember at the end of some of those old eighties shows, the guy says …"

Shayla laughed. "'Sit, Ubu. Sit.' Oh, I love it. What a fun name for him. He seems to like it."

In fact, the dog had plopped onto his hindquarters, obeying what he thought was her command when she'd said the word sit.

"You are such a good boy," Shayla said, cupping the dog's chin and scratching beneath it, earning several whacks with that big tail against her legs.

"Is that a bag from the bakery?" Bridger asked as they walked onto the porch.

Shayla took in an old wooden bench placed beneath a window and envisioned Bridger sitting there each evening, watching the sun drop into the horizon. The view of the lake from the cabin was nothing short of spectacular. She could well imagine the glorious scene the sunset on the water would create. Too bad she didn't have a single artistic cell in her body. It would have been a wonderful thing to paint or capture in a photograph.

Not that she'd be there at sunset. If Bridger didn't run her off before lunch, she assumed they'd be making great headway toward becoming friends.

Honestly, she'd been taken aback by his invitation. She might have declined it if she hadn't wanted to see the cabin so badly and spend time with Bridger.

"So, you own the cabin and the lake?" she asked. She'd never met anyone who owned a whole lake and was fairly certain she wouldn't again.

Bridger nodded and pushed open the door. Ubu trotted ahead, sniffing his way down a short hallway and disappearing. Shayla liked that Bridger had opened his home, and his heart, to the dog. She had a feeling they both needed the connection and companionship.

"Yep. My uncle passed in April. I inherited it from him. Actually, he's my great uncle, Wallace Holt. He brought me to the lake once when I was a kid. It was the best summer of my life."

Shayla glanced around the nicely furnished cabin, taking in big leather couches flanking the fireplace, heavy wooden tables, and lamps made of antlers. The furnishings gave the cabin a definite masculine vibe. The windows let in oodles of light, though. Combined with the Pendleton blankets tossed here and there and the homey touches, like family photos hanging on the walls, it felt warm and inviting.

She walked over to where three framed images hung above a small desk. They showed a soldier marching in front of a tomb in three different seasons. Shayla started to turn away, then noticed the man bore a striking resemblance to Bridger. If a growth of scruff didn't currently obscure his face, she would be better able to judge, but she was almost certain it was him.

"Is this you?" she asked, motioning to the photographs. Whoever had taken them had done a superb job.

"Yeah, it is." Bridger ran a hand across the back of his neck, as though he was embarrassed by the images.

"Where were they taken?"

"Arlington, Virginia. I, uh ..." He hesitated before he continued. "I spent two years as a tomb guard."

Shayla's eyes widened. "You were a guard at the Tomb of the Unknown Soldier?"

Bridger nodded. "That's right." He pointed to the bag she still held, abruptly changing the subject. "You mentioned sweets?"

"Oh, yes, I did. I brought some of Sunni's cinnamon buns, and some cookies to enjoy later."

"Sounds great. Do you want coffee, milk, water, juice, or tea with your bun?" Bridger stepped into a kitchen with pine cabinets and shiny new-looking appliances.

"Milk, please, and thanks." Shayla wanted to explore every inch of the cabin. She hoped Bridger would show her the rest of it before she left, or she might perish from curiosity.

He set two cinnamon buns on a plate and set it in the microwave to warm for a few seconds, then poured milk and set the glasses on the counter.

"Have a seat," he said, placing forks and napkins next to the milk glasses before he took the buns from the microwave. He slid one onto a plate and handed it to Shayla and kept the other as he settled onto a barstool next to her.

Much to her shock, he bowed his head and offered a brief word of thanks for the food and her presence at the cabin.

She waited until Bridger had taken two bites of the warm, gooey bun, then turned to face him. "Tell me what it was like. Being a guard. Are the stories true?"

"Stories?" Bridger asked, then took a long swig of milk.

"I read somewhere that once you become a guard, even when you finish your time of service, you have to live by a strict code of rules or get in big trouble. I also read that the guards live beneath the tomb and can't leave or talk to anyone while working as a guard."

Bridger grinned. "All rumors, started by goodness only knows who. Most of the guards live on the base that's within walking distance. Some are married and live in housing nearby. While we take pride and honor in our service as sentinels of the tomb, we don't have to pledge to live a certain way the rest of our lives."

"That's good." The article Shayla had read said the tomb guards lived like monks for the remainder of their lives or bore harsh consequences. She couldn't quite picture Bridger living a life of such strict seclusion.

Bridger grinned at her as he forked another bite of the bun. "I can almost see the wheels spinning in your head. What else do you want to know?"

"Did you really have to march in snow and rain or whatever came along?"

"Sure did. The tomb has been guarded continuously without exception since 1937. We walked in snow, sleet, rain, and searing sunshine. The worst was when we had a hailstorm. I got bruises this big," he held up his hand, holding his index finger and thumb together to indicate a circle about the size of a silver dollar, "all over my neck, back, chest, arms, and shoulders."

"That had to be rough." Shayla loved being outside, but she was admittedly a fair-weather girl. If the weather was too cold, too wet, too scorching, or too windy, she'd find something to do indoors to occupy her time. She couldn't begin to fathom what it would be like to have to stay out in a hailstorm. Not just be in it, but march back and forth without missing a step or changing expression.

Since she was one of those people who found it impossible to hide what she was feeling, she feared she'd never make it in the military, let alone as a guard.

She placed her hand on Bridger's arm, ignoring the spark the innocent contact sent skittering from her hand to her brain. "Thank you for your service, Bridger."

"Guarding the tomb was my pleasure. A great honor, actually."

She frowned. "An honor? How so?"

"You have to apply to be one of the guards. If you get accepted into the training program, it's rigorous and challenging. Many of the trainees drop out or fail to keep up. To earn a position as a guard is an honor, one I never took for granted. It's all about discipline and order, but I will never regret the time I spent doing it. It made me feel …" He paused, looking out the kitchen window at something only he could see.

Shayla wanted to prompt him but remained silent, waiting.

Bridger sighed and glanced at her before cutting another bite of the cinnamon bun. "It made me feel valued and needed."

Reluctantly, she lifted her hand from his arm and returned to eating her cinnamon bun.

"What were your shifts like?" she asked after a few moments of silence.

"Long."

When Bridger failed to elaborate, she playfully elbowed him in the side. "Long? How many hours did you work?"

"We worked twenty-four hours on, twenty-four off, but it was usually closer to twenty-six on. The twenty-four off is spent getting things in order for the next shift." He glanced at her, as though he knew what she was going to ask next. "Our uniforms had to be spotless, polished, precise. Everything is measured to within a miniscule fraction of an inch. When I first started, it took me thirteen hours to prepare my uniform for the following day. Polishing shoes to perfection took forever. Anyway, we did get a full day, sometimes two, each week to rest or do whatever."

"So, you had to march back and forth in front of the tomb for twenty-four hours straight?" Shayla gaped at him, wondering how he survived it.

"No. The guard changes frequently. In the summer, it's every thirty minutes. In the winter, it's every hour. Then at night, it's every two hours. When the guard changes, the commanding officer in charge comes out and inspects the guard coming on duty. If he meets approval, then he takes over guarding the tomb, and the other guard gets a break. There were generally a few groups of us, sorted by height, that worked on any given day."

At her confused look, he continued explaining. "Let's say I was on duty today and went on shift at eight this morning. Since it's summer, the guard changes every thirty minutes. If there were three of us on duty, I'd get an hour to rest between each turn. Then after we'd worked three or four hours, the second group would take over, and then the third. When the third finished, the first group would start over the rotation."

"Oh, I get it. You'd be on duty in two or so rotations in a twenty-four-hour period. I'm glad you didn't have to march for twenty-four hours straight." The moment she returned home, Shayla intended to look up videos about the soldiers who guarded the tomb. She had been sure Bridger had been, or remained, in the military, and she'd been correct.

"No one could do that and keep their sanity." Bridger took the last bite of his cinnamon bun, and finished his milk, then gave her an undecipherable look. "Thanks for bringing the sweets. I discovered Sunni's bakery on my first day in town. She has a talent for making delicious food."

"She does. I try to avoid going there often, or I'd never fit into my scrubs." Shayla slid off the barstool, carried her dishes to the sink, and started to wash them, but Bridger nudged her aside.

"I'll help. It will just take a second," she said, reaching for the soap bottle sitting on the edge of the sink.

"You can dry. The towel on the counter is clean." Bridger jutted his chin toward a blue-and-white-checked dish towel. It took no time for them to wash the few dishes they'd dirtied, dry them, and put them away.

Unable to curtail her curiosity, Shayla made a show of craning her neck toward the short hallway. "May I see the rest of the cabin?"

Bridger grinned and motioned for her to precede him.

"If I lived here, I'd feel like I was on a perpetual vacation," Shayla said, smiling at him as he showed her the storage closet beneath the stairs.

"It does feel a little like that. What about you? Where would you go if you could take a dream vacation?"

"Somewhere with flowers, and outdoorsy things to do, like hiking or boating, but also shopping and good restaurants. If it was near a beach, even better. Oh, my!" Shayla looked around a large, lovely bedroom decorated with a colorful Pendleton blanket bedspread on the king-sized bed and throw pillows. A bathroom located off the bedroom was spacious with a tub nicer than the one in her house, a big walk-in shower framed with thick timbers, a washer and dryer, and a bed by the door where Ubu slept.

Shayla didn't say anything, but she grinned as they moved past the dog and back into the living area. Bridger led the way up a set of stairs to a loft. He showed her the second bedroom and bathroom as well as the large open area where several boxes and trunks were stored.

"What's all this?" she asked, glancing at a trunk that had to be at least a hundred years old, if not more.

"My family history. Uncle Wally was good about preserving it, and he left me a note he wanted me to get to know my ancestors. I've been so busy getting settled in, I haven't had time to go through much other than a few boxes of photographs and three scrapbooks, but I'm looking forward to learning more about my Holt ancestors."

"Wasn't there a Doctor Holt?" Shayla asked, moving over to the window where she could look out at the lake. Three ducks landed on the water with such smooth, synchronized motions, it almost appeared choreographed.

"That's my ancestor. He grew up in Pennsylvania, where most of the Holt family, including my parents, still live. He came to Holiday before it was even a town and served as a doctor here his whole life. He had a house and practice in town. One of his early patients was a mountain man who gave him this property that included the lake when he passed. Evan wanted to preserve the beauty of Holiday Lake, so he set about buying as much property around it as he could."

"That makes sense," Shayla said, turning back from the window. "This cabin is new. Did he have a cabin out here?"

"Sure did. It's where my uncle and I stayed the first time I came to Holiday. According to Uncle Wally, several people in town came out and built that cabin for Evan when he announced his plans to wed his wife, Henley."

"That is so neat." Shayla walked back over to the stairs. "What happened to the cabin?"

"Between the age and the weather, and no one living in it for the better part of fifty years, it was falling down. Uncle Wally reclaimed as much of the wood as he could and used it in this cabin, like the cabinets in the kitchen and the timbers in the bathroom."

"It's so cool he did that." Shayla looked over her shoulder at Bridger as she made her way downstairs. The light shining in his eyes and the sheer breadth of his shoulders distracted her to the point she missed the last step and would have fallen if Bridger hadn't caught her around the waist and pulled her back against him.

The feel of his powerful arms around her made her experience, for the first time in her life, the inclination to swoon. Good grief! She'd obviously been listening to Ruth and Matilda with their matchmaking stories too often if the term swoon had now taken up residence in her vocabulary.

"Careful." Bridger's voice was barely above a whisper, but the deep timbre of his tone rumbled against her back where it touched his chest. A delighted shiver slid over her as she forced herself to move out of what could be considered an embrace.

Unsettled by his presence and his masculine, outdoorsy scent that pervaded her senses, she needed to put some distance between them before she did something completely stupid and insane, like throw herself back into his arms and kiss him. She'd been thinking about his kisses ever since the day they'd met. She wasn't wild about the scruff on his face, thinking it made him look brooding and dangerous, but there was no disguising the temptation of his full bottom lip.

When she realized she was staring at him, at his mouth, she whipped around and headed toward the door.

"Do you want to go for a walk?" Bridger asked as she opened the door and stepped outside.

"I do." Shayla turned and watched as Bridger whistled three sharp blasts. What sounded like a baby elephant stampeding through the house turned out to be Ubu as he raced out of the bathroom and into the living room.

Shayla laughed as the dog skidded on the floor and thumped into Bridger's legs.

"You are such a loveable, nutty mutt." Bridger patted the dog on the side.

Ubu gazed up at Bridger with a look of adoration. Shayla couldn't help but wonder if she'd borne the same expression when she'd looked at Bridger earlier. She hoped not. It was one thing for the dog to gaze at him with unbridled affection, but something else entirely for her to look at the gorgeous man that way.

It was unwise—crazy might be a better description—for her to entertain any thoughts about Bridger Holt. As far as she knew, he would be leaving soon and she'd likely never see him again. Pursuing any kind of a relationship with him would not end well. If she allowed herself to get any more involved with him, when she already felt such an inexplicable attraction to him, she knew her heart would be broken when he left.

Despite her head giving her loud, insistent advice, she blocked it out and smiled at him as he handed her a water bottle and stuffed a few things in the pockets of the cargo pants he wore.

Shayla recalled he'd worn something similar the day they'd met. Apparently, he was a man who liked to be prepared but wanted to keep his hands free. He also seemed to be a man who thought it necessary to iron his T-shirts and pants even though he was out in the woods. She'd seen an iron and ironing board tucked into the storage closet. Never had she met a man who not only knew how to iron, but apparently felt the need to iron everything he wore. The thought of him ironing his undies made her curious to see them.

Then thoughts of what that might lead to made her face flame with color.

Thank goodness, Bridger didn't seem to notice as he closed the door behind him.

"Ready to go?" he asked as they stepped off the porch.

"Lead the way," Shayla said, holding the cold water bottle to her face as she fell into step beside him. Together, they started up a hill that sat on one end of the lake.

As they walked, he asked about her job at Golden Skies, if Matilda and Ruth were making any headway in their current matchmaking efforts, and how she came to be in Holiday.

"I came for a job. Nothing too exciting. I loved it here, and now it feels like home."

"Where was home when you were growing up?" Bridger asked.

"Newberg, Oregon. It's south of Portland. My dad is a teacher at the middle school, and my mom is an accountant. I have one sister, Ciara; she's five years older. She and her very sweet husband, Jacob, live in McMinnville. He has his own roofing company. Ciara manages the books and appointments and takes care of their kiddos. Andrew is five, and Megan is three." Shayla sighed, missing her family. It had been a while since she'd seen them, and they'd always been close. "It's hard being away from them, especially the little ones, but we talk all the time, and do video calls once a week."

"That's great you stay in touch with them. I'm sure the kids miss you."

Shayla shook her head. "They barely know me, but we try to make a big deal about being together when I do get to visit them. In fact, Ciara and Jacob are planning to come for a visit this fall when work slows down for him."

"That's great." Bridger's long legs ate up the ground as they strode up a rise. Shayla was in good shape, but she felt out of breath by the time they reached the top.

She turned and looked at the spectacular view of the lake. "If I could see this view every single day, I would never get tired of it."

"I know. It's something, isn't it?" Bridger asked, standing just close enough she could feel the heat radiating from him. It wasn't even eleven yet, but the day was heating up.

In spite of the rising temperatures, it was about ten degrees cooler here than it was in town, due in part to all the trees and slightly higher elevation.

"If I owned this place, had this view, I don't think I'd ever leave." Shayla spread her arms wide and spun in a circle. "It's incredible!"

Ubu barked and bumped into her, knocking her over into the soft grass. She laughed and wrapped her arms around the dog, tilting her face so he couldn't land a slobbery canine kiss on her mouth.

Bridger held a hand out to her, and she clasped it with hers, feeling breathless when he easily tugged her to her feet.

"Over there is where the cabin used to be," Bridger said, pointing to a flattened area where a few rocks from the chimney's base remained.

"Do you ever come up here and wonder what it was like when your ancestors moved in? Maybe this is where he proposed to her? Do you think the cabin was a retreat for them? A place to get away from what I assume was a busy practice if he was the first doctor in town?"

Bridger shrugged as he toed over a rock. The only thing beneath it was a black bug that quickly skittered away. "I don't know. I assume they probably came out here to get away from the duties of serving the community. Henley was his nurse, I think, so she likely needed a break too."

"That's so neat she was a nurse," Shayla said, walking around. When something caught her eye in the dirt of what had once been the cabin's foundation, she used the tip of her fingernail to unearth a coin. After wiping away the dirt on the leg of her shorts, she held it up to try to read the date.

"What did you find?" Bridger asked, moving behind her.

"It looks like a dime." She squinted her eyes. "I think it says 1917."

Bridger leaned over her shoulder, and the scent of him made her mouth water. He stood so close, if she turned her head, she could easily press her lips against his cheek. She'd never kissed a man with a beard and wondered what that scruff would feel like against her lips. Before she crumbled to temptation, she handed him the dime.

He took a step back and examined both sides of the coin, then handed it back to her, placing it on her palm. That slight touch, when his fingers brushed across her skin, felt charged with sparks.

"Keep it. You found it. I think that's a Mercury dime. I have no idea what it's worth, but I know more than ten cents."

Shayla grinned and tucked the dime in her pocket. If nothing else, it would be a fun keepsake to remind her of a beautiful spring day spent in the mountains with a handsome man.

"What's back there?" she asked, pointing to an old building set back in the trees.

"A shop, of sorts," Bridger said. He followed when she started in that direction. "I think it was originally a small barn, probably somewhere to keep the horses if a team was driven out here, but Uncle Wally used it as a shop and a place to store tools."

Bridger pushed open the door, and Shayla stepped inside the large space. Light speared through the cracks in the walls and shone through a large window located high above the door. A workbench lined one wall, with shelves set above it holding an assortment of tools and cans filled with things like nails and bolts. Two stalls filled the back of the barn. One held an old two-seater sleigh in desperate need of repair. The second had an assortment of vintage tools and a few pieces of tack that looked like it might have belonged to Doctor Evan Holt for the way the old leather had cracked.

Shayla noticed a few stumps that appeared to have been burned; then she saw what she considered to be a masterpiece. A stump had been burned, sanded, sealed, and polished in such a way that it looked quite artistic.

"What's that?" she asked, pointing to it.

Again, Bridger rubbed a hand over his neck, like he was embarrassed. "It's a project I've been working on. I saw one in a gift shop in South Dakota. You basically take a stump, burn it, and shape it, and then seal it. I've been watching videos online. This is just a practice piece, but the idea is to add a piece of oval glass on top and turn it into a coffee table."

"You should order the glass and take this into town. Someone would happily buy it."

Bridger gave her a studying glance. "You really think someone would want it?"

"I do. And the perfect place to sell it would be one of the gift shops connected to the Lennox Historical Preservation Society. Kali Coleman is the director. Her husband, Trace, is part of the family that owns and manages Lennox Enterprises."

"I've heard of Lennox. It's run by the Coleman family?"

"Yep. I don't remember all the details, but Kali could fill you in. You really should go talk to her. She'd love to hear what you know about Doctor Evan and his wife. She lives and breathes Holiday's history."

Bridger stared at the artful piece of furniture he'd created, then looked back at Shayla. "Maybe I'll drop by to see her the next time I'm in town."

"You really should." Shayla ran her hand over the side of the table, the wood smooth beneath her hand. "Keep making these, Bridger. They are unique and fantastic. If you enjoy doing it, keep at it."

"I did have fun making it."

He waited for her to step outside, then closed the door behind him. Ubu chased a butterfly through the rich, green grass of the clearing, making Shayla laugh as she watched him.

"Shall we head back to the cabin?"

She hated to think of ending their time together so soon but didn't want to overstay her welcome.

They were nearly back to the cabin when a fawn trotted out of the trees and over to Bridger. He gave it a tender pat, and it leaned against him, offering Shayla a curious look.

"You have a pet fawn?" she asked, shocked to see the way the little deer trailed after the big man.

"That's Kit. He was here when I came to the cabin. I've kept a close eye out for his mother, but from what I can surmise, he doesn't have one. I've been feeding him and gentling him. I probably should do my best to keep him wild and wary of humans, but it's hard when he's so darn cute." Bridger rested his hand on the fawn's back.

A squirrel raced out to greet them as they approached the cabin, chittering excitedly as it sat on its back legs and looked like it was begging for a treat. Bridger pulled a peanut from his pocket and gave it to the squirrel. It took the treat and bounded off.

"That's Toby," Bridger said, then pointed to where two pheasants did a poor job of hiding in nearby brush.

"Tango and Crash are over there. The birds are Kit's self-appointed babysitters."

Shayla watched the pheasants for a moment, then gaped at Bridger. She pictured him as a loner, solemn and detached, but here he was with a woodland version of "Old MacDonald Had A Farm." Delighted, she smiled as she observed the two pheasants cautiously come out from beneath the brush, give a wide berth around her, then cozy up to the fawn on Bridger's other side.

"This is unbelievable," she said, kneeling in the grass and putting an arm around Ubu when he flopped down next to her.

"Believe it." Bridger grinned and winked at her as she scratched the dog's ears while he petted the fawn. "Is steak salad okay for lunch?"

"Better than okay," Shayla said, fighting back the urge to cheer that Bridger wasn't ready to get rid of her just yet.

He grilled steaks and cut the meat into thin pieces, then served it over tender baby greens with an assortment of toppings that included some of her favorites like cherry tomatoes, sliced avocadoes, and black olives.

"This salad is fantastic." She forked another bite. "Did you season the steak?"

"Marinade. A buddy in the Army came from a family that owned a steakhouse. He taught me all kinds of tricks and tips for getting the best flavor out of a piece of meat."

Shayla would have replied, but her mouth was full of the best steak she'd ever tasted.

After lunch, while Kit, Ubu, and the pheasants curled up in the shade of a maple tree to rest, she and Bridger lingered inside the cabin.

"Would you like to look through some trunks up in the loft?" Bridger asked, breaking the silence that had fallen between them. "I haven't opened them yet, so it could be a bit of a treasure hunt."

"I'd love to." Shayla practically raced upstairs, then stood with her hands held together in front of her, eager to dive in.

Two hours later, she looked around the keepsakes they'd unearthed in the first trunk they opened. They'd only gone through the one, but it was full of Evan and Henley's things. There was a porcelain-faced doll in a wooden box with a note from Henley about when she got it and where. There was also an outfit that had belonged to Henley's father who, according to Bridger, was a professional gambler. The brocade vest and fancy waistcoat with a silk tie certainly fit the image in Shayla's mind of a gambler.

There was also an old deck of cards, dog-eared on the corners, with a note from Henley saying it was a marked deck given to her by her father.

"How can you tell they are marked?" Shayla asked, afraid to touch the old, fragile cards.

"I have no idea. I'm not much of a card player." Bridger carefully turned the cards over, looking at the backs of a few, then he slid them back into the box they'd been in along with the note.

"You really should go visit Kali at the museum. If you have any inclination, I know she'd love to put some of these things on display. And if you don't want to do that, she'd still enjoy learning more about the Holt family. In fact, there's a photo of Doctor Holt that's going to be included in the auto museum."

"Auto museum? Where's it located? Is it open?"

"It's supposed to open in a few weeks. It's right across the street from the feed store. Rand Milton—he's Piper Ford's grandpa—owns the old garage. He has a collection of vintage cars and buggies. Kali convinced him to open a museum. He's been busy getting it ready, with the help of Kali and her staff."

"Sounds neat. I'll have to stop by when it opens."

Shayla fingered the dress on the doll, wondering if it was the original outfit as she set the fragile toy back inside the wooden box. "If you are looking for a job, last I heard, they were hiring."

Bridger didn't comment, so she let the thread of conversation drop. She rose from where she'd been sitting on the floor with the contents of the trunk spread all around them and went to look out the window.

"It's so beautiful here, Bridger. Like something out of a fairy tale."

"If it's a fairy tale, who are the characters?" he asked as he began repacking the trunk.

Shayla went over to help him. "I think you would be the beast. Tough and growling on the outside, but a big softie on the inside. The scruff on your face sort of feeds the beast theory."

Bridger brushed a hand over his jaw and smirked at her. "And you? Which fairy tale character would you be?"

"Hmm. That's a good question. I think I'd be Disney's version of Rapunzel. Did you ever see that movie?"

He tossed her a disparaging glance. "Even if I did, do you really think I'd admit it?"

She laughed. "Probably not. Anyway, Rapunzel was stuck in the tower, but once she got out, she was very social and outgoing. She loved to laugh and visit with friends, and she was good at connecting with people, even strangers. She was cheerful and upbeat. I guess I like to think of myself as being that way, at least most of the time."

"That's a good way to be, Shayla. From what I've seen, you are exactly like that. Open. Friendly. Easy to be around."

Bridger tucked the cards and a doll box back into the trunk, then closed the lid. "You really think the museum would want to have some of this stuff on display?"

"I really do. If you want a personal introduction to Kali, ask Sunni at the bakery. They are cousins. Sunni has three sisters and a brother. I work with one of her sisters."

"Good to know." Bridger headed down the stairs. "Can I interest you in a boat ride across the lake?"

"You certainly know how to sweep a girl right off her feet, don't you, big fella?" Shayla said in a teasing tone, batting her eyelashes at him in an exaggerated manner.

Bridger chuckled. "Romeo. That's me." He pushed open the screen door and followed her outside.

That evening, the two of them sat around a campfire, watching the last rays of the sun sink into the horizon. Bridger had roasted sausages on sticks for dinner; then they'd made S'mores. Ubu had tried to lick the sticky marshmallow residue off their fingers, while Toby the squirrel had made off with several pieces from a graham cracker.

It was one of the best evenings Shayla had ever experienced.

"I should get going," she said, reluctantly rising to her feet. "Thank you for the invitation to come out today."

Bridger stood and followed her over to her SUV. He opened the door for her, but Shayla wasn't quite ready to slide onto the seat. She leaned her back against the vehicle and smiled at Bridger. The man was complicated, quiet, and hard to get to know, but she had a feeling he would be worth every ounce of effort required to get past his lone wolf façade and to the intriguing man underneath.

Truthfully, he fascinated her. He didn't speak freely about himself or his life, but little by little, she was putting the pieces together. She'd found out more about him today than she'd anticipated. Then again, they'd spent the past twelve hours together and she'd enjoyed every minute of it.

It wasn't his outward appearance that enthralled her. Bridger could have been bald, homely, and short and it wouldn't have made any difference. There was something about him, about his heart, that spoke to hers in a way she'd never experienced.

Admittedly, it didn't hurt anything that he was tall, broad-shouldered, in prime physical condition, with haunting gray eyes, and a mouth simply made for kissing.

As though her thoughts became transparent, he moved forward and settled one big hand on her waist while the other gently cupped her cheek.

"You are something, Shayla Reeves," he said in a husky voice that caused a shiver to glide along her spine.

"Is that something good, bad, or weird?" She glanced up at him, wondering how shocked he'd be if she kissed him.

"Good. Very, very good," he murmured before his lips brushed across hers so softly, she thought she might have imagined it. Then the hand on her cheek slid to the back of her neck. He tipped her head back before he kissed her with enough heat it burned every other thought right out of Shayla's head.

She'd never been kissed like that. Never felt so alive, like every single cell in her entire being hummed with vibrant energy.

When Bridger finally raised his head, he gave her a slow, seductive smile, one that made her insides quiver.

"I'm glad you came out today, Shay. Maybe we can do this again sometime."

"I'd love that, Bridger. Thank you," she whispered.

With her knees weak and her thoughts muddled, she knew she needed to leave. Somehow, she managed to get into the SUV and settle behind the wheel without looking like a complete dork.

Bridger leaned in and kissed her cheek, grinning at her before he backed away. "Drive safely."

"I will. Good night."

Shayla's hands shook as she started the SUV and turned around. Even the bumpy, jarring drive back to the road did nothing to alter her euphoria. Bridger was an amazing kisser, and he tasted even better than she'd imagined, like chocolate and something dark and decadent.

Now that he'd kissed her, she had no idea how she'd continue to convince herself a relationship of any kind with him was senseless. Whether either of them wanted to admit or acknowledge it, a powerful attraction sizzled between them with enough force, she could practically see the sparks. When they'd kissed, she'd felt the electrical zap she'd experienced each time they'd accidentally brushed against each other all day, only with his lips crushed to hers the feeling had been intensified, magnified to an extreme.

Bridger had basically told her he'd be leaving, though. Besides, he was so quiet and withdrawn, so unlike her outgoing, friendly personality. Did they really have anything in common?

The best thing to do—the smart thing to do—would be to remain friends.

"Friends. Nothing bad can come of friendship," she assured herself as she turned onto the road and headed home. All she had to do was convince her heart of what her head insisted was the truth.

Chapter Nine

"Dude, you can't just spend all summer hiding out there by yourself, even if you have adopted a weird group of pets."

Bridger glanced behind him to where the two pheasants walked on one side of Kit while Ubu bounced around on the other, teasing Toby as the squirrel dashed back and forth from the stump he liked to sit on to the tree where he had a nest. Bridger turned his attention back to the computer screen and grinned at his friend Quinten.

"Seriously, man? If you could spend the summer here without having any responsibilities other than keeping the critters fed, would you want to leave?" Bridger turned his laptop around so Quinten could see the lake in all its glory with the morning light shimmering on the water.

Quinten whistled and shook his head. "You are so lucky, Holt. Okay, so maybe I would hang out there for a while and have no inclination to leave. But it's not good for you to be alone so much. Go into town. Make a friend. Eat dinner out. You need human interaction."

"Are you finally confessing you're an alien life form?" Bridger teased.

Quinten rolled his eyes and sighed. "Why do I even bother talking to you?"

"I've wondered that myself on numerous occasions." Bridger smirked at his friend, then grew somber. "I appreciate you, Quint. More than you know and more than I've expressed. You've been a true friend, and I'm grateful for you." He sighed. "And I know what you're saying. As a matter of fact, I have made a few friends that don't have four legs or feathers since I've been in Holiday."

"Really?"

"Yep. The couple who owns the feed store, Piper and Colt, are great. She takes in rescue animals, and he trains horses. Colt invited me to come over and ride sometime, and I will likely take him up on it. I miss being around the Caisson horses."

"That's good. Who else have you met?"

Bridger thought about the day he met Shayla, seeing her in a towel and hiking boots with that wild honey-brown hair in tangles. Even a glimmer of a memory from that day was enough to send his temperature spiking and his heart racing. A vision of those long legs as she walked out of the lake had given him more than one night of restless sleep.

Then there was last week when she'd come out and spent the day. It had been one of the nicest days he'd had in a long time. She'd looked so cute in a pair of hiking shorts, a bright pink shirt, and her hair in a ponytail as bouncy as her personality. He'd longed to reach out and catch the wavy tendrils of her hair in his hand to see if they'd be as silky as they looked.

He had hated to see her leave when the sun set, but knew it was for the best. Then he'd done something completely unwise and kissed her.

Not just a little kiss.

No.

Bridger had *really* kissed her, with his heart wide open. She'd kissed him back with enough passion and zeal that he'd forgotten everything but her until he'd felt Kit rub against his leg. That kiss had tormented and taunted him every time he closed his eyes.

However, Quinten didn't need to know all that.

"I met a nurse. She was camping here at the lake when I arrived. Before I chased her off, Ubu found us and she treated his cut."

"Did you seriously run her off?" Quinten asked in disbelief.

"I did that day, politely. When I ran into her at the grocery store, I invited her to come out to go hiking. We had fun."

"Hiking, huh? Are you going to *hike* with her again?"

The way Quinten emphasized *hike* made Bridger want to punch him in the nose. "Maybe. Haven't decided yet. She suggested I meet the woman in charge of the local museums and tell her what I know about my ancestors. Apparently, there is some interest in them."

"That sounds like a great idea. Didn't you say you found a bunch of historical stuff in your attic?"

Bridger nodded. "The loft. I found my great-great-great-grandfather's patient ledger and his wife's journal. According to both of those written records, Grandpa Evan regularly received payments in things like chickens, milk, baked goods, slabs of meat, and even tree saplings. I'm wondering if some of the trees planted here at the lake were those he received from patients. If I'm not mistaken, there are two pear and three apple trees up by where the old cabin used to be."

"That's cool." A noise in the background drew Quinten away from the screen. He was only gone a few seconds before he returned. "I need to go, bro. Take care and keep in touch. I expect a full report with more details about the hottie nurse the next time we talk."

Bridger scowled at the hottie nurse comment, then nodded to his friend. "Tell everyone I said hello and to stay out of trouble."

"Will do."

Bridger stared at the screen for a moment after Quinten disconnected the call; then he carried the laptop inside the cabin. He changed out of the shorts and tank top he'd been wearing into a pair of cargo pants, pulled on a pressed navy-blue T-shirt, then laced on a pair of hiking boots.

After he made sure all of his pets were squared away, he loaded a small trunk in the pickup and drove into town.

Grady Guthry had let him know he'd be able to get started on Monday with the road project. Bridger could hardly wait to be able to drive from his cabin to the main road without the threat of sustaining brain damage from hitting his head on the top of the pickup cab. It wasn't like he had an abundance of brain cells to spare.

He wondered how he'd be able to get in and out of his place while Grady did the work, then recalled the road Shayla had parked on when she thought she was at a different lake. He could always park there and walk over to his cabin if the need arose.

It might be a good idea for him to stock up on groceries before Monday. He could do that after church on Sunday. He'd met Pastor Ryan and liked him and decided he'd give the service a try.

At least he'd know a few people in the congregation. It was the church all of the Ford family attended, as well as Shayla. She'd mentioned attending last Sunday, since it happened to be her day off. He had texted her several times and had spoken to her once, when she'd called to supposedly check up on Ubu, Kit, and the other animals who'd adopted him. He could have spent hours listening to her talk, mesmerized by her voice, but she'd kept the call brief. Friendly.

If he had a functioning brain cell left in his head, Bridger would remain solely friends with Shayla Reeves. She was personable and outgoing, completely opposite of him. Shayla was the type of girl who had likely been a cheerleader in school and remained friends with almost everyone.

Shayla was lively and energetic, but caring and sweet. She'd have to be in her job as a nurse. He'd heard from Piper, who got news from her grandfather, a resident at Golden Skies, how good Shayla was with the patients in the dementia wing. Bridger assumed she probably excelled at her job, bringing joy to her patients, coworkers, and the residents.

Bridger smiled, thinking of the retirement home's nickname. It amused him the younger generation referred to the facility as the Hokey Pokey Hotel. From what he'd heard and observed, the name fit the place and the residents well.

When he reached Holiday, Bridger drove down Main Street, then turned onto Park Street and drove to the Depot Museum. He'd discovered that was where Kali Coleman's office was located.

He parked and got out of the pickup, lifted the small trunk, tucking it under one arm, then headed inside the old depot that looked like something from a movie set. He'd read about Trace Coleman initiating a huge restoration project of the depot and Lennox Manor, a mansion built by his ancestor George Lennox in the early 1900s. Seeing the restored, resplendent depot building in person was far different than viewing a photo posted online.

When he pulled open the door and stepped inside, he experienced a wave of gratitude for the person who decided the museum should have air conditioning. The cool air was welcome considering the rising temperature outside.

His gaze scanned a board fastened on the wall behind the front counter where train schedules were displayed. His attention shifted to the older woman seated behind the desk. She looked like a person who took charge and took no prisoners.

"Welcome to Holiday's Depot Museum. Would you like to purchase a tour ticket?"

"Yes, ma'am, but first I wanted to see if Mrs. Coleman was available. I probably should have called ahead for an appointment, but her cousin, Sunni, assured me it would be fine to drop by."

The woman studied him a moment, then picked up the handset from the telephone beside her. "May I give Mrs. Coleman your name?"

"It's Bridger Holt. Perhaps it would help if you told her I'm a descendant of Doctor Evan Holt and brought a few things to show her that might be of interest."

The woman grinned at him. "That'll likely do the trick."

Bridger glanced around him, trying not to listen to the one-sided conversation, then turned back around when the woman cleared her throat.

"She'll be down in a minute. She's finishing up an online meeting. You're welcome to take a seat while you wait."

"Thank you, ma'am." Bridger politely tipped his head to the woman, although he remained standing near the desk instead of sitting in one of the chairs lining the wall.

"Do you happen to know the Ford brothers?" the woman asked, eyeing him again.

"I know Colt and Piper through the feed store. I met Kaden the last time I stopped by the bank. His wife made the introduction."

The woman beamed. "Katherine is my niece. I'm Louella Harris, but everyone calls me Lou."

"It's nice to meet you, Mrs. Harris." Bridger reached out to shake her hand. At her scowl, he grinned. "Lou."

She shook his hand. "That's better."

"Katherine has been very helpful when I've been in the bank." Bridger had appreciated the banker's assistance and knowledge. She'd even helped him transfer money from one of his investment funds so he could open an account at the bank. He figured it would be helpful to have one there if he intended to stay very long in Holiday. "She told me a little about what Kaden does with his software. It's incredible he's developed such helpful agriculture programs."

"That boy has a mind that runs circles around mine." Lou smiled with pride. "He and Katie might just raise a genius if they ever get around to having children."

"Have they been married long?"

Lou shook her head. "Just a year, but I'm not getting any younger."

"You look plenty young to me."

The woman blinked her sparse eyelashes at him. "Aren't you a charmer, young man? You said you are a descendant of Evan and Henley Holt?"

"Yes, ma'am." Bridger shifted the trunk he still held. "I inherited the cabin out at Holiday Lake. I've been sorting through some things that have been kept in the family. It was suggested, more than once, that Mrs. Coleman might be interested in seeing some of the family heirlooms and hearing more of their story."

"She will be. I've never met anyone who loves history, particularly the history of Holiday, as much as that girl. Why, if it weren't for her brilliant planning, the town wouldn't be on the way to thriving. She organized a big holiday event that drew swarms of people into town for the Christmas season. When we reopened the museums in the spring, people started coming again and haven't stopped. I'm here to tell you, it's been a boon for the local economy. Everyone who has a business in town has benefitted from the tourism dollars, one way or another."

"That's great to hear." At least he hoped it was. There were always problems anywhere tourists gathered. He knew that from being a tomb sentinel and his duties in The Old Guard the last six months of his service. It seemed some people just caused trouble wherever they went. He hoped it would be limited here in Holiday. He'd hate to see such a nice little town change due to issues with the visitors who passed through.

Although he hadn't really thought about Holiday in terms of home up until that moment, he realized it was what the town had become for him, even in the short time he'd been there. When he thought of home, it wasn't the house where he was raised, or one of the military bases where he'd been stationed, but here in Holiday.

The notion of having a home, a permanent home, after so many years of being stationed around the globe, rattled him.

"You okay, hon?" Lou asked as he let the thoughts roll through him.

"Yes, ma'am." Bridger nodded at the woman and snatched his composure together as a lovely, dark-haired woman hurried over to him.

"Hello! I'm Kali Coleman. Lou said you have something to show me?"

Bridger shook the hand the woman extended to him. "It's nice to meet you, Mrs. Coleman. I'm Bridger Holt."

"As in Doctor Evan Holt's family?" she asked, appearing eager and interested. Even her body language, as she leaned slightly toward him, indicated her rapt attention.

"That's right. He was my great-great-great-grandfather. My great-uncle, Wallace Holt, recently passed and left me the cabin and Holiday Lake."

Lou gaped at him. "You own the whole lake?"

"That's what the deed says. Apparently, Evan wanted to protect it and bought up all the land around it that he could."

Lou whistled, then glanced at Kali. "I knew the Holt family had a cabin out there and access to the lake was prohibited, but I had no idea."

"Do you have a moment to chat, Mr. Holt?" Kali asked, motioning to a staircase.

"Call me Bridger, please. I do have a moment, as long as I'm not infringing on your time."

Kali shook her head. "Not at all. Come up to my office, and please call me Kali. I'd introduce you to my husband, but Trace is out of town right now. The headquarters for the family business are in Portland, and he had a few meetings he had to attend this week."

"At least Portland isn't too far." Bridger followed Kali up the stairs into a loft with windows on both sides. The furniture in her office made him feel like he'd stepped into a time machine that had taken him back to the 1940s. The pieces were old but looked brand new. Kali motioned to a couch, and Bridger took a seat. "This is amazing."

"Thanks. Trace and my cousin Matt hauled all this up here from the basement storage. It makes me smile every time I walk into my office." She sat beside him and watched as he placed the trunk on the floor between them. Bridger opened the lid, but before he could remove anything, Kali hopped up and hurried over to her desk. She pulled on a pair of white gloves, then resumed her seat beside him.

"May I?" she asked, hands poised above the trunk.

"Sure," Bridger said, sitting back as she carefully lifted out the box that held the deck of cards.

When she opened the box, a wide smile touched her lips. "Wow! I'd have to spend some time dating these, but I'd guess them to be from the 1870s."

Bridger nodded. "I figure that's about right. There's a note in there, written by Henley Holt. The cards belonged to her father, who was a professional gambler. The deck is marked, although I have no idea what to even look for."

Kali appeared quite excited as she carefully looked at a few cards, then read Henley's letter. When she finished, she carefully returned the cards and letter to the box, set it on the coffee table in front of them, and picked up a wooden box, balancing it on her lap. She opened it with a gasp.

"Oh, look at her!" Kali gently touched the painted cheek of the doll nestled into the box.

"The doll belonged to Henley. From what I've read in her notes, she received it as a Christmas gift one year and named it Amelia. Her father had the box made with a hiding spot in it where he kept money in case they needed it."

"Do you know how to open the hidden compartment?" Kali asked, turning her head at different angles to look into the box.

"No. I didn't want to mess with it and break something."

Kali closed the lid and set the box on the table with the cards. "I could have one of my antique experts take a look at it and see what they discover."

"That might be a good idea."

Kali looked like she might burst with excitement when she saw the gambler's outfit and a photo of John Jones with Henley tucked into the bottom of the trunk.

"Is this her father's attire?"

"Yep. To me, it looks exactly like something I'd envision a gambler wearing. Or maybe I've just watched that old Kenny Rogers movie one too many times."

Kali laughed. "No. It's perfect. Tell me his name again."

"John Jones was the name he went by, but when he died, Henley discovered his real name was Asher Tarleton. He grew up in Kentucky."

Kali set the antiques back into the trunk, yanked off her gloves, and picked up a tablet and pen. She began furiously writing notes and asking Bridger questions. He told her what he knew of Evan and Henley. He could fill in a lot more detail about the Holt family than he could Henley's relatives.

"This is all so helpful, Bridger. I'm thrilled you stopped by. If I promise to take the utmost care with these treasures, would you mind leaving them long enough for me to have them dated?"

"That's fine. If you want to include them in a display, I'd be happy to do that, as long as our family could have them back if they ever wanted them."

"Absolutely. We can fill out paperwork that shows the artifacts are on loan from the Holt family. Do you have other things we could include in the display, like any of Doctor Holt's tools, or, if I'm making wishes, something like his doctor's bag?"

"Not that I've come across yet, but there are still several trunks and boxes I haven't gone through. I did find one of his patient ledgers and Henley's journal from their early years together. From what they both recorded, people used to pay him in things like chickens, tree saplings, and baked goods."

"I think that happened more often than you'd realize, especially in rural areas." Kali retrieved her business card and gave it to Bridger. "If you find anything else you think might be of interest, call or text me anytime." She looked hesitant for a moment, then motioned to her doorway. "If you have time, there is something outside I'd like to show you."

"I'm not in a rush. Lead the way."

Bridger followed her down the stairs, through what was once a baggage storage area, and out the back door. In a large lot, a crew was working on what appeared to be an old house. It sat next to a smaller house that appeared to have been recently restored.

Kali waved to the work crew outside, then opened the door and stepped into the house where they worked.

"Don't mind the mess or dust. You might be encouraged to know this house belonged to Evan Holt. He had it built when he first opened his practice here in Holiday. This was the waiting room." She led him down a hallway, showing him what had once been exam rooms, then through another doorway at the end of the hall. "From what we know, this served as Evan's living quarters. I believe Henley lived here, too, until the children came along and they built a larger home. This house, and the property it sat on, became part of the hospital complex, although they didn't use the house for anything more than storage since the 1950s. When the hospital recently decided to tear the house down, I begged Trace to rescue it, so he had it moved here along with the house that belonged to Holiday's first sheriff. We hope to move more old houses that are in peril of being destroyed here and restore them. They'll become part of the museum; each house furnished to the period with as many details as we can glean about the original inhabitants. It would be wonderful to display some of Evan and Henley's things in this house."

Bridger glided his hand over the warped wooden counter in the kitchen. Had his ancestor built it or hired someone to create it? He knew Evan had been a farm boy who'd gone to medical school on a scholarship provided by a wealthy woman his mother had once worked for. He assumed the doctor had never completely abandoned his rural roots. Evan had proved that by preserving the lake and the land around it.

Goose bumps broke out on his arms as he thought of standing somewhere his long-ago relative had once stood.

"Take some time to look it over. I'll be outside when you're ready to go."

"Thank you." Bridger nodded to her, then wandered from the kitchen area into the bedroom, admiring the craftsmanship of the home. The fact that it had been built to last was likely one of the few reasons it had survived this long, especially when it had basically been left unused and without maintenance for years.

He returned to the living room, noting the fine wood trim, then made his way back into the other part of the house. He stood in the door of an examination room, closing his eyes and picturing Evan hard at work, helping a patient in need.

When he opened his eyes, he turned and walked out of the building over to where Kali appeared to be typing notes on her phone.

"Will you really open this as a museum? One that honors Evan and Henley?" he asked when he approached her.

Kali smiled. "I have every intention of doing just that. If you have photos or letters, anything that helps us get a clearer picture of them and their descendants, I'd love to include that in the displays. You could email me copies or drop off a thumb drive. Whatever works for you."

"My uncle left boxes of photos and some scrapbooks. One is of a Holt who served in the Great War. You'd be welcome to look at those. Also, I'll touch base with one of my cousins. She's the self-appointed historian in the family. She might have some photos or stories she could share."

"Wonderful!" Kali clapped her hands together, clearly elated. "I'm so grateful you decided to stop in today, Bridger. It's been wonderful to meet you and learn more about two of Holiday's prominent early citizens. I should …"

Her phone buzzing interrupted her. She offered Bridger an apologetic look and answered it. As he listened to the conversation, he got the idea there was trouble with a security camera system and no one was available to repair it until next week. She disconnected the call, appearing distressed.

"I could take a look," he offered without thinking.

Kali gave him a shocked look. "Do you have experience with security cameras?" she asked.

"A little. The place I was stationed five years ago had glitches all the time. They trained several of us to fix them so someone would always be available if there was a problem."

"And you'd really go take a look at it for me?"

"Sure. I'd be happy to. After all, you're rescuing a part of my history here." He waved his hand to the house behind them. "Is the system here at the depot?"

"No. At Lennox Manor. Have you been there yet?"

"Nope, but I've heard about it."

"My husband's ancestor George Lennox built the house. George's only child, Lorna, married Zach Coleman, so that's how the Coleman family, who was as blue collar as they come, ended up as billionaires."

Bridger hadn't heard the billions part of the story, but Piper had mentioned something about the Coleman family being associated with trains.

"So, Lennox Manor?" he asked, walking with Kali toward the depot.

"Yes. I'll call and let them know you're coming. Stop by the front entry, and someone will show you where to go. I can't thank you enough for this."

"Well, you might want to hold off until I actually fix the problem," he grinned at her. "I can't make any promises, but I think I know enough to not make it worse."

"It's not working at all, so anything would be an improvement." Kali shook his hand again. "I look forward to working with you, Bridger, to bring Evan and Henley's story to light. Perhaps when Trace is back in town, we could get together for dinner, and you could show me the scrapbooks."

"We'll plan on it. Thank you." Bridger tipped his head to her and headed toward his vehicle. In a town as small as Holiday, it wasn't hard to find anything. He soon pulled into the visitor parking area at Lennox Manor. The house was imposing and impressive. He had no idea anything so opulent had ever been built in Eastern Oregon, let alone Holiday.

Inside, the volunteer at the front desk directed him to the basement, where another volunteer showed him to the control room. The security cameras were definitely offline.

The system was one familiar to him. It didn't take long for him to reboot the system and adjust a few settings. Within fifteen minutes, the cameras were back in working order.

"It would have taken me a million years to figure that out," said the volunteer who showed him the room.

Bridger shrugged. "I used to work on something similar." He watched the cameras for a few minutes just to make sure they continued working before he followed the volunteer upstairs.

"Since you're here, feel free to take a look around, handsome," the older woman squeezed his bicep, then started back down the stairs.

Bridger spent an hour going through the rooms, reading all the placards, imagining the people who had lived and loved and died there.

"Be sure you go out to the gardener's cottage," one of the women said when he started to leave.

He followed her directions around the side of the house to a cottage that looked like something from a Thomas Kinkade painting. Flowers bloomed all around it in such profusion, the perfume of the blossoms filled the air with an almost exotic fragrance.

Bridger opened the door and stepped inside the gift shop. Before he could do more than pick up a pewter train ornament, two older women appeared in the room.

One of them looked like she belonged on a porch with a big straw hat, sipping a mint julep. Soft silver curls, a pastel dress, and pearls encircling her neck gave her a genteel appearance.

The other woman looked like she'd just left the circus as one of the side attractions. Her gray hair stood up on her head in stiff spikes, like she might have gotten a little heavy-handed with mousse or gel when she applied it. She wore a lime green shirt with pink flamingoes parading across it, and a pair of sunshine-yellow leggings.

Regardless of her attire, when she smiled at him, Bridger saw kindness in her eyes.

"Hello, handsome!" the colorful one greeted. "Welcome to Lennox Manor's Gift Shop. Is there anything we can help you find?"

"Just thought I'd browse around a bit. This is quite the place." Bridger motioned toward the mansion across the lawn.

"It is. We're just so happy Trace decided to open it as a museum. Have you met him yet? Trace Coleman?" the flamingo woman asked. As she tilted her head, studying him, Bridger noticed she wore big pineapple earrings. It was a wonder they didn't pull right through her ears for as heavy as they looked.

"I haven't had the pleasure, although I met his wife earlier today."

"Kali is a sweetheart and is dedicated to preserving Holiday's past. We're so fortunate to have her here," the grandmotherly woman said with a shy smile. "My name is Ruth Milton. This is my best friend, Matilda Dale."

Ah! The infamous matchmakers. Bridger didn't know whether to be amused or terrified after what he'd heard about them. Piper and Colt had told him some of the things the two women had done to get couples together, like faking fires and injury, and locking Kaden and Katherine in a storage closet.

He certainly didn't need them plotting with him in mind. Goodness only knew who'd they deem the perfect mate for him.

"I'm Bridger Holt. It's nice to meet you both."

"Holt?" Ruth's brow furrowed in thought. "As in Doctor Evan Holt?"

Bridger nodded. "That's the one. He was my great-great-great-grandfather."

"Well, imagine that." Matilda took a step closer to him and narrowed her gaze. "I've heard he had red hair and green eyes."

"Yes, ma'am. There are a whole bunch of Holt family members running around Pennsylvania who fit that description. My grandmother had black hair and dark eyes. Guess I take after that branch of the family tree, at least in looks."

"I see," Matilda said, although Bridger had no idea what she saw. She appeared to be puzzling over something as she gave him another glance, then rushed outside.

Ruth smiled and motioned him forward. He followed her as she showed him through the cottage. In the kitchen, he found a few things he was sure Madelyn would enjoy and decided to purchase them along with souvenirs for her girls.

"Are you, by chance, married to Rand Milton?" Bridger asked as Ruth rang up his selections.

Ruth smiled and glanced up at him with a dreamy look in her eyes. "I am married to Rand. Have you made his acquaintance?"

"Yes. The other day at the feed store. I've gotten to know Piper and Colt since I've been in town. Rand mentioned the auto museum he's opening soon."

"Mercy, but that has been a project." Ruth set his purchases into a gift bag with the Lennox Manor logo on the outside. The woman leaned toward him and dropped her voice conspiratorially. "He's loved every minute of it, though."

"I'll be sure to check it out when it opens."

Ruth walked around the counter and looked up at him. "So, you'll be staying in Holiday?"

"At least through the summer. My uncle passed in April and left me the cabin at Holiday Lake. I've been staying out there. It's peaceful and just what I've needed." Bridger rarely offered strangers that much information about his life. He had no idea why he was speaking so frankly with this woman he'd just met.

"I'm sorry about your uncle. How long were you in the military?" Ruth asked as they walked toward the door.

Apparently, even little old women could still guess his choice of career. "Almost ten years. I closed that chapter of my life in April."

"Thank you for your service, Mr. Holt. I'm glad you came to Holiday and hope your time here brings you exactly what you need."

"Thank you, Mrs. Milton. Please, call me Bridger."

"Bridger it is. Call me Ruth," she said, wrapping her hands around his bicep and giving it a light squeeze.

Before he could extract himself, Matilda hastened inside and glommed onto his other arm.

"Are you leaving so soon?" Matilda asked, planting her feet and giving him an inquisitive glance.

"Yep. Ruth helped me pick out a few things."

"For your wife?" Matilda pried.

Warning bells began clanging in Bridger's head, but he tried not to let his panic show. "No wife, ma'am."

"Girlfriend?" Matilda prodded.

"Nope. My cousin Madelyn. She enjoys kitchen stuff." He shrugged, feeling that was a sufficient explanation, not that he owed one to either of the women staring at him as though he was a prime slab of beef.

"Where does she live?" Ruth asked as they continued holding him captive near the door.

Just a few steps and he could escape. He didn't want to be rude, though. "Altoona, Pennsylvania. She and her husband have two cute little girls."

"That explains the toys you purchased," Ruth said, giving Matilda a knowing look.

"Well, I should get going. Thank you, Ruth, for your help. It was nice to meet you." He reached for the doorknob, but before he could touch it, the door swung open, and Shayla rushed inside.

She took one look at him, swiveled to Matilda and Ruth, and fisted her hands on her hips.

"Matilda Dale! How could you?" Shayla glared at the woman who didn't look the least bit remorseful over whatever it was she'd done.

"How could I what, darling?" Matilda asked, feigning innocence although Bridger had a strong idea she was guilty of something.

"You called in a panic, saying Ruth was experiencing all the symptoms of a heart attack. I ran three stop signs to get over here as quickly as humanly possible after you begged me to come take a look at her before you'd call the ambulance. You both look perfectly healthy to me." Shayla huffed in exasperation. "If you don't stop crying wolf, no one is going to come to your aid on the day you really do need help."

Matilda cozied up to Bridger and ran her bony fingers up and down the length of his arm. "Ruth nearly had heart palpitations when this hunky fella wandered into the shop. Have you met Bridger, dear?"

Shayla's face was red, lips compressed, and by the way her nose flared with each breath, he assumed she teetered on the edge of erupting. Bridger just wasn't sure if it was with anger or laughter. When her gaze met his, he had to work to hide his grin when he realized it was mirth he saw twinkling in the beautiful brown depths of her eyes.

In spite of her amusement, she glowered at Matilda. "As a matter of fact, I have made his acquaintance. Mr. Holt, it's nice to see you again."

"You as well, Miss Reeves. I was just on my way out, so I'll leave you ladies to, um …" He had no idea what they had planned. All he knew was that he needed to escape before it involved him.

"Oh, look at the time," Matilda said, making a show of checking the watch fastened around her wrist. "It's nearly time to close up and head back to Golden Skies for dinner. Ruth and I can't be late with our meals. Medications, you know."

Ruth's expression changed to one of delighted surprise, as though she'd just gotten a fabulous idea. Even Bridger could tell it was fake. Inwardly, he cringed, dreading whatever the old women were plotting.

"You two should go out to eat," Ruth said, giving Bridger a nudge toward Shayla. "Get to know one another better. I heard the special at the diner today is chicken-fried steak."

Bridger hadn't eaten chicken-fried steak in what seemed like years. Suddenly, he had an intense craving for it. Nevertheless, Ruth and Matilda didn't need to know that.

"Well, thanks again," Bridger said, reaching for the door with Matilda clinging to his arm. Would she hang on to him all the way out to the parking lot? How did one go about extracting an obnoxious octogenarian?

Thankfully, Matilda turned loose the moment he stepped outside. He soon realized that was only so she could have two hands free to shove Shayla out the door and into the back of him.

"Oof," Shayla grunted when her face connected with his back.

Bridger reached behind him and cupped her elbow to make sure she was steady on her feet, then turned around and raised an eyebrow. "Subtlety isn't high in their skill set, is it?"

Shayla laughed. "Not at all." She fell into step beside him as they headed toward the parking lot. "Are you hungry? I was busy working in the yard and lost track of time until Matilda called. I'm starving now that she mentioned chicken-fried steak."

Bridger grinned at her. "Me too. Meet you at the diner?"

"It's a date!" Shayla's cheeks turned bright pink, as though she'd said something she shouldn't.

Rather than comment, he winked at her and held open the door of her SUV. Fearful Matilda and Ruth might be spying on them, and reluctant to provide any fodder for their obvious matchmaking ploys, he stepped back before he surrendered to the need to kiss Shayla again.

The first kiss he'd shared with her had left him feeling like his world had spun in an entirely new direction. Would a second one turn him inside out and upside down?

The thought of finding out made his mouth water as he closed Shayla's door, jogged to his pickup, and followed her to the diner. He parked beside her, hopped out, and opened her door for her. Together, they made their way inside.

Bridger hadn't yet eaten at the diner, but it looked like a friendly mom-and-pop kind of place where the food would be plentiful and good.

He ordered chicken-fried steak with mashed potatoes and green beans. Shayla chose a breakfast skillet. When the server set their meals on the table, Bridger looked at the skillet with a little envy. Crispy hashbrowns were covered with sausage gravy, scrambled eggs, crumbled bacon, and gooey melted cheese.

"It's a heart attack waiting to happen, but so good," Shayla said, forking a bite and holding it out to him.

Bridger took the bite, then shared a sample of his steak with her. They talked little as they ate, focused on feeding their hungry bellies.

"I'm sorry about Matilda and Ruth," Shayla said when they'd finished their meals. "They mean well."

"I know. It wasn't a big deal, although I'm afraid of what they might do next time I see them."

"Did you at least tell them you have a girlfriend or something?" Shayla toyed with the straw in her glass of lemonade.

"No. I assured them I wasn't married and didn't have a girlfriend." Although Bridger thought more and more of Shayla in those terms. It was ridiculous to do so, but he couldn't help it. Being with her felt right. Good. Made him happy.

"Oh, it's open season now." Shayla grinned at him. "You won't have a moment of peace where they are concerned."

Bridger slumped in the booth where they were seated by a window. "Thanks for that encouraging news flash."

Shayla laughed, and the sound filled his heart.

He leaned forward and placed his hands over hers. "Maybe you could pretend you like me this summer. It would keep both of us out of their crosshairs if they think we're seeing each other, wouldn't it?"

Shayla turned her hands over and linked their fingers together. Such a perfect fit, her palms pressed to his. Even that innocent connection made his blood zing in his veins. When she looked at him across the table, he was sure he could see her heart in her eyes. They no longer snapped with humor, but sparked with affection.

"I don't need to pretend I like you, Bridger. I do. If I'm not mistaken, I thought the feeling was mutual. Aren't we friends?"

"Absolutely, we're friends. And as your friend, I'm telling you we should order a slice of pie to cap off this meal." He tilted his head toward a tall round refrigerated case, where slices of pie were displayed.

"You sure know how to sweet-talk a girl," Shayla said, overtly batting her eyelashes at him.

Bridger chuckled and caught their server's attention. "We'd like two slices of pie," he said, nodding toward Shayla.

"Is that huckleberry?" Shayla asked, pointing to the case and a slice of pie with dark filling.

"Yep. It's the last of the berries we had in the freezer from last year's harvest." The server looked at Shayla. "Two slices? Warm? With ice cream?"

"Yes!" Shayla looked at Bridger. "If that's okay with you?"

"Sounds great. Thanks."

He waited until the server was gone to take Shayla's hands in his again. "I've never had huckleberry pie. Does it taste like blueberry?"

"Not exactly. You'll have to taste for yourself and decide. I seriously shouldn't be eating anything else after that skillet full of calories, but who doesn't love pie?"

"Exactly." Bridger's conversation with Mrs. Parks about pie suddenly tripped into his thoughts. What had she said? Something about wooing the right girl with a slice of delicious pie. Well, he had no clear notion if he was wooing Shayla, or if she was the right girl for him, but the idea of it held a great deal of appeal at the moment.

"So, you had the day off?" he asked, observing her casual shorts and the tank top she wore that showed off tanned, toned arms.

"I did. One of the other nurses is taking a vacation, so we traded around days off to work with the schedule. I'm off today and tomorrow, then working the next five days."

"Won't it exhaust you to work five days in a row?" he asked, then sat back when the server returned with two plates. Scoops of vanilla ice cream melted on top and flowed in creamy rivers down the sides of the pie.

"Enjoy," the server said, then left them to eat in peace.

Shayla looked like a little girl on Christmas morning as she picked up her fork and waggled it at him. "Try it. I want to watch your face when you taste it."

Bridger cut off a bite and stuck it in his mouth. The crust was flaky, slightly sweet, and tender. The filling was fantastic, different than blueberry, and full of flavor. "So good," he said, forking a big bite.

Shayla grinned and took a bite of her pie. "The only thing better than their frozen huckleberry pie is when they have fresh berries. Usually in August, the diner features a week or two of huckleberry specials on the menu, like huckleberry pancakes and waffles, huckleberry lemonade, and huckleberry ice cream. It's all wonderful."

"I'll have to remember to come in then. Maybe you'd tag along so we could indulge together." Bridger tossed a quick glance at Shayla to see what she thought of his suggestion.

She smiled, looking only mildly surprised by his invitation. "I'd love that. If we ordered different menu items, we could share and get twice the huckleberry satisfaction that way."

"It's a date," he said, winking at her, enjoying the way a rosy-pink hue kissed the curve of her cheeks.

After they'd finished their pie and Bridger insisted on paying the bill, they walked back outside into the heat.

"What are you doing the rest of the day?" Shayla asked as she opened her car door.

Bridger shrugged. "I don't have anything planned. How about you?"

"Want to come over? You can see my place, and I'll put your brawn to good use digging holes for the flowers I'm planting."

Bridger straightened his posture and offered her a salute. "Sergeant Holt at your service, ma'am."

Shayla giggled and stretched up on her toes, kissing his cheek. "See you in a few, you goofball."

Bridger didn't even try to wipe the smile off his face as he followed Shayla to her rental house. He'd never been called a goofball in his life but decided he rather liked the sound of it coming from her.

Chapter Ten

Shayla settled back against the bench located beneath a snowball bush arbor. The branches had been trimmed to create a canopy of sorts over the bench, offering a shady place to rest in the courtyard at Golden Skies.

Although she only had fifteen minutes to enjoy the fresh air and sunshine before her break ended, she intended to make the most of every minute.

Eyes closed, she stretched out her legs and drew in a cleansing breath. She could hear three, no four, different birds singing a song around her. The air smelled of the pink and burgundy geraniums growing in containers to her right and the hint of roasting beef from the dinner the kitchen staff was preparing. Sunshine didn't reach her face, but it warmed her legs, even through the fabric of her scrubs.

Although she longed to sit in the sunshine, she'd known she'd get too warm before she was ready to return inside. This seat, tucked away in a corner, was secluded and quiet. Just what she needed after several busy hours of caring for patients.

Shayla drew another breath, and the scent she inhaled, one that carried a whiff of something masculine and rugged, made her think of Bridger.

She hadn't seen him since the evening he'd come over to dig holes for the flowers she was planting. Honestly, that had taken him all of five minutes. He'd helped her plant the flowers and water them, then they'd gone to the feed store and hauled home bags of bark they spread around the flower bed. It looked so nice when they'd finished, Shayla had snapped a few photos and sent them to her sister.

She'd invited Bridger in for something cool to drink. Instead of relaxing, he'd ended up fixing the leaky kitchen faucet, repairing the garbage disposal, and hanging a shelf for her in the bathroom.

When she'd commented on his handyman skills, he'd shrugged it off, saying he'd picked up a few skills here and there, but mostly from his uncle.

Getting information out of Bridger was like prying something out of a concrete block, but she kept trying. Each time they were together, he seemed less guarded and a little more open with her.

Given time, she was sure he would tell her about his past and what haunted him. He hadn't said anything, and she certainly hadn't asked, but it wasn't hard to figure out something had happened that left him troubled.

That night, as they lingered at the door, hesitant to say goodnight, Bridger had run his work-roughened fingers across her cheek, down her neck, and over the skin of her arm until her hand was clasped in his. The light touch had sent her senses into a tailspin.

Then he'd kissed her.

Shayla was glad he'd wrapped his arms around her, or she might have crumpled to a heap on the floor when her knees refused to hold her upright.

She had no idea if they'd kissed for minutes or an hour, but it was long enough that she felt completely boneless and breathless when he pulled away, gave her a tender smile, and then left.

They'd texted back and forth every day, and even had two brief phone conversations, but it wasn't enough. Not for Shayla.

She was coming to realize there would never be enough time with Bridger, and the thought terrified her. Never, not once in her life, had she been so besotted with a man she felt such an urgent, driven need to be with him. The strength of that need, like the need to breathe in air or have water to slake her thirst, was turning into something essential to her happiness.

Bridger was unlike anyone she'd ever met or known. The depth and power of her feelings for him left her unsettled and uncertain.

At the moment, what she felt for him didn't matter because she had no time to spend with him or dream about him. She'd worked five days in a row; then one of her coworkers had called in sick, and she'd been asked to work two additional shifts. After seven twelve- to fourteen-hour days, she was beyond exhausted. Tomorrow, she intended to do nothing but sleep.

A low woof and a bump to her leg startled her and drew her from her thoughts. Her eyes snapped open, and she glanced down at Ubu. The dog whined and placed a paw on her lap.

"What are you doing here, Ubu? Where's Bridger? I know you didn't come to town all by yourself." Shayla stood, keeping a hand on Ubu's head, when she noticed a familiar figure wandering through the courtyard, appearing to search for something, most likely the dog.

"Hey, stranger!" Shayla called, heading toward him with Ubu at her side. "What are you two doing here?"

"Matilda Dale called and asked if I'd put up a new curtain rod in her apartment. Matilda and Ruth discovered I can do odd jobs and have kept me busy. I hate to tell any of the senior citizens no, so I've gone along with it." Bridger held up a plastic resealable bag full of cookies. "The pay isn't bad either."

"You're as bad as your ancestor, accepting baked goods in lieu of payment. If I see you packing around a chicken, I might get worried."

Bridger chuckled and opened the bag, holding it out to her. Shayla took a cookie and bit into it. The buttery lemon cookie practically melted on her tongue.

"Ruth made these," she said, snatching another one from the bag before Bridger closed it.

He grinned. "She did. It was in thanks for the help I gave Rand at the museum yesterday. He's pretty excited about it opening this weekend."

"I've heard. Did you get to drive anything while you were there?"

"He let me move a few of the vehicles around. The snow car is really incredible. Have you seen it?"

Shayla nodded, brushing crumbs from her fingers. "At Christmas, they had it on display at Lennox Manor."

"I had Ubu with me when Matilda called. She said it was fine to bring him along. When I stepped off the elevator a minute ago, he dashed out here before I could stop him."

Shayla gave Ubu a good scratch along his back, noting his cut was completely healed. "It's no problem at all. He's a sweet boy. I'm sure it made the residents smile to see him. In fact, if you ever want to see how he does as a therapy dog, let me know."

"I don't think we're there quite yet, although he's been good therapy for me."

Shayla placed a hand on Bridger's forearm, surprised by the strength evident beneath her fingers. "If you ever want or need to talk about anything, I'm here. Anytime."

"Thanks, Shay. I really do appreciate it." Bridger gave her a perusing glance, then grinned. "Nice scrubs."

Shayla had forgotten she was wearing an eye-popping top with Minion cartoon faces plastered all over it. "Gift from my nephew when he was three. I only wear them when everything else is dirty. I'm always afraid these will disturb my patients."

"I can see why that would be a concern," he said in mock seriousness, then grinned. "How are you holding up?"

She sighed, unable to hide her exhaustion. "I'm so ready for my days off. It's been one incredibly long week."

"It's nice you stepped in to cover those extra shifts." Bridger walked with her when she glanced at her watch and headed toward the door that would take her back to the dementia wing. "Do you think you'd feel like doing something tomorrow or the next day?"

"Yes to tomorrow and the next day," Shayla said before she had time to consider how tired she was or how eager she sounded. She wanted to spend time with Bridger and get to know him better. To convince herself her attraction to him was a fluke that would fade, not something more. Something lasting.

Bridger's left eyebrow hiked upward. "Okay. Why don't I drop by in the morning, around ten, and we'll figure something out? I promised Kali I'd stop by and give her copies of photos I found of Evan and Henley, but that's all I have on my agenda."

"Great. It'll be nice to spend some time with you."

Bridger edged closer to her. He dropped his voice as he lowered his head until his lips hovered by her ear. She could feel the warmth of his breath against her neck when he spoke, causing goose bumps to pop up on her arms in response. "I'm looking forward to spending more time with you, Shay. I've been dying for more of your sweet kisses." He pecked her cheek, whistled to Ubu, then disappeared through a doorway before she could gather her wits enough to offer a comment.

Shayla hurried back inside and returned to work, hoping the blush on her cheeks soon faded. After six more hours of work, she arrived home, ate a banana, took a quick shower, and fell into bed. She slept soundly, dreaming happy dreams of Bridger.

Sunlight streaming through her partially opened drapes woke her the next morning. Lazily, she stretched in bed, still feeling tired, but not the bone-weary exhaustion she'd experienced most of the day yesterday.

Today, she could take her time getting up and around for the day, then she'd ...

Shayla bolted upright in bed, recalling Bridger's invitation to spend the day together. He'd said he would be there at ten. She gaped at the clock beside her bed. She had twenty minutes before he arrived.

Scrambling out of bed, her feet tangled in the sheet and she would have plowed face-first into the carpet if she hadn't grabbed onto the nightstand to regain her balance.

"Calm down," she instructed herself as she drew in a deep breath and then another before she hurried into the bathroom to get ready.

She'd showered and washed her hair when she got home last night, so it didn't take long for her to style her hair in a loose messy bun on top of her head, adding a few curls around her face. She applied mascara and lip gloss, rubbed on sunscreen, then hurried to dress in dark blue shorts, a white cotton top with tiny purple flowers, and a pair of dark blue sneakers. She assumed Bridger would want to do something outdoorsy rather than an indoor activity. If he wanted to go hiking, it wouldn't take her long to change into clothes more suited for that.

Grabbing her phone from her nightstand, she saw a text message from her boss, asking her to come in tomorrow morning to discuss a performance matter. Anxiety settled in her stomach like a rock. Had she done something wrong at work? A request for her to visit the boss's office was like being sent to the principal's office in school. Shayla always tried to be exemplary in her work, treating each patient with great care. What if she'd messed up? What if the boss planned to fire her?

Determined not to let her worries disrupt her joy in seeing Bridger, she walked into the living room and checked her purse to be sure she had everything she'd need for the day. She tucked her phone into one of the zippered pockets and left her purse on the entry table. On the floor just inside the door, a white envelope with her name written on the outside caught her eye. She picked it up and opened it, removing a letter from her landlord, letting her know he intended to put the rental house up for sale. He would give her until September to find alternate accommodations before he listed it.

Shayla sighed and sank onto her sofa. She loved this little house. It was comfortable and cozy and had been her home for the past several years. The landlord wasn't fabulous about small maintenance issues, like fixing leaky faucets, but he had kept the house maintained. In the time she'd lived there, he had put on a new roof, installed new flooring, and replaced the water heater.

The news that she would have to find somewhere else to live, somewhere she'd likely pay higher rent for a place she didn't like as well, cast a dark cloud over her day. Before she could give more thought to her housing situation, the doorbell rang. She dropped the letter on the coffee table and crossed the room to open the door.

Bridger stood on the doorstep, looking incredibly handsome with the sun backlighting the breadth of his shoulders. He had on a pair of cargo shorts, hiking boots, and a pressed T-shirt. Regardless of what he was doing, his clothes were always neatly pressed. She wondered again if he ironed his underwear.

Before the thought made her giggle, she lifted her gaze to his face and gaped at him. Bridger had shaved away the scruffy beard that had covered his face since she'd met him. She'd known he was handsome, but seeing him smooth-shaven with tantalizing, taut skin on display made her heart pitter-patter in her chest.

"Morning," Bridger said, smiling at her as he held up a bag from Sunni's bakery in one hand and a cardboard container with two steaming to-go cups in the other.

Although it was already hot outside, a caffeine jolt was exactly what she needed.

"Hi," she said, moving back so Bridger could step into the house.

He set the bag and drinks on the coffee table, then turned to her with open arms.

Shayla didn't hesitate to step into the warmth of his embrace. She felt him press a kiss to her temple and his arms tighten around her.

"What's wrong, Shay? You look like you lost your best friend." Bridger leaned back so he could see her face. "Something upset you."

Taken aback by his intuitiveness, she nodded. "My landlord left a letter stating his intent to sell the house. He's giving me until September to find a new place, which is good, but I hate the thought of leaving here. It's been my home for years."

"I'm sorry." Bridger hugged her close again, then led her over to the couch. When they sat down, he handed her one of the to-go cups. "May I offer you a hot beverage? Sunni was experimenting with some tea concoctions this morning and convinced me to take these two. One is raspberry chai, and the other is chocolate chai. My cousin Madelyn says a hot drink makes everything better."

Shayla accepted the cup he held out to her and took a sip of the chocolate-flavored drink. It was good, warm, and soothing.

Bridger took a drink from his, glanced at her, then handed her the cup. Shayla tried a taste, then another.

"Trade you," she said, handing him the chocolate drink, knowing he'd appreciate it more than the berry flavor, while she preferred the slight tang it offered. "This hits the spot, Bridger. Thank you."

"You're welcome." He leaned back and slipped his arm around her shoulders, pulling her closer to him. "I'm sorry about the house. I know you love it here. Would you consider buying it from your landlord?"

"I might, but I'm not sure it's a place I want to be locked into as a homeowner. It's one thing to rent, but something else entirely to buy. Besides, I'm not sure I'd have enough to make a down payment that would keep the monthly payments affordable."

Bridger nodded sympathetically. "At least you have all summer to figure it out. That gives you plenty of time to find a new place you'll love. I bet if you mention it to Matilda, Ruth, and Rand, they'll have a list of possibilities lined up before a week passes by."

Shayla snorted. "The houses will likely include single men looking for a wife."

"Tell them you're spoken for. You *are* my pretend girlfriend, you know," Bridger said in a husky tone that made Shayla feel languid as she rested against the solid strength he offered.

The languid feeling hastily departed, and irritation set in. She didn't want to just be his pretend girlfriend. Not when she longed to be the real thing.

"That's right. I'm supposed to pretend to like you. How could I forget? You excel at pretending to care about me." Her voice sounded sarcastic even to her own ears. She had no idea why, but she suddenly felt crabby and out of sorts. She didn't know if it was the shocking letter from the landlord, the text from her boss, or the fact that she was convinced she cared for Bridger far more than he cared for her.

He gave her an odd look and took another sip of his drink. "Maybe I should let you rest today. You look tired."

Insulted he'd not only noticed the dark circles beneath her eyes, but also commented on them, she scooted down the couch, out of his reach.

"Perhaps we should do this another day," she snapped, then set her drink on the coffee table.

Bridger gave her a studying glance, set his drink aside, and lifted her onto his lap. He held her close, comfortably, his hand rubbing gentle circles across her back.

Something about his kindness, his tenderness, made tears well and spill down her cheeks. Shayla wasn't someone who cried frequently. She couldn't be in her line of work.

Overwhelmed with emotions, she buried her face in her hands and cried while Bridger continued to hold her.

"Shh. It's okay, Shay. Everything will be fine. You'll see. Whatever it is, everything will be fine. Shh, baby. Shh." His soft murmurings finally calmed her. Her tears quieted and ceased, then she felt mortified she'd bawled like a baby and acted so snappish to Bridger when he'd been so kind to her.

"Excuse me," she said, jumping up and racing into her bathroom. She washed her face with cool water, repaired her mascara, and gave herself a stern lecture about not acting like a lunatic with the only man who'd piqued her interest in the past several years. Truthfully, she'd never felt like this about anyone. In ways that defied logic or explanation, he completed her.

She made a face at herself in the mirror. Now she sounded like one of those helpless women from the old romance novels Ruth foisted on her to read. She hated to admit it, but she truly did feel more complete, more content, and far happier when she was with Bridger than when they were apart. It wasn't like they'd gone on a real date yet, or spent weeks getting to know each other, but the time they'd spent together had been enough for her to realize he was a special person who filled her heart in ways she'd never expected.

He'd certainly earned bonus points for being patient with her earlier when she'd been cranky and then burst into tears. Her father ran at the first sight of emotion, and so did her sister's husband. But Bridger had held her and let her cry instead of racing out the door.

Before she succeeded in pushing him away with her emotional outbursts, she returned to the living room to find he'd carried their drinks and the bakery bag to the kitchen. He was just removing a plate of warm cinnamon buns from the microwave when she walked into the room.

She waited until he set the plate on the counter to wrap her arms around his waist and hug him. "I'm sorry about earlier. You didn't do anything wrong. I guess I'm just tired and a little on the cranky side today. On top of the house thing coming up, my boss sent a text that she wants me to come in for a talk tomorrow about a performance matter. It's never good if they call you in on your day off to talk. I'm praying she's not planning to fire me."

"Fire you? Why on earth would she do that? You're one of the finest nurses I've ever met. I spent enough time in hospitals to know. Maybe it's something good, not something bad. Think positively."

Shayla wanted to ask about his mention of hospitals. When and how had he been hurt? How much care had he required?

Rather than pelt him with questions, she offered him a grateful smile. "If you think you can endure my somewhat intolerable presence, I'd still like to hang out with you."

"You aren't intolerable, even if you are a crabby Abby today."

When she glared at him, he winked and kissed her nose. "It's okay, Shayla. I'm sure exhaustion combined with the unexpected news of the house and the summons to report to your boss tomorrow threw you off your game. We can hang out and watch movies if you want or go for a drive. I was thinking about driving around to see some of the places mentioned in Evan's ledger and Henley's journal. They both talked about an explosion at a mine not long after Henley had arrived in Holiday."

"Thank you for being understanding." Shayla slid one of the cinnamon buns onto a second plate and gave it to Bridger, then picked up the other plate and took a seat at her small dining table. After Bridger asked a blessing on their meal, she looked over at him. "The

Coleman family owns the Yellowbird Mine. It might be the mine Henley mentioned. It's where the old steam engine Hope was buried for years. Have you had a chance to ride one of the trains yet?"

Shayla thought it was neat the museum offered train rides each Saturday. There was a morning excursion or one in the afternoon, and tickets could be hard to come by if not purchased in advance.

"Not yet, but Kali promised, if I ever wanted to go on one, she'd make sure I had a seat."

"That's good. It seems like you've been busy working as a handyman around town. I heard you've done everything from replacing windows to hanging rain gutters. Is that something you plan to continue to pursue?" Shayla cut off a bite of cinnamon bun, savoring the soft, yeasty roll and delicious filling.

Bridger shrugged. "Maybe. For now. It's a good way to earn money. I had a few women, including Matilda Dale, offer to pay me to do their ironing. The rate they offered almost made me consider doing it."

A vision of Bridger in his pressed cargo pants and T-shirt with a frilly apron tied around his trim waist as he bent over an ironing board smoothing the wrinkles from one of Matilda's garish tunics made her laugh.

"What's so funny?" Bridger asked, scowling.

"I was picturing you in an apron ironing the flamingoes on Matilda's shirt."

Bridger shuddered. "Not going to happen. Those demented birds would give me nightmares."

The mood lightened, and Shayla set aside her concerns about work and her house to enjoy the time with Bridger.

They ended up driving up to the Yellowbird Mine to look around, then followed the notes left behind by his ancestors to check out a few other locations in the mountains around Holiday.

Despite their breakfast of tea and cinnamon buns, Shayla was starving by the time Bridger pulled into a public campground and parked.

"Ready for a break?" he asked.

She didn't take time to answer as she hopped out of the pickup and made a beeline for the restroom.

When she emerged, Bridger was sitting at a picnic table with a *Paw Patrol* lunch bag propped up, taking a photo of it with the mountains in the background.

"*Paw Patrol*? Seriously? I'd have taken you for more of a *Dinosaur Train* guy," Shayla teased as she walked up behind him.

He pushed a button on his phone, set it on the table, and then turned to her. "My cousin Madelyn gave it to me when I drove out here. I thought her kids would get a kick out of seeing it, so I sent her a photo."

"Is there anything to eat in the bag, or should I dig all the change out of my purse and raid the vending machine over there?" she asked, pointing to a vending machine encased in a wire cage to keep anyone from tampering with it.

"I've got you covered." Bridger grinned and Shayla felt her heart do a backflip in her chest. She still hadn't gotten used to seeing him without hair on his face. Now that she had, she hoped he would never let the scruff grow in again.

It was all she could do not to press her lips to the newly exposed skin. As it was, the scent of his aftershave had driven her half-mad the entire time they'd been in the pickup. The cab even smelled like him, and she'd drawn in big, deep breaths of the scent she'd forever associate with Bridger.

He was unlike anyone she'd ever known. At a glance, he might appear uptight, solemn, even stoic. But once a person got past the surface, he was witty, funny, intelligent, caring, and sweet.

Bridger was the type of guy who would always do what was right and honorable. He was the kind of man who would willingly give his life if it meant saving someone else's. She'd never met anyone like him and felt blessed to be considered his friend, even if she wanted to be much, much more.

"Sandwiches and salads from Sunni's bakery," Bridger said, opening the lunch bag and setting out the food. He retrieved two water bottles from the pickup and handed one to her before he took a seat beside her.

Together, they bowed their heads, and Shayla offered thanks for the meal; then they both dove into their sandwiches.

They'd just finished eating when Bridger's phone rang. He looked at Shayla, picked up his phone, then turned so all that was visible from the phone's screen was the mountain landscape behind him.

"Hey, cuz. What's up?" Bridger asked as he answered the FaceTime call.

"The girls were so excited to see you are using the lunch bag. Where are you?"

"Just went for a drive up in the mountains today. I thought the kiddos would get a kick out of seeing it. How's everything there?"

"Good. Nothing new to report, other than a reminder about Jen's wedding next month. You'll be here, won't you?"

Bridger nodded. "I didn't forget, and I'll be there, Maddie."

"Will you bring a plus one?"

Bridger scowled. "No. Why would I subject anyone to our family?"

The woman he'd called Maddie giggled. "Because I can see an arm beside you and unless one of your buddies likes purple flowers, I'm guessing that arm belongs to a woman. Perhaps you should invite her to the wedding."

A deep, long sigh rolled out of Bridger, but he shifted slightly and held the phone out so Shayla could see he was on a call with a beautiful woman who looked a lot like him.

"Madelyn, this is Shayla. She's a nurse in Holiday. Shayla, this is my bossy, annoying, favorite cousin, Madelyn."

Shayla and Madelyn both laughed.

"It's so nice to meet you, Madelyn. Bridger has mentioned you several times."

Madelyn made a face at Bridger, then smiled at Shayla. "I wish I could say the same, but he's never mentioned you. The fact you are with him, obviously on a *Paw Patrol* picnic, is huge news."

"That you'll keep to yourself," Bridger warned. The fierce look on his face might have been frightening if Shayla hadn't known he was all bluff.

Madelyn must have known it too because she merely stuck out her tongue at him. "Whatever, Bridge. Now, go play while I talk to Shayla."

For a moment, it looked like he considered disconnecting the call before he finally handed the phone to Shayla and got up from the table. While he disappeared into the restroom, Shayla had a brief but pleasant visit with his cousin. Madelyn didn't give away any of Bridger's secrets, but Shayla did get a sense of how much the woman seemed to adore him, which spoke well of both cousins.

Shayla glanced up as Bridger approached and returned her gaze to Madelyn. "He's back, so before he takes the phone away, I'll just say it was lovely to chat with you and I hope to speak with you again sometime."

"Same here. It was so nice to connect, Shayla. Now that you have my number, call me anytime."

Bridger groaned, loudly, and took the phone. "I don't need you two sharing secrets about me."

Madelyn shook her head and made a "tsking" sound. "Your conceit is hanging out there, cuz, for all the world to see. Who said we'd talk about you? Maybe we hit it off and want to be friends."

Bridger's left eyebrow hiked upward, and Madelyn laughed.

"Love you, Bridger. Have fun."

"Give the girls hugs from me and behave." He disconnected the call and dropped the phone into his pocket.

"Madelyn is awesome," Shayla said as she gathered up their trash and tossed it into the garbage, then turned to look at Bridger. He studied her, as though he tried to figure out how much information she'd gained from his cousin.

Without a word, he returned the lunch bag to the pickup, then motioned to a footpath that went around the campground. "Want to take a walk?"

"I'd like that." Shayla started down the path. She'd only taken three steps when Bridger caught her hand in his, lacing their fingers together. Surreptitiously, she glanced up at him, wondering what thoughts tripped around inside his handsome head.

They'd walked for several minutes in silence when Bridger glanced down at her. "What did Madelyn tell you about me?"

"Just that you tend to be quiet and close yourself off. Nothing I didn't already know." Shayla shrugged. She didn't want Bridger to feel uncomfortable because she'd talked to his cousin. To her, it seemed silly to worry about it, but she had the distinct idea it was bothering him. "Madelyn mentioned you had some things in your past that might hold you back from your future until you dealt with them. That's all."

Bridger's jaw clenched; like he was doing his best to hold onto his anger or irritation.

Shayla stopped walking and placed a hand on Bridger's arm, concerned by his reaction. "Honestly, Bridger, I don't know why you are upset. Madelyn didn't divulge anything. Besides, I know you spent nearly a decade in the Army, two of them as a tomb guard. I looked up some information about what it takes to become a guard. Just meeting the requirements to apply for a position is impressive. Also, you mentioned this morning about hospitals. It's not that hard to put all the pieces together and figure out that you spent time in a war zone. Whatever happened there has impacted your life in a big way. Am I right?"

Bridger stared at her for so long that she felt like squirming. Finally, he ran a hand across the back of his neck and started walking again. Shayla hurried to catch up with him, taking his hand in hers. When he gently squeezed her fingers, she knew he wasn't upset with her.

"I was nineteen the first time I went overseas. Ended up in a war zone and learned far too many terrible ways to die within the first month I was there. I did two more tours. My best friend, Keith, and I had gone through it all together. We met at boot camp and just hit it off. Three years ago, we were doing a routine check when we were attacked out of nowhere. Our assailants, terrorists, hit us with a hail of IEDs and gunfire. Keith took an explosive to the chest. One minute, we were fighting side by side, and in the next he was dead. Six of my men were hit, so I did what I needed to and got them all to safety. In the process, I ended up hurt and spent months in hospitals, rehab, and physical therapy."

"If you spent that much time recovering, you were more than a little hurt." Shayla knew injuries, knew the human anatomy and a body's ability to heal.

Bridger yanked his T-shirt up on his back. She gaped at the ridged scars that crisscrossed his skin and traveled around his left side. Shayla could see they went down below the waistband of his pants. The pain he'd endured had to have been excruciating. Gently, she trailed her fingers over one of the scars before he jerked his T-shirt down and tucked it into his pants.

"What happened? The scars, Bridger. Most people wouldn't…" Emotion choked out her words, leaving her unable to speak.

Bridger slipped his arm around her shoulders and guided her to a bench that sat on an overlook offering a spectacular view of the mountains and the river below them winding through the trees.

It wasn't until they were both seated that he cleared his throat and spoke. "I don't know exactly what happened. According to my team, those that survived, I turned into a fighting machine, taking out as many terrorists as I could while getting my men behind cover. The reports said I carried out four of them, two after I'd taken a bullet to my thigh. I remember my shirt catching fire and one of the guys ripping it off but not before I was burned. I also took several hits from shrapnel. When I finally came to my senses, I was in a hospital bed in pain unlike anything I'd ever known. My body healed, but I had a hard time accepting the fact that Keith and the others were dead. It haunted me, and still haunts me. My commanding officer was the one who suggested time spent working as a guard might be helpful. Healing, he called it."

"Did it help?" Shayla asked, cradling Bridger's hand between hers.

"Yes, and no," he answered cryptically, pulling his hand from hers and bracing his forearms on his knees as he leaned forward. "Being one of the sentinels at the Tomb of the Unknown Soldier changed me. I've always been what most people would refer to as patriotic. But it wasn't until I became one of the guards that I gained such incredible respect for those who went before us. They sacrificed everything they had, right down to their identity."

Shayla didn't speak but thought about what he said. She'd never visited the cemetery, but just from what she'd read and the videos she'd watched, she'd experienced wave after wave of emotion over the sacrifices made by the soldiers that went, for a large part, unnoticed and unappreciated by most Americans.

"Did you know the sentinels have a creed? It was written by a sentinel years ago, but it's something we memorize, something I'll never forget. 'And with dignity and perseverance, my standard will remain perfection.' That's part of the creed and part of who I am now, who I try to be. I told you about our uniforms. It's one way to honor that standard of perfection. I know none of us are perfect, that perfection is in Christ alone, but that creed and standard pushes me to strive to be a better person."

Shayla felt tears sting her eyes. "You are one of the kindest, best men I've ever met, Bridger Holt. What is it you think is so lacking in you? What haunts you so much that Madelyn thinks you'll never move forward with your life?"

"I feel like I failed Keith and the others. If I'd only pulled back a minute sooner, he might still be alive. If …" He stopped and drew in a ragged breath. "It should have been me that died. Not him. It should have been me."

Bridger dropped his head and Shayla knew he was battling demons she couldn't begin to imagine or understand. She placed her arm around him and slid so close she could feel his breath blowing on her leg; then she murmured words of comfort to him as he'd done to her that morning.

"Everything is going to be okay, Bridger. I promise it will all be okay. Don't dwell on things you can't change. Thinking in terms of 'if only' gets you nowhere. Believe me. I know. I've lost patients and played that game. You just have to accept what is, let it go, and move on. Beating yourself up because of something you have no control over, no power to alter, is useless. Reclaiming your life from those doubts and fears that you failed or let people down takes courage. Courage I know you have. If you let it, everything is going to be all right. Just let go of the past that's holding you captive." Shayla rubbed gentle, comforting strokes across his back. "For the record, I'm incredibly grateful you are here with me."

Bridger lifted his head and looked at her. His eyes held anguish and years of pain, but she saw a flicker of hope in their depths. "Me too."

For a long while, they sat in silence on the bench, absorbing the peacefulness and resting in the presence of someone who eased the wounds in their spirits.

Bridger slowly rose to his feet, then pulled her up beside him. "Come on. I'll buy you an ice cream cone."

"How about ice cream on top of a piece of pie from the diner?" Shayla grinned at him as they started back toward his pickup.

"Deal."

On the way back to Holiday, Shayla pulled up a song she sometimes listened to when she was having a hard time. As the two of them listened to Kenny Chesney sing about everything being alright, Shayla could tell Bridger was starting to believe it.

They'd just parked at the diner in Holiday when Bridger pulled his phone from his pocket. "I guess I accidentally turned it off after we talked to Maddie." He turned on his phone as they walked toward the door, then stopped just before they reached it. "Oh, no."

"What's wrong?" Shayla asked, moving beside him so she could see the phone's screen. He had two voice mails and three messages from the veterinarian.

Found Ubu's owners. They are excited to get him back. Please call when you get this! The dog's name is Woofer.

"Oh, Bridger. I'm so sorry," Shayla said, unable to keep tears from rolling down her cheeks. She'd grown attached to Ubu just from the little time she'd spent with the dog. It was going to be devastating for Bridger to give him to his owners.

He called the vet and promised to bring the dog to the office right away.

"I'd like to go with you, if you don't mind." Shayla hurried to keep up with Bridger when he headed toward his pickup.

"Okay," he said and didn't utter another word as they drove out to the cabin.

At least Grady Guthry had finished working on the road. Not only was it smooth, but he'd dumped enough gravel on it to keep it from getting rutted like it had been before.

"Grady did a great job on the road," Shayla commented as they neared the cabin.

"He did. Grady's a nice guy. Glad I met him," Bridger said, as though he didn't think he'd see Grady again. Shayla knew from past conversations that Grady had discounted the cost of the road project when Bridger had agreed to let him come fishing on the lake.

Before the pickup rolled to a stop, Ubu and Kit raced around the corner of the cabin. Toby the squirrel stood on the bottom step of the porch, while the two pheasants trailed after the fawn.

"Kit has really grown since the last time I was here." Shayla got out when Bridger parked. She watched as he dropped to his knees and pet both the dog and deer.

"He has a hearty appetite," Bridger said, burying his face against Ubu's fur.

"Is there anything you want to take into town with the dog?"

"Probably just his leash. Maybe that Frisbee he likes so well." Bridger continued focusing his attention on the dog.

Shayla couldn't blame him. She knew Ubu was the first pet he'd ever had. She just hoped the pain of returning the dog to his rightful owners wouldn't keep Bridger from getting another dog down the road.

She found the Frisbee and gathered the dog's leash from just inside the door of the cabin where Bridger told her she'd find it. When she returned outside, Bridger stood, gave the fawn a few gentle pets, then motioned to the pickup.

"Ready to go, Ubu?" he asked, opening the back passenger door of the pickup. The dog barked and sailed inside, settling onto an old blanket Bridger had placed on the seat for him. He closed the door, then looked at the pheasants as they protectively flanked Kit. "You two keep an eye on things while I'm gone."

Bridger opened Shayla's door and gave her a hand inside, then hurried around to slide behind the wheel.

Ubu seemed happy to go for a ride, although the two humans in the vehicle were silent the whole trip back to town.

When Bridger pulled into the veterinarian clinic parking lot, Shayla thought her heart would break at the look on his face. He was back to being stoic. Silent. Retreating into himself.

She wanted to comfort or reassure him, but had no idea what to say.

He picked up the leash and Frisbee she'd set on the floor between them, then hopped out, opened the back door, and clipped the leash on Ubu's collar.

They'd only taken two steps toward the door when a little girl rushed outside, heading straight for them.

Pigtails flying, her face radiated joy as she called, "Woofer! My Woofer!"

The dog barked excitedly and lunged against the leash. Bridger let it go, and Shayla placed her hand on his arm as they watched the dog and child reunite.

It was clear the two of them were best friends as the child laughed and hugged the dog between having her face licked.

A couple Shayla guessed to be near her and Bridger's age hurried out of the clinic, followed by the vet.

The man walked over to Bridger while the woman knelt down beside their daughter and lavished the dog with affection.

"Thank you for finding Woofer. It means the world to us to get him back. I'm Cory Billings, and that's my wife, Linette."

"Bridger Holt," Bridger shook the man's hand. "This is Shayla Reeves."

"Nice to meet you folks. I'm so grateful you found our dog. We live in Pendleton and passed through the area on a Sunday drive. We stopped at a campground for a picnic lunch, and Woofer disappeared. We spent hours looking for him, calling to him, but he never came back, and we had to head home. We've been asking everyone to keep an eye out for him. A few days ago, we decided to try calling all the veterinarian offices in the towns around the campground to see if anyone had found a stray dog. When this office said someone had reported finding a dog and had adopted him, I emailed photos so they could confirm it was Woofer. Vicci, our little girl, has been heartbroken about the dog. We all have been."

Before anything else could be said, Mrs. Billings stood and walked over to Shayla, giving her a hug, then surprising Bridger by giving him one as well. "Thank you, thank you, thank you for taking such good care of Woofer. Vicci was inconsolable when we lost him. We got Woofer when we moved to Pendleton, to give her a companion, and she'd never been separated from him before. She's just four and so attached to him. We can't thank you enough for bringing him back to us."

"My pleasure," Bridger said, his voice rough, as though he struggled to keep his emotions in check.

Shayla was trying to balance the sense of loss she felt at knowing she'd never see Ubu again with the look of happiness on the child's face as she hugged her dog.

"If there is ever anything we can do for either of you, please let me know," Mr. Billings said, shaking Bridger's hand again.

"Thanks," Bridger said, then handed the man Ubu's Frisbee.

"Vicci," Mrs. Billings called to her little girl, motioning her over to where the two couples stood. "Tell Mr. Holt thank you for rescuing Woofer."

"Thank you, mister. You brought my doggy back, and I missed him whole bunches." The little girl threw her arms around Bridger's knees and squeezed, looking up at him with a wide grin that melted Shayla's heart.

Bridger smiled at the child and hunkered down so he was looking her in the face instead of towering over her. "You take good care of Woofer. He's a great dog."

"I will. Thank you!" The little girl hugged him, then stepped back when the dog bumped against Bridger's side.

Bridger ruffled the dog's ears and grinned at him. "You be good to your family, Woofer. I'll miss you, buddy."

The dog woofed and wagged his tail, getting in one more lick across Bridger's chin before he stood, nodded to the couple, then turned and headed toward the pickup.

"It was nice to meet you both. I think Woofer and Bridger have been good for each other." Shayla shook their hands, then hurried to catch up to Bridger. He opened the pickup door for her and drove her home in silence.

He walked her to her door, kissed her cheek, and left without a single word.

Shayla leaned against the door and watched him drive away, her heart breaking for one more loss he had to endure.

Chapter Eleven

Bridger set down the heavy coffee table he carried in the depot's gift shop, then stepped back.

"It's incredible," the gift shop manager said, running a hand over the smooth wood on the side. "I like this one even better than the last one you brought in."

Bridger smiled as he pulled on a pair of gloves to set the glass top onto the table, doing his best to keep from smearing fingerprints over the glass. "Maybe it will sell as fast as the last two."

"It likely will. I'm so glad you started letting us carry your furniture, Bridger."

He nodded and adjusted the glass until it was perfectly aligned. "Me too. Between you and the florist shop, I'm having to hustle to keep up with orders."

The manager grinned. "From what I hear, you keep busy even without making furniture. Rand Milton was in yesterday and said you've been assisting him at the auto museum a few days a week."

Bridger removed the gloves and tucked them into his pocket. "I enjoy working with Rand. If you ask the right questions, he'll start talking about his years in the service. I never get tired of hearing those stories."

"Speaking of service," a voice said from the doorway, drawing Bridger's gaze to Kali Coleman as she breezed into the gift shop. "Could I talk you into participating in the Fourth of July parade? We're lining up as many military members as we can to either ride on a float or walk around it. Would you be willing to do it, Bridger?"

"Sure. I'd be happy to. Just tell me what time and where to show up." He had plenty of experience from his time in The Old Guard marching in parades. A month ago, he wasn't sure he would have agreed to participate, but after the day he bared his heart and soul to Shayla, he'd felt like he'd been making headway in moving beyond his past. Not only that, but he truly liked being part of the Holiday community. No one pressured him or pushed him, other than Matilda and Ruth, to do anything that was beyond his comfort zone. He'd also found a sense of camaraderie with the other veterans in the area. At Rand's suggestion, he'd even attended a few meetings where the attendees shared about their military experiences. Some had gone through similar experiences as his and it helped to know he wasn't alone.

"Perfect," Kali offered him a pleased smile. "I'll add your name to the list. The parade starts at ten on the morning of the fourth, so please be there by a quarter to ten at the latest. The float will be parked across the street from the hospital."

Bridger added the info to his phone and set a reminder so he wouldn't forget, not that he would. He turned to the gift shop manager. "Thanks again for letting me bring in the tables and furniture to sell."

"Anytime, Bridger. I'm sure I'll be calling soon to have you bring in another piece when this one sells."

He nodded to the manager, then walked with Kali into the lobby.

"People seem to love your furniture, Bridger. It's such a clever idea to use old stumps and logs and fence posts to turn into unique, artful pieces. The chair you made that's on display at the florist shop is unbelievable. I think Trace wants to talk to you about having a few pieces crafted for Lennox Enterprise's headquarters."

"I'd be happy to do that." Bridger had been shocked yet inordinately pleased that people seemed to want to buy his furniture. At first, he had no idea what he was doing, but the more he worked, the more confident he felt in his talents. The first table had sold for nine hundred dollars, and the last two had far exceeded that. He'd let Kali suggest a price and gone with it, fearing the hefty price tag would shock people, but it hadn't.

He had plenty of raw material available on the land around the lake. Working on the furniture gave him something to keep his hands and mind occupied.

The past few weeks had been hard. He missed Ubu—Woofer—more than he thought he could miss an animal, but he did. Instead of bottling up his emotions and shoving them into a compartment in the back of his mind, he allowed himself to feel and to grieve the loss of a pet he'd adored. He even considered what Shayla had shared the day he'd told her about Keith and his past.

Just as she'd been there to help and encourage him, he'd tried to do the same for her. She'd been so worried that her boss might be planning to discipline or fire her, but the woman had commended Shayla on all her hard work and given her a raise. They'd celebrated with pie at the diner that evening.

When Shayla wasn't working and Bridger wasn't doing handyman projects around town, they spent time together. In fact, hardly a day had gone by that he hadn't seen her. Sometimes it was out at the lake, other times they did nothing more than sit on her couch and watch movies. One afternoon, they'd binge-watched an entire first season of a police drama he'd never seen but she'd loved. He couldn't wait to watch the second season with her. He'd met her for lunch at the Hokey Pokey Hotel a few times, and twice they'd taken a picnic supper with them and gone for a drive. They'd even ridden the train one Saturday, and he'd loved every second of the experience.

The more time they spent together, the more he wanted to be with her. When they were apart, all he could think about was being with her again.

Although they hadn't said the words, Bridger had fallen in love with Shayla. With the light that seemed to radiate from her soul and shine into his. With the joy she shared in every smile and laugh. With the kindness she spread to those around her. With the hope she gave him each time she assured him everything was going to be fine.

Bridger still didn't feel like he had his act together enough to declare his feelings for her, but he was sure she cared for him. He could see it in her gorgeous brown eyes every time she looked at him. He could feel it in her touch when she placed her hand on his arm or brushed her fingers across his jaw.

Since he'd shaved off the scruff he'd worn for weeks, he'd kept it off. Shayla seemed challenged to keep her fingers and lips from touching his skin when he greeted her with a freshly shaved face. Who was he to discourage her? He grinned, thinking about how those sweet kisses to his cheeks led to kisses that made him consider what it would be like to love her forever.

Kali said something that he missed, pulling him from his daydreams of Shayla back to the moment. He offered her a sheepish look.

She motioned toward the stairs that led to her office. "Do you have a minute before you rush off?"

"Yep."

Kali led the way upstairs to her office. She walked over to her desk, pulled on a pair of white gloves, then motioned for him to take a seat on one of the two chairs in front of it. She sat in the other, picked up Henley's journal, and held it between them.

"I can't thank you enough for allowing me to read through Henley's journal and Evan's ledger. They've been so helpful in getting a better picture of their life here in Holiday. We finished making copies of them, so I can return them to you today, but there was something I wanted to show you." Kali opened the journal and carefully turned to a page where she'd inserted a white slip of paper. "When I was going through them, I realized there were two pages stuck together. It took me longer than you want to know to separate them, but I'm so glad I managed to get them apart. Did you know Evan purchased a piece of property here in town, in addition to the lot where he had his office and the one where they built their new home? According to what Henley wrote, it was on the east side of Holiday, not far out of town."

"What? I had no idea." Bridger allowed Kali to hold the journal while he read the entry. From what Henley had noted, Evan had indeed purchased land not far from town.

"Wow. Do you know where it might be located? With some of the street names changing since then, how would I go about finding it?"

Kali smiled and pulled a sheet of paper off her desk, handing it to him. "I did a little research and then asked Trace to have his legal team verify the location. The land is now within the city limits, but it's an empty lot. If you have the deed, you own a piece of property in a residential area that would make a great place to build a house, if you ever wanted to do that. Or sell it for a nice profit. I don't think it would be hard to sell because of the location."

"Huh." Bridger felt too surprised to say more.

Kali handed him a copy of a city map with a spot circled in yellow and a red X drawn in the middle of it. "In case you want to go check it out."

Bridger grinned at her. "Thank you so much for doing the legwork on this. I really appreciate it, Kali."

"My pleasure. It's always fun to unravel a mystery from the past. Thank you for letting me see the ledger and journal and allowing me to make copies of them." Kali set the journal inside an archival storage box with Evan's ledger and handed it to him. "I hope you can locate the deed."

"Me too!" Bridger nodded at her in thanks, then hurried from her office, down the stairs, and out to his pickup.

He drove to the bank and asked to see his safe deposit box. Katherine gave him a curious look as he plopped down at the table in the room where the boxes were kept and began poring through the documents he removed from the box. Near the bottom of the stack of papers he'd inherited from Uncle Wally he found a sticky note that read, *not sure what this is for. Haven't been able to find it yet.* The paper the note was attached to was an old deed, made out to Evan Holt, for property he purchased from a man named Wagner.

Bridger fought the urge to whoop in excitement as he read over the deed a second time.

He asked Katherine if he could have a copy of it, which she made for him; then she waited as he tucked everything back into the box and stored it in its slot before locking the room.

"Good news?" she asked as she walked with him to the door of the bank.

"Great news, actually. Thank you." He offered her a rare, unbridled smile, then rushed out to his pickup.

Instead of driving to the property, he went to Shayla's house. She had the day off, and they'd made plans to get together for lunch. As he turned onto her street, he hoped he'd find her at home. When he saw her watering her flowers in the yard, he grinned, rolled down his window, and leaned out with his elbow braced on the door.

"Hey, beautiful! Want to go for a ride? I found out something kind of incredible today and would love to show you."

"I'll be right there. Keep the A/C running!" She turned off the water, dashed into the house, and soon returned with her purse in one hand and two bottles of water in the other.

Bridger smiled as he watched her rush toward him, dressed in one of the flowered, girly tops she seemed to prefer when she wasn't wearing scrubs. She might enjoy the outdoors and love to hike and fish, but she had a soft, feminine side that he found entirely enchanting.

He knew she loved flowers of all kinds. Purple and dark pink were her favorite colors. She thought butterflies were magnificent creatures. She loved to dress up when she had a chance to attend church services or go somewhere nice, like the Italian restaurant where they ate dinner one evening. Pie was her preferred form of dessert, and huckleberry was her favorite. She'd rather read a murder mystery or watch a police drama than dive into a romantic comedy. Shayla was a tender, gentle soul, full of joy and fun.

And he loved her. Loved her more than he'd ever thought himself capable of loving another.

He got out and ran around the pickup, opening her door for her, breathing deeply of her enticing fragrance that put him in mind of wildflowers and summer sunshine. As she settled onto the seat, he inhaled a second breath, tantalized by the perfume and the mesmerizing aura of her. Before he lost himself to the passion bubbling inside him, he jogged back around and slid behind the wheel.

"Where are we heading, soldier boy?" Shayla asked, tossing him a coy smile as she buckled her seat belt.

"To find a treasure."

She smiled, and the glory of it filled him with light and warmth. "Treasure? Like a treasure hunt? Is there a map?"

He picked up the map Kali had given him and handed it to her.

Shayla laughed. "X marks the spot. Let's see …" She turned the map around and studied the streets. "Okay. Here's Main Street. Then you turn east onto Park, jog over onto Birch, then head east again on Mistletoe Drive." She glanced at him. "I didn't know there was a street named Mistletoe in Holiday, and I've lived here eight years."

"I think the name changed when a subdivision went in. Kali said it used to be Cleveland. Several of the streets had presidential names when Holiday was newly incorporated as a town." Bridger turned off Main onto

Park, excitement building the nearer they got to the destination.

"What will we find on Mistletoe Drive?"

"Property, I hope. Kali discovered Evan had bought a piece of land from a man named Wagner. If I'm not mistaken, he was one of the patients who used to pay him in chickens, ham, and slabs of beef."

"Really? Wow!" Shayla gave him a shocked look, then studied the map again. "How much land are we talking?"

"The deed says two acres." He handed her the copy of the deed, which listed the address on Cleveland Road.

"Two acres of land that's just been sitting empty all this time?" Shayla gave him a studying glance. "What will you do with it?"

"I don't know yet. I want to see it first. Confirm for sure it's mine before I get my hopes up or make any decisions."

"Good plan." Shayla looked out and pointed to a street sign. "Turn left there."

Bridger followed her directions. A few minutes later, they parked in front of an empty lot at the back of a dead-end street. Weeds grew waist-high in places, but the property held promise.

"Ready to explore?" he asked, pleased when Shayla beamed at him and then hopped out of the pickup before he could even get his door open.

"Come on, slowpoke," she teased, grabbing his hand after he stepped out of the pickup, and tugging him forward.

The houses that lined the two sides of the street varied in age from a turn-of-the-century home to newer-built houses, but they all appeared to be maintained with care. Lawns were green and trimmed. Flowers bloomed. There wasn't a bit of peeling paint or any weeds in sight, other than the empty lot behind them. The neighborhood had a peaceful feel to it. One Bridger immediately liked.

Together, holding hands, he and Shayla walked around the perimeter of the lot. At the back of it, they discovered what might have at one time been an orchard. A variety of fruit trees grew wild next to a small creek that meandered through the property.

"Can't you picture a big Victorian house with a porch that wraps all the way around?" Shayla asked, holding up her hands with her index fingers and thumbs forming a screen to peer through as she closed one eye and squinted the other.

Bridger could envision the house, painted a soft shade of yellow with white trim. "A gazebo could sit in the backyard and a shop over there for woodworking projects. Maybe a garage that looks like a barn or a carriage house."

"Exactly!" Shayla said, clearly as enthused as he felt. "The house should be yellow. A pretty, buttery yellow, with flowers growing out front and a big garden in the back. You could even put in a small pasture to have a few animals. I'm sure the city would give you a permit since the lot is barely within city limits and on a dead-end street with nothing but woods behind it."

Bridger settled his hands on her waist and swung her around. Laughter spilled out of her, pouring over him like a healing balm.

When he set her down, he didn't let her go. Instead, he pulled her into a hug. "I can hardly believe it, Shay. Do you really think it's mine?"

"You've got the deed to prove it. If you're worried about it, why don't you have an attorney look at it? Or you could check with the county tax assessor. Someone would have paid taxes all these years, wouldn't they?"

Bridger felt a sinking feeling in the pit of his stomach. If he owned the property and taxes hadn't been paid since Evan and Henley were alive, he could owe a fortune in back taxes.

As though she read his thoughts, Shayla pushed back so she could better see his face. She bracketed his cheeks with her hands, gave him a quick kiss, and smiled in that reassuring way that calmed him. "Let's go talk to the assessor so you won't have any reason to worry."

"Okay," Bridger said. The sooner he found out about the property, and money potentially owed, the better. "Where's the county seat?"

"Baker City. We should probably call to make sure someone is there before we drive all that way." Shayla pulled her cell phone out of her pocket, looked up the number, and called, while Bridger walked all the way around the property boundary a second time. He couldn't explain, couldn't begin to find words to describe it, but something in him felt like he'd finally come home. Arrived at the place he'd always belonged. He glanced over at Shayla as she spoke animatedly on her phone. Maybe it wasn't so much this place but the idea of building a home here with her.

Bridger didn't feel like he had a lot to offer a woman, especially this energetic, vibrant female who kept him on his toes yet so often left him off-kilter. He didn't have a high-paying job or any interest in working in an office. He enjoyed making furniture and doing handyman jobs around town for people, working at his own schedule and pace. Would that be enough to support a wife and family?

In the last month, he'd made more money doing those two things than he'd earned in three months in the Army. Perhaps he could provide for a wife and a family, even if he earned money in an unconventional way.

Shayla rushed up to him. "The person we need to speak with will be at the courthouse until noon today."

Bridger glanced at his watch, grabbed Shayla around the waist, and sprinted to his pickup. She laughed as she wrapped her arms around his neck. His heart felt like it might burst with love as he set her on the pickup seat.

"You'll go with me, won't you?" he asked as he put the pickup in gear and headed back toward Main Street so they could connect with the highway that would take them out of town.

"Of course. I want to see your face when you realize everything is going to be just fine. That, and I'm kind of hoping you'll agree to take me to lunch in Baker City. There's a grill there that makes the best sandwiches. There's also a fabulous kitchen store. And a place that sells the most decadent fudge. Oh, I almost forgot about the ice cream shop." Shayla took out her phone and sent a text. "We need an ice cream shop here in Holiday. I'm sure Kali can find someone to open one."

"If she can't, sic Ruth and Matilda on it. Those two women are relentless." Bridger knew the mention of the two meddling octogenarians would make Shayla smile. Since the day Matilda called Shayla, insisting Ruth was having a heart attack, the two old women hadn't employed further matchmaking tactics.

Bridger attributed that to the fact that he and Shayla spent so much time together without anyone forcing it. He genuinely enjoyed being with Shayla. She not only set his blood on fire, but she'd also become a good friend. Someone he trusted and, on occasion, even confided in.

The conversation was lively and lighthearted as they drove to Baker City. Shayla directed him to the courthouse, an early 1900s building constructed of gray volcanic stone that had been quarried a few miles out of town, or so Shayla read from a website she'd looked up as they drove through Baker City.

Bridger parked, got out of the pickup, and nervously wiped his damp palms on his pants before he took Shayla's hand in his. Together, they went inside to the tax assessor's office, where Bridger discovered Uncle Wally had been paying the taxes for decades. No back taxes were due. Bridger's name and the post office box he'd started using to collect mail were added to the information so he could make the annual property tax payment going forward. Assured everything was now legally his, he relaxed for the first time since Kali had pointed out the details about the lot in Holiday earlier that morning.

"Are you ready to celebrate now?" Shayla asked as they returned outside.

"I sure am. Where's this grill you were bragging about?"

Hours later, after they'd eaten lunch, sampled fudge, wandered through the downtown shops, and purchased ice cream, they returned to Holiday, content and happy. Shayla had even talked Bridger into speaking with the owner of the Baker City furniture store to see if the man would be interested in carrying some of his pieces. After seeing photos of the coffee tables, the owner agreed to have Bridger bring in a table and two lamps, just to see if there was any interest in them.

Excited about the work, about the plot of land that belonged to him, and about what suddenly seemed like unlimited possibilities for his future, Bridger felt carefree and full of life when he walked Shayla to her door.

"I had a great time today," she said, lingering in her doorway with her arms wrapped around his neck, standing on tiptoes as she kissed his cheeks, his chin, and then settled on his lips.

After several passionate kisses, he rested his forehead against hers. "It was a great day, Shay. Thanks for coming with me, for always being there when I need you. You're a great friend. One of the best I've ever had."

The smile dropped from her face, and she stepped away from him. Her eyes went from glistening with love to snapping with irritation. "Great friend. That's me," she said in an annoyed tone. "Listen, Bridger, I'll talk to you later. I just remembered I need to run over to HPH. I'll see you later."

Bridger had no idea what he'd said or done to alter the loving, tender moment they'd been sharing. He wanted to press her, to ferret out what was wrong, but decided to give her space.

He kissed her cheek, then backed away. "Thanks again for today. I really do appreciate you."

"Yep. Got it. You can always count on me, ol' pal."

He took two steps away from the house and jumped when she slammed the door behind him.

Bridger had several visions of how the afternoon would end, and the scenario of Shayla upset with him wasn't one of them.

Maybe he'd call Madelyn and ask her for input on what he'd done or said to upset her.

Before he headed home to the lake, he drove back to the lot and sat staring at the property—his property—dreaming big dreams.

Chapter Twelve

Shayla gave herself a long, observant look in the full-length mirror in her bedroom. She'd dressed with extra care in a new dark red dress dotted with little white flowers. The fabric was light and breezy, making her feel utterly feminine.

She'd spent far too long styling her hair, braiding a navy-blue ribbon into the strands around her face, forming a woven headband, then leaving the back to hang in long waves. She'd added a few little curls that bounced around her cheeks and ears, making her feel even more womanly.

A touch of makeup and a few dabs of her favorite perfume placed in strategic points that would release the scent for several hours left her ready to take on the day and the exasperating man who had stolen her heart.

Would Bridger notice her efforts? Or give her another inane line about friendship.

Honestly, there were moments she was sure he'd traded in his brains for a box of hopelessly tangled fishing tackle.

"You're a great friend, Shay. One of the best I've ever had," she said in a deep, mocking tone, mimicking what Bridger had said the day he'd discovered he owned a two-acre lot in one of the nicest neighborhoods in Holiday.

She was a good friend to him. Bridger had been a fantastic friend to her as well. But that wasn't enough for Shayla. Not when she wanted so much more. Not when she wanted a future with Bridger.

Well, to amend that, she wanted a future with him if he'd stop being such a lunkheaded, clueless guy.

She expelled a frustrated sigh, slipped her feet into a pair of cute navy and white polka-dot wedge sandals, grabbed a small leather crossbody bag where she'd tucked her phone, wallet, and a few essentials, then headed out the door.

Rather than drive to the Fourth of July parade and festivities happening in the heart of town, Shayla decided to walk. From her house, it was only about six blocks. If Bridger didn't infuriate her before the afternoon was over, she hoped he'd bring her home.

Due to her residual perturbed state after his friendship comment, she hadn't seen him in four days. Four unbearably long, lonely days. Then again, she'd been busy working her four-day shift, and she had volunteered to help with the Golden Skies float. She'd stayed late after work last night to help Sage and Justin

James, Fynlee and Carson Ford, and a few others add the finishing touches to the float; then they'd all gone out for pizza.

Although she'd enjoyed time with her friends, Shayla missed Bridger. He wasn't a big talker around other people, but the absence of his quiet, steady presence had left her unsettled.

Shayla knew she loved him. Of that, she had no doubt. She just wasn't certain how he felt about her. She was waiting to see if he ever moved beyond the "let's be friends" stage into the "let's build a life together" notion that she hadn't been able to get out of her head.

The day he'd taken her with him to see the lot he'd inherited, it had been as if their thoughts were in sync as they'd envisioned the house that he could build there. The place they'd described was Shayla's dream house, and from the way Bridger talked, it was his too.

If they built a house on the two-acre parcel, they could use the cabin at the lake much like Evan and Henley had—as a place to escape when they needed the calm peacefulness found there.

Before Shayla could entertain any dreams of a future with the quiet, often reserved soldier, she needed to know for certain, without a single question, that he was truly hers.

Shayla arrived on Main Street hot and thirsty, so she ducked into Sunni's bakery and ordered a large lemonade. Because it was a holiday and she felt indulgent, she also ordered one of Sunni's delicious strawberry brownies. She nibbled on the treat and sipped the drink as she stood among a boisterous crowd as they waited for the parade to begin.

A loud pop down the street sounded the beginning of the parade. The sheriff's posse rode by on horses, several of them carrying the American flag or the Oregon state flag.

Mayor David Coleman was next in line, riding with his wife in a vintage auto from the 1940s driven by his grandson Trace. Kali sat in the front seat next to her husband, waving to the crowd and tossing out handfuls of candy. Shayla waved at Kali and caught the Tootsie Roll she tossed to her.

Right behind the mayor was a float full of veterans and members of the military. Shayla waved at Rand Milton as he proudly stood on the float in his uniform, looking quite dapper. Then she caught sight of a familiar figure marching beside the float.

Although she'd seen a few photographs of Bridger in uniform, they did nothing to prepare her for what the sight of him, resplendent in his dress blues, did to her system. Her breath caught in her throat while her heart raced in her chest and her pulse pounded in her ears.

Sunlight glinted off the brass on his uniform, polished, like his shoes, to a high shine. His hat rested at a perfect angle on his head, and even the sunglasses he wore added to the overall appearance of masculine strength and appeal. He stood so straight and tall that he seemed to tower over most of the others walking around him.

Love for him, for the good, caring, honest man that he was, filled her heart so full it felt like it was overflowing, washing over her in waves.

When he saw her, for the briefest moment, his step faltered, but he quickly corrected it. Then he tugged down his sunglasses and winked at her.

Shayla smiled so broadly her cheeks ached. From that point onward, the President or the Queen of England could have been in the parade, and she wouldn't have noticed. All she could think about was Bridger.

She forced herself to focus on the high school band as they played a rousing tune, clapping along with the crowd although her thoughts lingered on her handsome soldier.

The parade was nearly at an end when the back of her neck tingled about the time a familiar scent tickled her nose. Bridger settled his hand on the curve of her waist as they watched the final float roll by before the crowd began to disperse, heading for the park near the depot for a day of arts and crafts booths, games, and musical performances.

Shayla turned and smiled at Bridger. He looked even more imposing and handsome up close than he had in the parade.

"Hey, you. I'm not sure it's safe for you to be walking the streets dressed like that. You'll have half the single women in town chasing after you."

Bridger grinned. "I already had three of them ask me for a date, but I politely declined. I already have a special girl. At least I think I do." He looked at her over the rim of his sunglasses. The heat flickering in his eyes made her mouth water. "If she's ready to speak to me again."

"She might be," Shayla said with a carefree grin, looping her hand around his arm and heading down the street with no particular destination in mind.

"I'm going to go change. Can I meet you somewhere?" he asked as they waited for cars to pass so they could cross the street.

"Did you bring your clothes with you?"

Bridger nodded. "I did."

"Why don't we go to my house? You can change, and then we can have lunch in the park."

"Sounds like a good plan to me." Bridger slipped his arm around her, and they made their way to where he'd left his pickup parked near the hospital. He drove to her house. Before she'd let him inside to change, Shayla begged him to let her take a few photos of him in his uniform. She sent one image of him looking fierce to her parents and sister, then her favorite photo of him grinning to his cousin Madelyn.

Shayla had developed a friendship with the woman, and connecting with her, hearing snippets of stories about Bridger from Madelyn, helped Shayla better understand the complex man. From what his cousin said, he'd always been someone who was quiet. A loner. A person who felt it his duty to protect others. It made sense he'd gone into the military. It also explained why he spent so much time alone.

Lately, though, she'd seen him interacting more, becoming part of the Holiday community.

Shayla had no idea he'd planned to walk in the parade today, but she was glad he'd participated. Not just so she had a chance to see him in his full-dress uniform, but because he'd clearly enjoyed being among fellow soldiers, even if most of them were Rand Milton's age.

Bridger stepped out of the house wearing a pair of dark blue cargo shorts with a gradient print polo shirt that was deep red on the bottom and faded into dark blue on the top. Of course, both shirt and shorts were neatly pressed and crisp. He wore a ball cap on his head, had his sunglasses dangling from the V of the shirt's neck, and wore, to her surprise, dark blue sneakers instead of hiking boots. She had no idea he even owned a pair since he typically wore hiking boots or cowboy boots when she saw him.

"You look great, Bridger. Very patriotic."

"I could say the same about you, Miss Betsy Ross." Bridger playfully wrapped one of her loose curls of hair around his index finger, then kissed her cheek. "You are beautiful, Shay. An amazing all-American girl. Is that a new dress?"

She hated to admit she'd gone online shopping and paid extra for express delivery, but it was the truth. She'd gone out of her way to look her best today. At least Bridger had noticed. From the expression of approval on his face and the gleam in his eye, he'd definitely noticed.

"It is new." She stepped away from him and did a few twirls, making the skirt swish and flare out. "Like it?"

"I do. More importantly, I like the girl wearing it. Truly, you look amazing and that scent is fantastic." He bent close to her and pressed his face to her neck, drawing in a breath that made a shiver of anticipation shimmy down her spine. "You smell and look luscious."

Before she shoved him inside the house and forgot all about the celebration in the park, she grabbed his hand, and they walked back downtown.

That evening, they sat on a blanket at the park and watched fireworks burst against the night sky. After the show ended, Bridger walked her home. Fireworks exploded behind her closed eyes when Bridger kissed her so deeply, so passionately, she couldn't think of anything except how much she loved him. How much she wanted his kisses for a lifetime.

"Sweet, sweet Shay," Bridger whispered, brushing his thumb across the curve of her cheek as they stood in her living room near the door. "You do things to me I never expected. I love you, but there are some matters in my life I need to get squared away before we take this relationship to the next level. Do you think you can be patient with me a little while longer?"

Shayla wanted to stamp her feet in frustration. Shout that she was tired of waiting. Pound some sense into the stubborn, loveable, maddening man holding her so tenderly in his arms.

Instead, she ignored what she wanted and focused on what Bridger had said. He loved her. He'd finally said he loved her.

For now, that was enough.

"I love you, too, soldier boy. When you get yourself together, I'll be here. Well, maybe not here in this house, but here for you."

His gaze met hers. "You'll end up in a house you love. Don't get in a rush about leaving here. You still have two more months, right?"

"Two months that will pass far too quickly," she said, not wanting to talk about her housing situation when they'd just made a declaration of love. She moved a little closer to Bridger, slowly trailing her fingers up his arms, lingering on his bulging biceps. "Tell me again, Bridger."

"Tell you what? Not to get in a rush about finding a house?" he teased, knowing exactly what she wanted to hear.

"Ooh!" She smacked his arm, and he laughed, then nuzzled her neck.

His lips hovered above her ear, his breath warm against her skin. "I love you, Shayla Addison Reeves. I love you so much. More than I've ever loved anyone. Don't ever forget that, okay?"

"I won't, as long as you remember how much I love you, Bridger Evan Holt. Do you think it's odd you are the only one of your family members to be named after Doctor Evan, and you're the one who ended up back here in Holiday, where he and Henley built a beautiful life together?"

"I don't think it's odd. I think maybe it was meant to be. How else would I have met you?"

"Good point," Shayla whispered, pulling his head down to hers for another long, lingering kiss.

Bridger held her close, kissed her neck, her temple, her cheek; then he let her go with a measure of reluctance. "I need to leave before I find it impossible to go, Shay, but thanks for today. I had a great time. It's been the nicest Independence Day celebration I've had in a long while."

"I enjoyed it too. Thank you, Bridger, for everything." She hated to see him leave but knew it was for the best. "Drive safely home. Text me when you get there."

He kissed the tip of her nose and opened the door, stepping out into the night air scented with the fragrance of the flowers blooming around her porch. "It's cute how you worry about me. Now that Grady fixed the road, I can at least arrive home without my brain and insides scrambled."

"I think the damage has already been done, my friend," Shayla joked, then squealed in delight when he lunged for her, making growling noises.

It took three more impassioned kisses before Bridger pulled away and hurried down her porch steps.

"Happy Fourth of July!" he called, waving to her before he stepped into his pickup and drove away.

Shayla wondered if he realized he carried her heart with him.

Chapter Thirteen

Bridger shifted the carry-on bag to his other hand and grinned when he saw Madelyn waiting for him near the baggage claim area at the airport. He'd flown to Pennsylvania for his cousin Jen's wedding, and Madelyn had offered to give him a ride from the airport.

Although Madelyn had begged him to bring Shayla along, he hadn't invited her. He needed time away from her to get his thoughts aligned. He had plans for the future, but he wanted a few days to sort them out, to discuss them with Madelyn, who always gave him good advice. When he was with Shayla, it felt like he couldn't think straight, or sometimes think at all. Not when all he wanted was to be with her.

He also needed time to speak with his parents. He knew he'd never be able to move into his future until he made peace with his past, and his parents were part of that. Madelyn had encouraged him many times to start a journal where he shared his feelings, since that was not something he readily did with anyone. The first two—or ten—times she'd mentioned a journal, he'd scoffed at the idea and brushed it off as silly. She'd even given him a blank journal with a fancy pen when Uncle Wally had died. He'd kept it because it was a gift from someone who loved him, but he'd never intended to use it.

A few weeks ago, he'd been sitting on the porch at the cabin, staring out at the lake and thinking about Keith and those who'd died that day, when he felt an overwhelming wave of emotion, like he was about to drown in it. Uncertain what else to do, he'd gone into the cabin, dug the journal out of the storage box where he'd tossed it, and sat down at the table. He wrote until his hand cramped, then took a short break and wrote some more. He'd filled pages and pages with memories of what had happened, how it made him feel, how he blamed himself, how hard it had been to keep on going without Keith and the others. Somehow, writing it down, putting pen to paper to release his thoughts and emotions, had made him feel better.

Bridger was developing the habit of writing in the journal every day, usually right before he turned in for the night. Now, he wasn't just writing about the pain of the past, although that was a large portion of it. He was also writing about his hope for the future. His joy in each day.

Despite how he thought he'd spend the rest of his days mourning his losses and blaming himself for them, he felt as though he was finally reclaiming his life. He had stepped into the light and the land of the living, instead of just muddling through one dark day after another.

Now that he'd started moving forward, he held no intention of ever returning to his former existence of sorrowful days filled with pain.

Once he spoke to his parents, made an attempt to set things right with them, he would finally be free from the weight of his past. Free to pursue his future. A future he hoped and prayed would be spent with Shayla.

Bridger had never allowed himself to think about marriage, settling down, or raising a family. Not until he'd met Shayla.

Lately, it seemed to be all he wanted to think about. Building a home with her, having a few babies. Settling into a life he'd not even dared to dream could be a possibility. Somehow, in the midst of the healing he'd found in Holiday, he'd also discovered love—true love. The kind that made him think of porch swings and pots of colorful petunias and picket fences surrounding a big yard where his kids could play ball.

If he could convince Shayla to marry him and they did have children, Bridger hoped they looked like her, with her beautiful honey-brown hair and lively brown eyes. Truthfully, what they looked like didn't concern him all that much. Mostly, he wanted them to have Shayla's vibrant spirit. Her smile could brighten any room and warm any heart. It certainly had illuminated his world and left him changed for the better.

Before he could further contemplate his future with Shayla, Madelyn raced up to him, throwing her arms around him in a tight hug.

"You made it!" she said, pulling back, then giving him a second hug. "Any luggage?"

"Nope. Got what I need right here." He held up the bag in his hand. "Did the wedding gift I sent arrive?"

Madelyn nodded and, wrapping her arm around his, guided him outside into the bright July sunshine. "It did. I'm impressed you sent it already wrapped. Jen said the box was too lovely to open, but she did anyway."

Bridger grinned as he walked with Madelyn to where she'd parked her car. "Shayla gets credit for wrapping the gift. She offered when she found out I intended to ship it so I wouldn't have to cram it in my bag."

"I'll have to ask her how she made that bow. Jen showed me a picture of it. And the vase! My word, Bridge! I had no idea you had such talent with wood. I suppose you got that from Uncle Wally."

"Maybe." He shrugged. "It's just something I've found I enjoy."

"Jen said the note you included about it mentioned the vase was once a rotting fence post. How did you get the sides so smooth? They look like glass."

"Lots of elbow grease and sealant." Bridger smirked as he held Madelyn's door for her, then jogged around to the passenger side of her SUV, tossed his bag into the back, and took a seat in the front. "Where are the kiddos?"

"With Mark's mom. She's watching them today, thank goodness. I needed a day without them underfoot to finish up a few wedding details I volunteered to take off Jen's plate. If you aren't otherwise occupied, you can help."

"Happy to do what I can," Bridger said. "What's going on with all the family?"

"Did I tell you about the clause in Uncle Wally's will?"

Bridger shook his head. "Nope. What did it say?"

Madelyn looked like a cat that had just discovered a bowl full of cream. "If anyone disputed the will, attempted to declare him insane or incompetent, or tried to alter his wishes in any way, their inheritance would be revoked and given to you."

"What?" Bridger gaped at his cousin. "Is that why all the rumblings of lawsuits dropped as quickly as they started?"

"Exactly. The only thing worse than not inheriting what they thought they deserved was having you inherit everything. Uncle Wally loved you dearly. He often talked about you, especially the last few years."

"I miss him so much, Maddie. He was one of a kind."

She nodded in agreement. "He was."

Bridger leaned back in the seat and looked out the window. Nothing had changed since he'd been there a few months ago, but he felt like everything in his life had shifted in a much better direction.

He glanced over at Madelyn to find her watching him. "You look different, Bridge. It isn't the deep tan or the civilian clothes. For the first time in a long, long while you look happy and at peace."

"I am happy, Maddie. Happier than I think I've ever been. Moving to Holiday was one of the best decisions I've ever made. I love it there. The cabin is so peaceful, and I've got Kit and Toby and the nutty pheasants to keep me company."

"I can't believe you have wildlife as pets. I hope you are ready to share a bunch of photos because my two demanding youngsters will want to see them."

Bridger chuckled. "I do have several. They can look all they want."

"Tell me more about what makes you happy. I'm assuming it's not just the cabin at the lake."

He knew his cousin was fishing for details about Shayla, but he wasn't quite ready to bite. "The town of Holiday is great. It has so much character and history. Some of the buildings in town have been there for more than a century. There are also families that have been there that long or longer. The Coleman family, for instance, started the Elk Creek Ranch before Holiday was even a town. I don't know if I told you about them or not."

"No. You just mentioned working with Mrs. Coleman at the museum."

Bridger nodded. "Kali is great. Passionate about history, and super nice. She recently had Evan and Henley's house, the one that had the doctor's office in it, moved to the depot grounds, where she plans to turn it into a museum with old medical equipment and information about our ancestors. I've been giving her copies of photos I've found, that sort of stuff. Anyway, she's married to Trace Coleman. Have you ever heard of Lennox Enterprises?"

"Don't they have something to do with shipping or international business?" Madelyn cast a glimpse at him as she merged onto the freeway.

"Yes. George Lennox started the empire with railroads and built a multi-billion-dollar business from there. They have offices all around the world, but the headquarters are in Oregon, and at one time they were run from Holiday, where George Lennox built a mansion. His daughter married a Coleman, and that's where the Coleman connection comes into play. Trace is the vice president of the company now."

"And his wife is the museum lady?" Madelyn asked as she took an exit.

"Yep. I didn't mean to give you a history lesson on the Coleman family, but they are part of what people would call an old family in town, like the Milton family. Even the pastor at the church, Rogan Ryan, is a descendant of the first pastor in Holiday."

"Wow. That is cool. It sounds to me like you've gotten to know people in town and have become quite smitten with the community."

Bridger wasn't sure he liked her using the word smitten where he was concerned, but he supposed it accurately described how much he enjoyed being part of Holiday's community. "I do enjoy working around town, getting to know people there. It's a nice place, Madelyn. Small town America at its best."

"So, you've been doing handyman jobs and making furniture out of old stumps and fence posts?"

"I have. Not only do I like the work, but it also pays better than what I was earning in the military. I get to set my own hours and work at my own pace. It might seem like I'm being lazy or crazy, but I really and truly like what I'm doing."

"Then keep doing it, Bridger. Don't you dare listen to whatever nonsense your parents are going to say. I've seen the photos of the coffee tables you've created. They are works of art. When you said one of them sold for almost two thousand dollars, I choked on my coffee. However, I can see why someone would pay that much. They are truly masterpieces. What made you decide to start creating them?"

"I needed something to do to earn money and something to keep my hands and mind busy. One day, I was walking in the woods by the lake and came across a tree that had been struck by lightning. The stump was just so cool, and I thought it would be neat to try to do something with it. So, I dug up the stump and wrangled it back to the cabin. I spent hours online looking up tutorials and watching how-to videos before I dove into working on it. After that, I guess you could say I was hooked. There are several stumps and dead trees around the lake. I feel like I'm giving the wood a second chance at life this way."

"That's a great way of thinking about it, Bridge. Now, before we get to the house, you have to tell me about Shayla. I think she's wonderful and has been so good for you, but I want to hear your thoughts."

Bridger had known Madelyn was eventually going to ask about Shayla, prodding into matters of his heart. If it had been anyone else, he would have told them to mind their own business, but Maddie was more like a sibling to him than his own brother. He knew she only asked because she cared.

"Shayla is amazing. Unique. Intelligent and smart, witty and fun. She takes such great care of her patients and is so patient with the elderly people at the retirement center where she works. She's a happy person who tends to lift people up and brighten their lives with her laughter and smiles. She's beautiful, with these incredible eyes that just snap with life and energy. Shayla loves the outdoors and hiking and fishing, which are major marks in the plus column with me. Even though she does that stuff, she's also very feminine and girly. When she isn't wearing scrubs or dressed in what she calls her mountain clothes, she wears floral shirts that are soft and pretty or dresses that seem to float around her. She loves flowers and cop shows, and she laughs at my inane jokes. She drinks lemonade by the gallon, and her favorite dessert is pie. You know how much I appreciate a good piece of pie. Most of all, she loves me. Faults and flaws, she loves me."

Madelyn smiled at him, her eyes glistening with tears. "How do you feel about her?"

"I love her," Bridger said without a second of hesitation. "I mean, I really, really love her, Maddie. I'm talking the step-in-front-of-a-bullet-for-her kind of love."

Madelyn laughed. "You'd step in front of a bullet for a total stranger, or even someone you disliked because that's the kind of guy you are, Bridger, but I know what you're saying. For the record, I'm so happy for you. Happy that you've finally allowed yourself to grieve and move forward, and especially happy you've let yourself fall in love. Shayla is perfect for you. She'll keep you on your toes, but your heart is safe with her."

"Exactly." Bridger smiled at Madelyn as she pulled up at her house and they dove into helping with wedding preparations.

The day after the wedding, Bridger stood in front of his parents' home and knocked on the door. His father opened it with a shocked expression on his face.

"Bridger. Didn't expect to see you today. Aren't you supposed to be with Madelyn's family?"

"I am, but I wanted to speak with you and Mom. May I come in?"

His father nodded and moved back. Bridger stepped inside the house, gently closing the door behind him.

"Rosalind is in the kitchen. We just finished breakfast. Have you eaten?" His father led the way down the hallway to the kitchen.

"I have eaten, but thank you."

"Roz, look who stopped by," Jason said as the two of them walked into the room.

Bridger met and held his mother's gaze as she stared at him over the rim of her coffee cup. Although she had a few more wrinkles on her face than she'd had when she was young, she was still a beautiful woman. It was too bad the beauty was only skin deep.

When he compared her to Shayla, who was so good and kind, his mother seemed shallow and selfish. Probably because she'd always been that way.

"Bridger. What are you doing here? I thought I heard you were spending the day with your cousin, then leaving tomorrow." His mother lifted her chin slightly, as though evaluating him and finding he fell far short of her expectations. "It doesn't surprise me in the least you're heading back to that nowhere town in Oregon. You had a promising career in the military, and you just cast it all aside to do what? Play with wood?"

"Gee, good morning to you too, Mom." Bridger took a seat at the table across from his mother and accepted the cup of coffee his father handed to him. He glanced from his mother to his dad, wondering what made them the way they were. So concerned about their images and money, about what others thought of them, instead of caring about the things that truly mattered in life.

"Is there something you needed, son?" Jason asked, studying Bridger, clearly attempting to unravel the mystery of what brought him to visit, since he generally avoided spending time with them.

"No, Dad. Not really. For the first time in a long, long time, I'm happy. Holiday is a great community and the peacefulness at the lake has helped me get past some hard things I needed to work through." He took a long sip of coffee. "The woodwork I started for fun, but it's been therapeutic. I make more selling the furniture I create than I earned in the Army. I also help around town with different things and I like doing that. None of that is why I'm here though. I just wanted to say I forgive you both."

"Forgive us? For what?" his mother asked in a shrill tone. "You're the one who ran off and joined the Army without giving a thought to the future we had planned for you. Then you got hurt, just like I told you would happen. The next thing we knew, you were one of those strange guards at the cemetery, and then you raced off to Holiday where your loony uncle had that deplorable old cabin."

"Exactly, Mom. I served my country with honor and have the medals to prove it. Being one of the sentinels at the tomb in Arlington was the greatest privilege of my life. The time I spent doing that is something I'll always be proud of and will never regret. For the record, Uncle Wally wasn't loony. He was good, and honest, and caring. He was always there for me when I needed someone because you two weren't. You never understood me and never tried, but that's not why I'm here." Bridger ran a hand over the back of his neck and took a deep breath. "Before I can step into my future, I need to let go of everything holding me back in my past, and you are a big part of that. You never showed me love or compassion or acted like you cared if I lived or died. I used to think it was because of some flaw in me, but I've recently realized it was never about me. I'm not angry at you. I don't hate you. I don't wish either of you any ill will. I just needed to tell you I forgive you for the past. If you want to be part of my future, you have my number and know where to find me."

"Well, I never!" his mother ranted, slamming her coffee cup on the table, sloshing liquid on the pristine white cloth.

Bridger rose to his feet, nodded once at his parents, and headed to the door. A hand on his arm stopped him before he reached for the knob. He turned around and looked at his father.

The older man had tears in his eyes. "It might not seem like it, but we do love you, Bridger. Go wherever makes you happy and have a good life."

"I intend to, Dad. Thanks." Bridger pulled his father to him, and they shared a warm hug before he stepped back. "Maybe you'll get in touch once in a while?"

"Maybe I'll do that, son." Jason smiled at him as Bridger walked outside and waved once before he got into the SUV Madelyn had let him borrow.

It had been challenging to face his parents, to speak bluntly with them, but he felt better for having done it. He doubted his mother would ever change, but that moment of connection with his father as he stood at the door gave him hope.

Bridger spent the day with Madelyn and her family. The next morning, his cousin dropped him off at the airport. She hugged him, kissed his cheek, and shed a few tears as they said goodbye.

"Promise you'll come visit sometime?" Bridger asked as he gave her one more hug.

"I promise. I'll be thinking good thoughts for you and Shayla. Do you have everything?"

"I do." Bridger stepped back and smiled at Madelyn. "Thanks to your bossy interference in my life, I feel like I'm finally getting the past squared away so I can think about my tomorrows."

"I'm here anytime you need someone to give you a kick in the pants, cuz." Madelyn squeezed his hand. "Be happy, Bridge. Be ridiculously, joyfully, immeasurably happy because you deserve it."

"I'm gonna try, Maddie. I'm gonna try."

He turned and rushed into the airport before emotion got the best of him.

He spent the time waiting for his flight writing in his journal. Yesterday, he'd been too tired after a full day with Madelyn's family. They'd gone to the zoo and the park and ended the evening with a barbecue in the backyard and watching a kid-friendly movie on a screen Mark had set up outside.

If Shayla went along with his plans, if she was willing to share his dreams, perhaps by the time Madelyn and her family came to visit, he and Shayla would be living in their dream home on the property in Holiday. The cabin would be great as a guest house for their family and friends when they came to visit.

Quinten had already promised to fly out next spring. Bridger intended to hold him to it.

On the return flight, Bridger rehearsed what he wanted to say to Shayla when he returned home. He grinned to himself. Holiday was home because it was where his heart remained. With Shayla.

He landed in Boise, ran a few important errands, then headed for Holiday. Anticipation filled him with each mile that took him closer to the woman he loved.

Chapter Fourteen

"You did so well today, Mr. Johnson. I'm so proud of you," Shayla said, patting the arm of the older gentleman who had willingly done his exercises, even if his mind had wandered elsewhere. She settled him in his favorite chair in his room, then glanced at her watch. Past time for her break.

She poured lemonade into her reusable water bottle from the pitcher she'd left in the break room fridge, then went outside to the courtyard for a few minutes of fresh air and peace. Shayla settled on a seat that caught some of the afternoon sunshine, leaned back, and closed her eyes, thinking about Bridger.

He'd called last night and talked for a few minutes, telling her about going to visit his parents. She couldn't imagine how his parents could treat Bridger with such cold indifference and disgust.

He was such a good man. He was caring and gentle, smart and funny. Admittedly, Shayla appreciated his good looks and strength. Those muscles were the stuff of romance legends.

Regardless of his outward appearance, it was his inner strength and resilience, his ability to not just survive his past but thrive in spite of it, that she truly admired. Bridger had seen terrible things and experienced horrible situations, but he hadn't let it change the fine person he'd been, the fine man he still was. If his parents were too blind or stupid to realize they had an honorable, wonderful son, then that was their loss.

As soon as Bridger returned, Shayla intended to tell him just how much she admired him, and how deeply she'd missed him. He'd only been gone five days, but it seemed like a thousand.

She'd grown so accustomed to spending time with him nearly every day, even if it was just a quick moment of hello when she got off work. It felt like she'd been deprived of something essential and vital with him out of town.

She had no idea what the future might bring. No idea if they had a future together, although she couldn't picture hers with anyone other than Bridger. Just for today, though, it would be enough to see him. To see the love in his fascinating gray eyes and feel the warmth of his touch.

She sighed, dreaming about Bridger as she rested in the sun with the scent of flowers all around her.

A bump to her leg startled her, and she straightened, opening her eyes to see an adorable chocolate lab puppy with a purple collar around his neck sitting at her feet.

"Hey, little guy. What are you doing out here?" Shayla set her bottle of lemonade beside her and picked up the puppy, cuddling him close. He licked her chin, making her think of Ubu and his slobbery kisses. She looked around to see if someone was looking for him, but she couldn't see anyone in the courtyard, other than a few elderly people who sat beneath an umbrella playing cards.

"Did you get lost, buddy? Huh? Shall we go find your owner?" Shayla stood and turned to go back inside. She almost dropped the puppy when she noticed Bridger standing a few feet away, smirking at her.

"You're home!" she said, rushing over to him. He gave her a hug, careful not to squish the puppy, then brushed his lips over hers. She wanted to deepen the kiss, but with a dozen sets of eyes watching them, now wasn't the time.

Bridger shifted and she noticed he held a box in his hand. "What's that?"

"Pie. I stopped by the diner and bought a whole huckleberry pie. Just for you. Want a piece?"

"Sure, but first I need to find out who this puppy belongs to."

Bridger's grin widened to a smile. "He belongs to you, and maybe me, if you want to share. I picked him up in Boise on my way home. You seemed to really enjoy Ubu when I had him, and I thought you might like your own puppy to love."

"You know I can't have pets at my place."

Bridger nodded. "I do know that, which is why he can stay with me, for now. I figure he's a good reason for you to come see me more often." He motioned to a nearby bench. Shayla took a seat, and Bridger sat so close to her she could feel the heat of him radiating through her scrubs.

"Let's trade. I'll hold the puppy, and you take the pie." Bridger set the box on her lap, then took the puppy in one of his big hands. The dog made a contented grunt and snuggled up against Bridger's side, as though he'd found his perfect human.

Shayla might have been jealous if she hadn't been so pleased by Bridger's gift. She and her sister had pets growing up, but it wasn't until she spent time with Bridger and his animals that she realized how much she'd missed having a dog in her life.

"He's wonderful, Bridger. Does he have a name?"

"Nope. You get to name him." Bridger rubbed a gentle finger over the puppy's head.

"I'll come up with something just right for such a special little guy." Shayla glanced down at the box on her lap. "How do you propose we eat the pie? Are there forks and plates in the box?"

"Just open it and see." Bridger looked like he would tear off the lid if she didn't open it soon.

She smiled and lifted the lid, then sucked in a shocked gasp. There was a pie in the box, but someone had spelled out the words "marry me," with huckleberries. A velvet ring box sat on a folded square of parchment in the middle of the pie.

Hands trembling, Shayla picked up the box, but before she could open it, Bridger took it from her. He opened it, removed the ring, and held it out to her. A brilliant round cut diamond on a platinum band sparkled in the sunlight. It was beautiful, something she'd have chosen for herself if she'd been looking.

Shocked by Bridger, by his proposal, she just stared from the ring to him.

He shifted the puppy so he had both hands free, took her left hand in his, and slid the ring onto her finger.

"I came to Holiday broken, thinking I needed time alone to heal. Then I saw you, and everything changed. The first time I laid eyes on you, wearing nothing but a towel and your hiking boots, I knew it was game over. I hate to admit it, but I saw you walk out of the lake that morning. When I caught sight of those long, sexy legs of yours, it was enough to leave me struck dumb. I hope you don't think it's crazy, but I fell in love with you that day, and I knew even then my future was wrapped up in you. I've never felt like this before and know I won't again. Will you take my ring, Shayla? Will you take my hand? You've already got my heart. Take my name, if you'll have it. Take my time, if you want it. Take my days as my friend, and my nights as my lover. I don't want to waste a minute, not a single minute, that I could spend beside you. I want to start my tomorrows today. With you. I want you entwined in my heart and my world forever. Will you marry me, Shayla? Will you do me the great honor of becoming my wife?"

Tears blurred her vision, but Shayla nodded, overwhelmed by Bridger and his love. "It would be my honor to marry you, Bridger. You tell me when, and I'll be there."

"Bam, baby! Let's do this!" Bridger set the pie on the bench along with the puppy, hopped up, and lifted Shayla in his arms. "I love you."

"And I love you!" Shayla was laughing and crying when his mouth claimed hers in a kiss of passion and promises. A kiss that set her heart on fire.

Whistles and claps finally drew them back to the moment. She turned her head, cheek pressed to Bridger's as they looked at friends and staff members who'd come outside to see what the commotion was about.

"She said yes!" Bridger boomed as Shayla held out her hand. Fynlee, Sage, Matilda, Ruth, and Rand were among the first to swarm around them, offering congratulations and well wishes.

Two weeks later, on a sunny August afternoon, Shayla glanced in the mirror in the downstairs bedroom at Bridger's cabin. Their cabin, she amended. She'd finished moving her things there that morning. What wouldn't fit, they'd left in a storage unit in town while they waited for their house to be built on the empty lot in town. It would be another month before the construction crew could start breaking ground, but she and Bridger had already chosen the design for their future home. They'd known the moment they saw the house plan it was the one they both wanted.

By next summer, they'd be living in their dream home.

Although everything seemed to be happening so fast, Shayla was ready. She didn't want to delay her future happiness with a long engagement. Not when she knew right down to her very bones that Bridger was the man she was meant to love for a lifetime.

Today would make their love and plans to spend forever together official. She couldn't think of anywhere more fitting for their wedding than at the lake where they met.

Much to her surprise, Matilda, Ruth, Sage, and several of their friends had volunteered to take care of everything. All Shayla had to do was choose her wedding colors, flowers, and the flavor of cake she wanted.

She'd spent last weekend with her sister and mom, shopping for a dress. The first bridal shop they'd entered had a gorgeous dress on display. It was as though a spotlight had shone on it the moment Shayla laid eyes on it. She didn't need to look at another gown. It was *the* dress, and it had looked even better when she'd tried it on than she'd dared to hope. Her sister had talked her into trying on several other dresses, but Shayla's mind was made up. She bought the gown she loved and couldn't wait for the man she loved to see her wearing it as she walked down the aisle.

"Ready for this?" her sister asked as she swept into the bedroom with Shayla's bouquet in her hands.

"So ready." Shayla grinned at Ciara, and the two of them looked in the mirror, smiling.

"Did you know Bridger called Dad and asked for his permission to marry you before he proposed?"

Shayla couldn't hide her shocked expression. "No. He never mentioned a word about it, but it doesn't surprise me. He's a traditional kind of guy."

"We all think he's wonderful, sis. Dad and Bridger have been talking about home repairs and woodworking tools. They really hit it off. Mom said you'd be nuts not to marry a hot hunk like him."

Shayla blushed as Ciara adjusted her veil. "I'm glad you all like him. That means a lot to me, Ciara."

"Dad said if anything ever happens, he's keeping Bridger and you are on your own."

Shayla laughed. "He's stuck with both of us because I'm never letting anything come between me and the man I love."

"Spoken like a besotted bride," Ciara teased, then gave Shayla a tight hug. "I'm so happy for you. He really is terrific, and I hope you have a long, happy, beautiful life together."

"Me too. Thank you." Shayla sniffled as she drew back. "If you make my makeup run, I'll have to end you, you know."

"I know. Come on. Let's get this show on the road."

Ciara served as Shayla's lone attendant, while Bridger's friend Quinten had flown in for the wedding along with several members of the Holt family. Madelyn had earned huge points with Kali Coleman when she'd hand-delivered Evan Holt's old doctor's bag to be used in the museum. Madelyn's parents had it in their attic, and she'd retrieved it. No one had mentioned if it was with permission or not.

The two sisters moved into the living room, where their father waited to walk Shayla down the aisle.

Shayla took a deep breath, squeezed Ciara's hand, then took her father's arm. He kissed her cheek, emotion shimmering in his eyes, brown and full of life like her own.

"I'm happy for you, honey. Bridger is a great guy, and I think the two of you will have a joyful life together."

"Thank you, Daddy. I've never felt like this, so happy and just about to burst with love." Shayla stepped outside and walked with her father down the steps to the creek, then over the footbridge to the clearing where their wedding ceremony would take place. The reception would be held in the courtyard at Golden Skies, catered by Sunni's bakery.

Because the location for the ceremony was hard to access, there were only a few dozen people gathered at the lake to watch as Shayla walked down an aisle that was flanked on each side with white chairs and carpeted by white rose petals.

Bridger, resplendent in his uniform, stood beneath a wooden arch covered with pink, purple, and white flowers. Quinten stood to his left, while Pastor Ryan waited to his right.

The look on Bridger's face when he saw her, one of awe and adoration, made her smile and all her nerves dissipate as she made her way to him.

"Who gives this woman in marriage today?" Pastor Ryan asked.

"Her mother and I do," Brian Reeves said, looking over at his wife, Mary, before he faced Bridger. "If you ever hurt her, I will hire a brute squad to take you down since we all know I couldn't manage it on my own."

Everyone laughed, and the ceremony progressed on a lighthearted note. Shayla had been pleased to see Bridger's parents in attendance since his mother had initially refused to come. She didn't know if the couple would ever be able to mend all that they had destroyed with their son, but their presence at the ceremony was a start.

After vows and rings were exchanged, Shayla felt nerves stirring inside her when the pastor proclaimed them husband and wife and told Bridger to kiss his bride.

She'd spent considerable time pondering the type of first kiss they would share as a married couple, whether he'd give her a light peck, or a sizzling kiss that would shock her parents.

Bridger cupped her chin and gave her a sweet, tender kiss that held just enough heat to make the women sigh before he lifted his head and smiled at her with his heart in his eyes. "I love you so much," he whispered as he took her hand in his.

"I love you, Bridger. For always." She kissed his cheek; then they turned to face their family and friends, who cheered and clapped.

Across the creek, Shayla caught a glimpse of Kit watching from the safety of the shadows of a tree with Crash and Tango, his pheasant guardians, beside him. The deer wore a wreath of flowers around his neck. She wondered who had gotten close enough to put it on him. The most likely suspect was her husband and Madelyn's girls.

Life with Bridger was going to be one remarkable, incredible adventure.

Hours later, after they'd enjoyed a delicious meal and cut into a decadent layered cake baked and decorated by Sunni, and danced until Shayla was out of breath, Bridger gave Trace Coleman what appeared to be a secret hand signal.

"What was that about?" she asked as Bridger guided her off the dance floor and slipped out a side door. "Are we leaving?"

"Yes. If I don't engage in a few covert tactics, I'm not sure I'll ever get you all to myself."

Shayla laughed and stopped long enough to give Bridger an impassioned kiss before they continued down a hallway that took them out to the parking lot.

They'd just stepped outside into the bright sunshine when Trace pulled up in an old car that had belonged to one of his ancestors. Kali grinned at them from the front seat as she rolled down the window.

"Need a ride?"

"We sure do," Bridger said, opening the back door and helping Shayla inside before he settled beside her.

"I don't have my purse or my suitcase or anything," Shayla said, looking at Bridger in a panic.

"Your purse is here. Suitcases are in the trunk, and you can change on the plane if you are so inclined," Kali said, smiling as she handed Shayla her purse.

Shayla had asked Bridger if he would plan the honeymoon. She didn't care where they went as long as they could be together. He'd told her it would be a surprise, and she'd agreed, but now she wanted to know what was going on.

"Where are we heading?" she asked.

Bridger held her hand with his and offered her a teasing grin. "I thought you didn't want to know."

"I do now." She leaned forward and touched Trace's shoulder. "By the way, this car is fabulous. Thank you for letting us ride in it."

"My pleasure. Gave me an excuse to drive it today." He grinned back at them. "As for your destination, I may have taken over the plans a bit."

"Don't believe him, Shay," Bridger said, shaking his head. "When I asked Kali if she'd ever been to Vancouver, BC, Trace not only volunteered his private jet to take us there, but he also offered to let us stay in one of the Coleman condos on a private beach. How does that sound?"

"Amazing! Oh, my goodness. I've always wanted to go to Vancouver, mostly to see Butchart Gardens, but this is incredible. Thank you, Trace. Thank you so much!"

"You're welcome. That condo sits empty most of the time, so enjoy it. Besides, Bridger promised the first project he's going to work on when he gets back is a table for my office." Trace glanced over his shoulder again. "After that, I'm thinking a big piece of art, maybe a tree trunk about ten to twelve feet tall, for the lobby of corporate headquarters."

"I'll get started on that as soon as we get back." Bridger gave Trace a grateful look.

"I hope you two have a great time," Kali said. "We wish you all the best for a future full of happiness."

Trace smirked at his wife. "She's mostly just excited your cousin found Doctor Evan's old doctor's bag. I've heard her raving about that for three days."

Kali swatted his arm, and they all laughed as Trace pulled up at a tiny airfield. It turned out the pilot was Trace, and Kali went along for the ride. He, or one of his pilots, would be back in a week to pick up Bridger and Shayla when they were ready to return home.

"Thanks again, man." Bridger shook Trace's hand and then Kali's before he helped Shayla out of the plane when they'd reached Vancouver.

They both could have changed and sent their clothes home with Kali and Trace, but had decided to leave them on. Shayla wanted to get a few photos while they were still dressed up at the beach.

As they rode in the car Bridger had arranged to meet them at the airport, Shayla turned to study the man she'd married. He was nothing like she'd expected, but everything she wanted and needed in a husband.

"Have I mentioned how handsome you look today?" she asked as they rode toward the condo.

"Only half a dozen times, but feel free to expound on that all you want." Bridger winked at her.

She smiled and squeezed his hand as it held hers. "When you said you'd take care of your clothes for today, I assumed you'd rent a tuxedo, but I'm so glad you wore your uniform. I love seeing you in it."

"Enjoy it while you can. Now that I'm married, I can just let myself go." He patted his flat stomach. "It might be the last time I'll fit in it." While his voice sounded serious, the mirthful sparkle in his eyes assured her he was joking.

"It would be a shame to let all this go, Bridger." She leaned so her lips were close to his ear, and she brushed against his side. "I intend to love every inch of you before the day is through."

"Are you sure we need photos on the beach?" he asked, not giving her a chance to answer as his mouth claimed hers in a kiss full of yearning.

"Just one or two," she whispered.

"Two tops, then I'm not leaving our room until it's time to go home."

She lifted her head and gave him a doubtful look. "Really?"

"Fine. I didn't schedule anything tomorrow, but there might be a kayaking trip, a seaplane ride, and a few other surprises, including an afternoon tea at Butchart

Gardens on the week's agenda. I hope the fact that I'm willing to sit through a tea party is proof enough of how much I love you."

"Complete and total proof," she said, kissing him again. "I do love you, so, so much, my soldier boy."

"I love you, Shay. Today, tomorrow, and forever, I'm yours."

Are you as excited as I am about Bridger and Shayla finding their happily ever after? Keep reading for a preview from another sweet romance!

Recipe

Huckleberries can be hard to find, but boy are they tasty!
Here's a recipe for Shayla's favorite pie!

Huckleberry Pie
2 9-inch pie crusts
5 cups huckleberries
2 tablespoons lemon juice
1 cup white sugar
4 tablespoons quick-cooking tapioca
1 tablespoon butter

Combine huckleberries, sugar, tapioca, and lemon juice in a large bowl. Toss to evenly distribute the sugar, then let the mixture rest for 20 minutes so the tapioca can soften.

Preheat oven to 425.

Line pie plate with one crust.

Stir the filling, then spoon into the crust-lined pie pan. Dot filling with butter. Roll out the top pie crust and set it over the huckleberry filling. Fold the edges under and crimp in a decorative manner. Finish by cutting a few lines or designs in the top of the crust.

Bake for 20 minutes, then decrease the oven temperature to 375 degrees and bake for another 25-30 minutes until the top crust is golden brown and the filling is bubbly. If the edges of the pie darken too quickly, cover them with strips of foil to keep from overcooking.

Remove from the oven and let cool slightly. Serve with vanilla ice cream or freshly whipped cream.

Serves 6-8, depending on the size of your pie slices.

Author's Note

The idea for this story started in a rather unusual place.

My dad's cousin, JJ, frequently sends him emails with funny memes, or interesting stories. Dad often shares those he likes the best with me. One of the emails he sent was about the soldiers who serve as guards at the Tomb of the Unknown Soldier at Arlington National Cemetery in Arlington, Virginia.

Up until that email arrived, I hadn't given the cemetery, the tomb, or the soldiers who so faithfully serve as guards more than a passing thought. Had I heard of them? Yes. But did I know anything about them? Nope.

Intrigued by that email, I dug a little deeper into the cemetery and what it was like to be one of the sentinels there, why the tomb was guarded, and how it all started. It was amazing to read about the history of the cemetery and the tomb, and I tried to incorporate some of the pertinent details into the story.

I think it took me all of five minutes to decide I had to write a story about a man who was a guard at the Tomb of the Unknown Soldier. I knew I wanted him to be at the end of his service there. I knew there had to be some trauma in his past. I just didn't know the rest of his story at the time.

Fast forward several months to when I was working on my sweet historical romance *Henley*. There's a scene with Henley Jones and Doctor Evan Holt near the end of the story that takes place at Holiday Lake. As soon as I started writing it, I knew the lake would be the perfect place for my tomb guard to go and decided he'd be one of Evan and Henley's descendants.

So that's why I chose to write about a tomb guard and why he ended up inheriting a cabin in my fictional town of Holiday.

If you've never heard of the Tomb of the Unknown Soldier or watched a video with the guards marching in front of it, I encourage you to check it out. There's a wonderful commemorative guide available free online. I also recommend reading *Twenty-One Steps: Guarding the Tomb of the Unknown Soldier* by Jeff Gottesfeld. It's a children's book, but it tells the story of the tomb and the guards beautifully. It also includes the Sentinel's Creed.

I confess, the first time I read it through, it gave me chills. Just thinking about the unknowns in those tombs, who gave everything they had to give, including their identity, in service to their country just touches my heart and fills me with emotion and gratitude for those who have sacrificed so much for our freedoms.

My heartfelt and deepest thanks to those who have served and protected. You are appreciated so much.

Also, I thought I'd give just a brief mention of the Caisson Platoon of The Old Guard. The respectful, dignified service they provide for military funerals is extraordinary.

After doing all the research for this book, I have added Arlington National Cemetery to the list of places I intend to visit someday. I hope to maybe visit in the fall to see the leaves changing color much as Bridger experienced that October day. And if I see the Korean War Memorial Contemplative Bench, I'll think of his conversation with Mrs. Parks.

In fact, I gave that character the last name of Parks as a tip of the hat to the first caretaker of Arlington, a man named James Parks, who is buried there.

The cover for this book came together before I actually started writing the story. When I found a piece of digital art I could use with the fawn and pheasants, I decided they had to become part of Bridger's story. He loves animals, so it only stands to reason that would include the wildlife at the cabin.

The name for the fawn comes from my childhood. When I was a little girl, one of my dad's friends had a pet fawn named Kit. I loved getting to see it and even have a few photos of me petting it. Thank you, Jack, for those fun memories!

As for Ubu the dog, I once had a puppy named Ubu (named for the same reason Bridger gave his dog that name). Oh, he was the smartest little guy, except when it came to chasing vehicles and nipping at tires. Yes, the story of Ubu's fate has a sad ending, but I adored Ubu for the short time I had him.

When I was thinking about how Uncle Wally might have decorated the cabin, I was browsing through Pinterest (one of my favorite ways to generate inspiration and ideas). I happened upon some images of a cabin decorated with Pendleton blankets and loved the way it looked. When I happened upon a blanket in the Alta Lakes pattern, I knew it was perfect for Bridger's room.

Do you ever have days when nothing seems to go right and you just feel overwhelmed? After a couple of those in a row, I was so stressed I could hardly think straight. Then I woke up one morning with a song in my head. It's titled "Everything's Gonna Be Alright" by Kenny Chesney and David Lee Murphy. That song in my thoughts first thing in the morning sure put a different spin on my day. Now, when I feel that stressed, overwhelmed feeling coming over me again, I just listen to that song, take a deep breath, and remind myself everything really is going to be alright. I thought it would be nice for Shayla to share that song with Bridger.

A song that had meaning to her, and one she hoped would be meaningful to him.

I had to throw in a reference to *Paw Patrol* because it is my little nephew's favorite thing right now. Well, that and dinosaurs, hence the reference to *Dinosaur Train*. It just made me giggle every time I thought of big, tough Bridger packing around the *Paw Patrol* lunch box. I hope it gave you a grin too!

The inspiration for Bridger's tree stump art came from my niece's husband and his incredible talent. We were at their house right before I started writing this story, and Marc had just finished creating a fantastic work of art made from a tree stump that had been struck by lightning. I don't even have words to describe what a cool thing it was he created. But seeing it gave me the idea for Bridger to create furniture from old pieces of wood. The vase he gave his cousin for her wedding came from one Captain Cavedweller gave me for my birthday a few years ago. It's made from an old fence post and is absolutely stunning!

I've talked all about Bridger and not much about Shayla. She's a nurse (which is a profession I admire so much since it isn't something I am programmed to be able to do), and she's one of those amazing people who have sunshine in their soul and let that glow spill onto those around them. Bridger needed that so much, just like she needed his quiet, steady presence in her life.

Although it might have seemed like they were an odd couple at first, I think they were meant to be, and I'm so happy I could give them their happily ever after.

A special thanks to Katrina, Allison, Alice, Linda, and all of my Hopeless Romantic readers who helped make this book the best it can be. I'm so grateful for each one of you!

Thank you for reading this book and taking another adventure to the town of Holiday. Who would you next like to see have a story set in this fun small town?

Thank You

Thank you for reading about Bridger and Shayla's journey to a happy ending. If you enjoyed the story, I'd be so grateful if you'd consider leaving a review so other readers might discover the book, too.

Read more about Bridger's ancestors in the sweet historical romance *Henley*. You can also read more about the town of Holiday in the Holiday Bride series. Start with Valentine Bride when the characters of Matilda, Ruth, and Rand are first introduced.

Two unlikely matchmakers
bring love and mischief to the town of Holiday…

Holiday Express
Four generations discover the wonder of falling in love and the magic of one very special train in these sweet romances.
Find them on all Amazon

Also, if you haven't yet signed up for my newsletter, won't you consider subscribing?

You'll receive a free book or two, and what I call The Welcome Letters with exclusive content and some fun stuff! My newsletters are sent when I have new releases, sales, or news of freebies to share. Each month, you can enter a contest, get a new recipe to try, and discover details about upcoming events. Don't wait. Sign up today!

Catching the Cowboy Preview

Reins held loosely in his right hand, Hudson Cole rested his crossed wrists on the saddle horn and surveyed the sea of red and white cattle below him from the nearby hilltop. In the middle of spring calving season, he kept a close eye on the cows, watching for any trouble. He'd already moved five cows into the pen closest to the barn, sure they'd all give birth before morning.

He scanned the herd again, his gaze resting on a cow that had moved off by herself, bag full and heavy.

"Come on, Ajax, let's bring that ol' girl in. I think she's trying to sneak off to drop her calf when nobody's looking." Hud clucked his tongue to the horse.

Ajax carried him down the hill in a smooth, unhurried gait, one that wouldn't disturb the cows as they milled around, grazing on the hay he'd tossed out for them earlier. He'd be glad when spring fully arrived, and they could turn the cattle out to pasture for the summer.

Hud tipped back his head and gazed up at the bright yellow orb inching across a clear blue sky. He sure wouldn't complain about the nice weather they'd had the past week. Unseasonably warm, the temperatures reached into the mid-sixties each day and quickly dried the soupy mud left behind when the snow melted.

At least he wouldn't have to worry about any new calves suffering from frostbite. He'd lost a dozen calves two years ago when winter had lingered clear up until April. A shudder rolled over him just thinking about the miserable days and nights he spent trying to tend the cows and care for the calves in below-freezing temperatures. He sent a prayer of thanks heavenward for the mild weather that made his job of ranching so much easier.

When he neared the cow, Hud flicked the end of his reins, making a popping sound against the leather of his chaps that sent the cow into a slow saunter along the fence.

Twenty minutes later, Hud shut the gate behind her in the small pasture next to the barn with the other expectant mothers. "You girls don't do anything crazy until I get back to check on you," Hud said, taking the horse's reins in his hands and leading him to the barn. A glance at his watch made him hurry as he unsaddled Ajax and left him in the pasture on the other side of the barn with three other horses.

Cricket would soon be home from school, and Hud liked to be there when she raced off the bus, full of excitement and news from her day. Although his daughter was only six, he sometimes worried she was maturing way too fast as she talked about the boys she liked and fussed about her clothes and hair. Other days, he'd find her playing with a doll or lugging around her kitten, telling it a silly story, and think maybe his precious child wasn't so grown up after all.

Hud drove his mud-splattered all-terrain vehicle toward the house. He'd just rounded the bend in the lane when he noticed a shiny black luxury car stop at the end of the front walk.

Unexpected visitors rarely showed up at the ranch, and certainly not in cars that cost more than he'd make all year. The possibility existed that his grandmother had invited someone and forgot to mention it to him. It wouldn't be the first or last time.

As he approached the house, Hud observed a driver getting out of the car, then two older men exiting the backseat. One of them looked familiar, but he couldn't place why. A slim young woman slid out and stood between the men. His breath caught for a moment as he watched the afternoon light create a halo around her, making her skin glow and her hair sparkle like each strand was spun with gold.

Painful recollections from his past, of another golden-haired woman, slapped over him with the force of a tidal wave. He brought a gloved hand to his chest, rubbing at the ache that suddenly began to throb in the region of his heart. Determined to ignore the tumultuous feelings generated by his thoughts, he shoved the memories back down in the fortress buried deep in his soul where he kept them. He parked the four-wheeler and made his way over to the visitors.

The driver noticed his approach and looked at him uncertainly as he pulled luggage from the trunk.

Before Hud could say a word, his grandmother barreled out of the house and down the porch steps, wiping her hands on a pink-flowered apron that contrasted sharply to the blue and green plaid flannel shirt and faded blue jeans she wore.

She wrapped her arms around the taller of the two men, giving him a hug.

"Land sakes, Henry Brighton! It's been too long since you've come to visit. Welcome, welcome!" Nell Cole said, smiling at the man. "And it's good to see you, again, James. It's so nice to have you all here."

For a moment, Hud studied the men his grandmother spoke with, noting the resemblance between them. He assumed they were brothers. Suddenly, the name jolted something loose in his memory. Henry Brighton had been a good friend to his grandfather and used to come hunting every autumn. But Henry hadn't been to the ranch in years, not since before Grandpa passed away.

Curious as to what brought the judge and his brother to Summer Creek Ranch, Hud stowed his gloves in his back pocket and walked over to offer a word of welcome.

"Hud, honey, you remember Judge Henry Brighton, don't you?" Nell said, tugging on his arm to pull him closer to where she stood with the men and young woman.

"Welcome, sir. It's been a while, but I'm pleased to see you again." Hud shook Henry's hand then turned to his brother. "You must be Henry's brother. I'm Hudson Cole."

"That's right. James Brighton. Last time I saw you, you were about this big," the man said, holding his hand about two feet off the ground. He smirked and his eyes twinkled with mirth. "You've grown a bit since then."

Hud grinned, aware his size could be intimidating to some. "Yes, sir, I suppose I have." Slowly, his gaze drifted over the young woman, taking in her delicate beauty, perfectly styled hair, and makeup that appeared to have been applied by a professional. Intriguing blue eyes held a guarded look behind unnaturally long eyelashes. Rosy cheeks could have been from the slight wind or too much blush, he couldn't tell.

Her oval face was flawless, gorgeous, and therefore of no interest to Hud.

From the top of her head to the toes of her designer shoes, she reeked of money. No doubt her diapers had been made of hundred-dollar bills. Most likely, she'd spent her entire life spoiled and pampered, indulged and coddled.

Years ago, a pretty little rich girl had turned his head, entangled his heart, and caused him enough pain to last ten lifetimes. He certainly wasn't stupid enough to make that mistake twice.

"This is my daughter, Emery," James said, nudging the woman forward. "We can't thank you enough for taking her in like this. If there is ever anything I can do to repay your kindness, I hope you'll let us know."

Hud's right eyebrow hiked upward so high, it disappeared beneath the brim of his dusty cowboy hat. He swiveled his head around until his gaze clashed with his grandmother's. She looked only slightly guilty as she smiled pleasantly and clenched his arm with both hands, as though she intended to restrain him from saying anything about James' announcement that took him completely by surprise.

His grandmother's elbow connected with his ribs. "We're more than happy to have Emery stay with us for as long as she needs to. Isn't that right, Hud?"

Rather than answer, he offered a noncommittal grunt and gave the woman another once-over. He'd be surprised if she lasted a day on the ranch before she hightailed it back to Portland or wherever it was she'd come from. From experience, he figured the first nail she broke or the first waft of manure blowing around her face would send her running for civilization.

The rattle and screech of the school bus diverted his attention and that of their guests to Cricket's arrival.

Hud watched as his little girl hopped off the last step of the bus, shifted her pink backpack on her shoulder, then raced toward them, waving a hand over her head. He hurried out to greet Cricket, swinging her up in his arms and kissing her cheek.

"How was school today, baby girl?" he asked, relishing the feel of her arms around his neck as she gave him a hug. He received several a day but cherished each and every one as a special gift. Before long, she'd deem herself too old and grown up to give him hugs. Hud felt depressed just thinking about it.

"Great, Daddy! Miss Sullivan asked me to read to the class today. She said I did a good job. I got a sticker!"

"That's wonderful, sweetheart." Hud carried her over to where his grandmother waited with the Brighton family. He set Cricket on her feet but kept a hand on her shoulder. "Cricket, this is Judge Henry Brighton, his brother, Mr. James Brighton, and Emery Brighton. My daughter, Cricket."

"Why, Nell, she looks just like Jossy," Henry said, hunkering down and shaking Cricket's hand. "It's nice to meet you, Cricket."

"Do you know Aunt Jossy?" Cricket asked, tipping her head to the side and studying the stranger.

"I used to, when she and your daddy were your age." Henry stuck his hand in his pocket and pulled out a wrapped piece of candy. He glanced at Hud for permission to give it to Cricket.

Hud nodded and grinned when Cricket accepted the candy with a big smile. "Thank you, Mr. Judge. I love peppermints."

"You are welcome, Cricket. And you can call me Uncle Henry if you like." Henry straightened and took a step back. "Is Jossy here?"

"No. She married the rancher across the road and runs the Lazy J now. Her husband passed away the year before last," Nell said, glancing to the east. "That girl is always on the go."

Hud didn't bother to offer his comments on the matter of his sister trying to resurrect a run-down ranch or how hard she worked to keep the Lazy J afloat. Goodness knew he'd tried more times than he could count to help her, but she generally refused, claiming he had enough to deal with at Summer Creek Ranch. She wasn't wrong, but he hated to see his only sibling work herself to death. Then again, who was he to talk when all he did was toil on the ranch and occasionally help out in town when an extra pair of hands was needed.

"You're pretty," Cricket said, beaming at Emery like she was a fairy princess who'd dropped onto the ranch out of the sky. "You smell good, too."

To her credit, Emery Brighton didn't snub his child, but bent down until she was on eye level with Cricket. "Thank you very much, Cricket. Is that a nickname or your real name?"

Cricket tossed her head and glanced back at Hud. "My name is Caitlyn Amorette Cole. I'm six, and my favorite color is pink, and my daddy says I sound like a summer cricket."

Emery smiled. "I'm not sure I know what a cricket sounds like."

"Nonstop chatter," Hud said, tenderly ruffling his daughter's tangled black curls. With big blue eyes and milky skin, she held no resemblance to her mother, a blessing that filled Hud with gratitude every time he looked at his child. The Cole family genes were definitely dominant in Cricket's DNA.

"Where are my manners?" Nell wrapped her arm around Emery's and guided her up the steps. "Let's go inside. I just took a batch of cookies out of the oven."

Hud helped the driver carry in three large suitcases, three leather traveling bags, two duffel bags, and a box full of footwear, most of which appeared to be tennis shoes. After removing his boots so he wouldn't track manure across his grandmother's clean floors, he packed everything upstairs to one of the guest rooms. If any of the baggage belonged to Henry and James, they could sort it out later.

On quiet feet, he went down the back stairs to the mudroom and washed up, then wandered to the front room. His grandmother perched on the edge of a chair like she was serving royalty as she poured glasses of iced tea and passed around a plate of lemon cookies. Cricket sat on the floor in front of the coffee table with a glass of milk, a cookie, and her kitten, Luna.

Emery watched his daughter and sipped from a glass of tea while her father and uncle engaged in an animated conversation with Nell.

The driver had disappeared so Hud could only guess he'd gone back outside. He took two glasses of tea and set a handful of cookies on a plate then stepped outside. The driver sat on one of his grandmother's wicker porch chairs, eyes closed, and face turned to the sun.

"Care for some cookies and tea?" he asked, setting a glass of tea and the cookies on the table beside the man.

"Thank you, sir," the man said, sitting up and straightening his tie before he took a long sip from the tea.

"What's your name?" Hud asked then bit into a cookie.

"Drew. Drew Daniels."

"Nice to meet you, Drew. Have you worked very long for the Brighton family?"

Drew nodded. "I've been Mr. Brighton's driver for about ten years. He's a generous employer and a good man, a rare combination."

"I'm sure it is. If you've been with him ten years, then you must enjoy working for him."

Another nod. "I do. I mostly drive Mr. Brighton around for business matters, not a personal trip such as this one. Miss Brighton means well, but she sometimes … " Drew glanced around to see if anyone was listening. Assured they weren't, he continued, "is impetuous. It's not my place to say anything, but someone should warn you that she can't handle alcohol. Two sips and she's plastered."

Hud's eyebrow hiked upward again. "Good thing our ranch is dry, then. Does she often get into trouble drinking?"

"No. In fact, this is the … " Drew snapped his mouth shut. "I've already said more than I should. I believe Judge Brighton or Mr. Brighton would happily answer any questions, though."

"Then I reckon I'll ask a few. Do you know their plans?"

"Mrs. Cole invited us to spend the night, then we'll be on our way back to Portland in the morning."

"All four of you?" Hope filled Hud that Emery Brighton would soon be out of his hair.

"No. Miss Brighton has to stay here. It's part of the terms of her release and community service. I thought … " Drew gave him a studying glance. "I think it will be a learning experience for everyone."

"No doubt about that." Hud drained the tea from his glass in one long gulp then returned inside. He yanked on his boots and had his hand on the doorknob to escape when he felt a presence beside him.

"Mind if we tag along?" James asked. He and Henry had changed from suits into jeans and cotton shirts with work boots that appeared to have been worn many times. Not exactly what Hud had expected to see a billionaire tycoon wear.

"I'm just heading out to take care of the evening chores and check on a few cows." Hud pulled open the door and waited for the two men to precede him outside.

Drew hopped up, but James waved him back into his seat.

"Enjoy the quiet while you can, Drew. I'm sure Mrs. Cole would be happy to have you join them inside, if you like."

"Thank you, sir," Drew said, then appeared to relax as he soaked up the sunshine. The temperature had started to drop as evening approached, but it was still enjoyable out.

Hud motioned toward the lane that would take them to the barn.

"I know you must have a hundred questions for us," James ventured as they walked along the graveled path. "I get the distinct impression you had no idea we were coming."

"I didn't, sir. Would you tell me what your daughter did to get herself exiled to Summer Creek, and how I'm expected to be involved with matters while she's here?"

James and Henry relayed the story of Emery's arrest and Henry's sentencing.

Hud stopped at the barn and stared at the two men. "You mean her mother has no idea what happened?"

"No, and we plan to keep it that way, at least for now." James gave Hud a pleading look. "I love my wife more than anything, but she has pampered and spoiled our daughter to the point she's become … "

"Decorative," Henry supplied. "Emery is a smart girl, has an MBA and a few other degrees, but she's squandering her time and her talents. I think she's bored with life and needs to be challenged."

"What will your wife do when she finds out you left your daughter here?" Hud asked, checking the water tank outside the barn then turning to look at James.

The man shrugged. "Most likely pitch one of her famous southern belle fits, but don't worry about it. She won't be back from Georgia for almost a month. By then, I hope Emery is settled into life here. We truly do appreciate your allowing her to stay at Summer Creek Ranch. I'd like to promise she won't be any trouble, but I'm not sure I can."

"At least you're honest, sir." Hud wondered what his grandmother was thinking to agree to take a troubled young woman into their home. According to what James and Henry shared, Grammy had offered Emery a job as Cricket's nanny. Not that he couldn't use someone to keep an eye on his daughter while he and his grandmother took care of ranch work, but Hud wasn't sure he wanted to entrust his child into the care of a woman who planned to steal a police officer's horse. What other questionable behaviors did she have? What if she corrupted Cricket? Then again, perhaps she was merely spoiled and clueless.

A sigh of resignation escaped before he could suck it back in. "What do you need me to do?"

"I've cut off Emery's funding, so she'll be required to work for any money she receives." James gave Hud a long glance. "I will happily provide whatever you think is fair, but I do want to pay for her room and board, and leave enough extra to cover a minimum wage job, whether that's here on the ranch or somewhere in town. I don't expect anyone to come up with the funds to employ her."

"You don't need to pay me, sir. She'll be our guest. I can hire her to do some things on the ranch."

"No. I insist on paying for her keep and her wage. And if any incidentals arise, you've only to let me know, and I'll take care of the expense." James held up his hand when Hud started to protest. "My daughter is stubborn, opinionated, and sometimes downright challenging. I can't, in good conscience, leave her here and not at least offer something for the inconvenience this will be to you and your family."

Taken aback by the man's blunt assessment of his daughter, Hud didn't know what to say.

James placed a hand on his shoulder. "Just take the money, Hud. You could use it for Cricket's college fund, or something along those lines."

Henry smirked at him. "Yes, think of it as bonus money for Cricket's future."

The Brighton brothers sure knew how to be coercive. Hud would do anything for Cricket and money to put in the savings account he'd started for her college fund was too important to refuse.

"Okay, you talked me into it, but I'll only accept a fair amount for room and board and Emery's wage. How many hours do you want her to work and how many community service hours does she need to put in?"

"She ought to work at least thirty hours a week for her wage and room and board. I'd prefer she not know I'm paying for it, by the way," James said.

Hud nodded. "I gathered that much. Is there a specific type of community service she needs to complete?"

"No. It can be anything as long as it is helpful, and she isn't getting any benefit from it beyond building her character," Henry said.

"I'll figure out something." Hud wished he'd stayed out with the cows that afternoon instead of coming home to this disastrous state of affairs.

Later, after their guests had retired to the guest rooms upstairs for the night, Hud cornered his grandmother in the kitchen as she prepared overnight oatmeal to serve for breakfast.

"What in the world were you thinking, Grammy? Bringing that drunken ninny here?" he asked, helping himself to a slice of chocolate cake left from dinner. He took a bite as Nell added ingredients to the oatmeal concoction she layered in a slow cooker. "Have you lost your mind? She can't stay, Grammy."

"I promised her father and Henry we'd keep an eye on her, Hudson. You've got to do this. She's a young lady in need of our help."

"I don't have to do anything. I wasn't the one making promises when I had no business doing it." Hud sighed, thinking about the way Miss Emery Brighton had turned up her nose in disgust earlier when the ranch dogs wandered over and sniffed her legs. "From what I've seen, she is no lady, and the only help I foresee giving her is a swift kick to her designer-covered backside. What kind of influence do you think she'll be over Cricket?"

"A good one, I hope," Nell said, glancing at Hud as she set the lid on the slow cooker and adjusted the cooking time. "Just give her a chance. I think you'll find she's not nearly as horrible as you expect."

"Come on, Grammy. Who are you trying to kid? She got drunk at breakfast, tried to steal a horse, and attempted to bribe a police officer before threatening him. I don't want her around my daughter."

"Well, she's staying whether you like it or not, so you better get used to the idea. Henry and James have been good friends for years and years. I won't disappoint them." Nell wiped her hands on a dish towel then gave Hud a look he knew all too well. One that sized him up and found him lacking. "If you'd stop comparing that girl to your former wife, you might notice she's lovely and sweet. She and Cricket are already getting along famously."

"That's exactly my point, Grammy. I don't want her around Cricket. There's no telling what kind of foolishness Emery will plant in her impressionable young mind." Hud took a last bite of the rich cake, then pointed the fork at his grandmother. "You could have mentioned earlier that Henry called last night."

"I could have," his grandmother said with a sassy grin. "But you would have refused to let Emery come, and there's not a good reason for it, except when you look at her you see Bethany."

Hud scowled and set his empty dish in the dishwasher. "I thought we agreed to never mention that name again."

"You agreed; I didn't. Besides, the day will arrive when your daughter will want to know more about the woman who gave birth to her even if Bethany never acted like a mother." Nell filled a thermos with coffee and set it on the counter next to him. "Will you please just try to go into this situation with an open mind, rather than deciding you dislike Emery based on your experiences with your wife?"

"I'll try, but I don't have time to babysit her, not in the middle of calving season. Until we get a better idea about the kind of person she really is, please keep her away from Cricket. Henry mentioned a video circulating online of what she did. Did he say anything to you?"

"He emailed a link, but you know half the time our Wi-Fi signal is too weak to connect. The first time I get into town, I'll see what he sent. For now, though," Nell pointed toward the back door, "you've got a date with half a dozen expectant mamas. Want me to sit up with you?"

"No need for both of us to lose sleep tonight. The way things were moving along when I checked an hour ago, it shouldn't be too much longer before they get down to the business of birthing calves."

"You're a good man, Hudson Cole." Nell patted his cheek with affection. "I don't know what I would have done without you and your sister all these years."

He kissed her cheek, then pulled on his coat. "I'm glad we had you, too. Now get to bed, you troublemaker."

Nell grinned at him as he took the thermos of coffee and stepped outside into the chilly night air. He hoped her decision to welcome Emery Brighton into their home wasn't one they'd all come to regret.

Available on Amazon

More Sweet Romances

Summer Creek is one of *those* small towns—the kind brimming with quirky inhabitants, pets with personalities (like a meandering goat named Ethel), meddling matchmakers, tumbling-down old buildings, and dreams. So many dreams. These sweet, uplifting romances explore the ties that bind a community together when they unite for a common purpose and open their hearts to unexpected possibilities. Heart, humor, and hope weave through each story, touching the lives of those who call Summer Creek home.

Enjoy this sweet, romantic, funny series:

Catching the Cowboy – She's fresh out of jail . . . he's fresh out of luck.

Rescuing the Rancher – Her hero has arrived, even if she doesn't realize it . . . yet

Protecting the Princess – He wants to protect her. She needs him to love her.

Distracting the Deputy – Trouble is coming . . . but for whom?

Grass Valley Cowboys Series

Meet the Thompson family of the Triple T Ranch in Grass Valley, Oregon. Three handsome brothers, their rowdy friends, and the women who fall for them are at the heart of this sweet contemporary western romance series.

About the Author

PHOTO BY SHANA BAILEY PHOTOGRAPHY

USA Today bestselling author Shanna Hatfield is a farm girl who loves to write. Her sweet historical and contemporary romances are filled with sarcasm, humor, hope, and hunky heroes.

When Shanna isn't dreaming up unforgettable characters, twisting plots, or covertly seeking dark, decadent chocolate, she hangs out with her beloved husband, Captain Cavedweller, at their home in the Pacific Northwest.

Shanna loves to hear from readers.
Connect with her online:
Website: shannahatfield.com
Email: shanna@shannahatfield.com

Manufactured by Amazon.ca
Acheson, AB